Acknowledgements

First, I thank God for my life and for the gift of the written word. Thanks so much to my husband and children for their love and support. I thank my mother and father for their unrealized dreams, which were their gifts to me. Thanks go to my entire extended family and loving teachers who made me feel like I had something special to offer. The list goes on.

SOJOURNER'S DREAM

A NOVEL

ANGELINE BANDON-BIBUM

SOJOURNER'S DREAM

Published by

Bandon Press, Inc.
P.O. Box 10310
Silver Spring, MD 20914

First Edition
ISBN 0-9777586-0-5

AUTHOR'S NOTE
This novel is a work of fiction. Although aspects of the story were
inspired by actual events, the characters, names, places, and incidents are
either the product of the author's imagination or are used fictitiously.

SOJOURNER'S DREAM

For My Mother

PROLOGUE

As she dreamed, she saw a handsome man walking through a tropical rain forest. The man wore military fatigues, and his boyish face glistened with sweat. Carrying an AK-47, he walked in a direction parallel to a stream. She noticed that the stream was red with blood. There was a primordial greenness and moistness about the forest. She could feel the thick, warm air. A monkey, sitting on a tree branch, yawned lethargically, as it watched the man walk by. The man started to run, and it seemed that he was pursuing someone. Suddenly, the forest gave way to a clearing. She saw the man stop running and look around. Green hills were everywhere. Then she saw the corpses of men, women, children, and babies. Some were clothed, and some were partially clothed. It was like a sea of human corpses, covering the hills; the people were so freshly killed that she hoped and anticipated that the bodies would move at any moment. However, to her despair, the bodies did not move. They just bled and began to rot. She wanted to call the man in her dream, as she saw him looking down at his military boots; blood had splattered over his boots. He looked up to the sky. Then he grasped the rosary around his neck and prayed. She heard him whispering the prayer of St. Michael the Archangel.

CHAPTER ONE

Washington, D.C., September 1990

Sojourner Brown felt giddy as a tall, dark brown complexioned attorney approached her in the law library of Livingston and Richards, a corporate law firm. Livingston and Richards was located in Washington, D.C., in an office building on Pennsylvania Avenue across the street from The Old Post Office Pavilion. The location was in walking distance to The White House, The Capitol, and The Supreme

Court. That she was in close proximity to these institutions made Sojourner feel like she was in the center of the world's most important location.

The attorney approaching Sojourner was a lean man with an angular, boyish face and an aquiline nose. As the attorney approached Sojourner, he seemed to grow with each step. Sojourner estimated that he was about six foot four inches tall. She stood behind the counter of the law firm library, where she worked part time as a library assistant. The attorney's name was Joseph Kalisa, and he was a new associate attorney at Livingston & Richards. Joseph's name was included in the monthly employee newsletter, along with a note about the universities from which he had graduated, and his native country in Africa, Rwanda.

"Good Morning, Miss," Joseph Kalisa said. His voice was low and soothing.

Sojourner detected a rich foreign accent.

"Hi, Mr. Kalisa, how are you?" Sojourner said.

"Fine, thank you. I would like to check out these books, please," Joseph said, glancing quickly at the books he held in his arms.

Joseph wore a chocolate brown three-piece suit, which seemed to be fresh from the racks of a couture designer's studio, and a cream-colored dress shirt with a matching cream-colored silk tie. The cream and brown colors accented his smooth complexion, creating a vanilla and chocolate effect that made Sojourner's mouth water. However, on the outside Sojourner was cool and professional.

Sojourner opened the circulation binder and proceeded to show Joseph how to check out books from the library. Joseph signed his name for each book that he checked out, and she watched him. Joseph's long, elegant fingers curled delicately around his expensive looking gold pen, showing clean, well-groomed fingernails. Ostensibly, Sojourner watched Joseph as if to help him in case he had questions about checking out the books.

Standing near Joseph, Sojourner absorbed his scent, a light, clean, woody fragrance. His hair was closely cropped and neat, with a healthy sheen. Joseph carried himself with the dignity of royalty, and his disposition was serious and reserved. Although he made eye contact with Sojourner, his facial expression was almost blank. His dark eyes gazed, not at her, but through her. She was transparent to him, she thought. Sojourner was intrigued.

Quickly glancing at her clothes, Sojourner thought about what she wore that day, a pale yellow oxford shirt, beige gabardine pants, and brown penny loafer shoes. The faux pearl necklace that she wore matched her faux pearl earrings. She was glad that she had taken some extra time that morning to style her hair in a chignon.

When Joseph Kalisa was hired six weeks earlier, Sojourner was pleased. Before he arrived, there were five black attorneys in the law firm, which had a total of one hundred and twenty attorneys, as well as about two hundred other staff employees. When she had first seen Joseph Kalisa, he was reading in the firm's posh and elegant two-level library, replete with oriental carpets, rows of cherry wood bookshelves, heavy lacquered reading tables, high-back black leather chairs, and some private rooms for research.

"Carol, is that the new attorney from Africa?" Sojourner said to her co-worker, whispering.

Joseph was sitting at one of the reading tables. Sojourner and Carol Jones, who was also a library assistant, were shelving books together.

"Yeah, that's him," Carol said, also whispering.

"A very good looking man, huh?" Carol said, smiling.

Sojourner nodded in agreement.

Sojourner was a full-time graduate assistant at Howard University. She enjoyed working part time in the large private library of Livingston and Richards. Watching the seemingly haughty attorneys, young and old, glide in and out of the library entertained her. The money that Sojourner earned in her part-time job in the law library supplemented the modest stipend that she received for her graduate assistantship, and it helped her to pay her share of the rent for the apartment that she shared with her roommate, Rose Johnson.

As Sojourner worked, she daydreamed of Joseph Kalisa. Sojourner imagined holding Joseph's hand. She wondered what it would be like to kiss him. Joseph's lips would be soft and fragrant as they pressed against her lips. His long arms would embrace her and press her firmly against his chest. Then she would ride with Joseph in a Range Rover through a rural, tropical area, somewhere in Africa. Sojourner was so lost in her reverie that she tripped over a footstool in the library.

Sojourner took the Metro bus home that evening.

"Hey, Rose?" Sojourner said, entering the small living room of their apartment.

"Yeah, Soj, what's up?" Rose said.

Sojourner saw Rose sitting on their small tan sofa, eating shrimp fried rice and watching a rerun episode of the TV series Dynasty. It was the episode when Krystle and Alexis Carrington brawled in the Carrington Mansion. Rose was immersed in the fight, cheering for Alexis. Rose had a light beige complexion and light brown hair, which hung to the center of her back, in a ponytail. Sojourner thought that Rose had a pleasingly plump figure, although Rose often complained that she wanted to lose weight. Rose worked part-time as a sales associate at Woodward & Lothrop, better known as Woodies. At night, Rose pursued her career as a singer in a local band.

"I'm going to Founders Library to do some research," Sojourner said. "I'll see you later."

"Dang, girl. You're always studying. You work in a library during the day, and you come home and go back to another library on campus. You're gonna go library crazy," Rose said, shaking her head.

"You sing, and I study," Sojourner said.

"So true. Be careful, girl," Rose said.

Sojourner intended to spend the evening researching in the Founders Library on Howard University's main campus. She needed to research some African novelists for one of her Graduate classes, Contemporary African Writers. It was a dark and chilly night, and she was cautious and careful as she walked south down Georgia Avenue. Just before Sojourner reached the Howard campus, a large, dark-complexioned man approached her. He called her by her childhood nickname, "Ann." Many of Sojourner's family members found her name odd and formal, so they didn't use it. Instead, they called her Ann, which was her middle name. Sojourner was shocked that this person knew her nickname. She was not from D.C., and she was sure that no one in the area knew her by this name. How did he know, Sojourner thought? Sojourner didn't stop to speak to the man. She slowed down and stared back at him. A flicker of recognition entered her mind, and she realized that she'd seen this man before, many years before. However, she still didn't remember who he was. He called her "Ann." That brought back her past, the past that she'd been trying to escape. She walked past him, and he called her name again, like a sinister whisper in the dark. The derelict called out her nickname again.

"Hey Ann!" the man said.

Ignoring him, Sojourner walked faster.

She heard the man's lumbering footsteps behind her, and she increased her walking pace. The man sped up, and Sojourner could hear his heavy breathing, as he tried to catch up with her. After following her for a block, the man stopped. Sojourner looked back as she walked past the School of Business building, and she was relieved when she realized that he was no longer following her.

Sojourner walked diagonally across the main quadrangle of the campus. Although she couldn't see him well at night, he still seemed very familiar, Sojourner thought. She wouldn't allow herself to think too much about him though. He was a part of her past. She wanted to focus on her future. The Founders Library loomed large before her, a beacon of hope for African Americans, for more than one hundred and twenty years. Like many before her, education would be her ticket to a better life.

Entering the library, she went to the second floor, passed the circulation desk and entered the high-ceilinged Graduate Library. The old, oak paneled book shelves in this large reading room spoke of the longevity of the library and the institution itself. Sojourner felt secure in this old library. She read the inscription over the fireplace in the center of the reading room. "The noblest mind the best contentment has." Sojourner liked that quote from Edmund Spenser's Faerie Queene. Finding a table, she placed her navy blue canvas tote bag down on it.

Harold Westwood, a graduate engineering student who sat nearby at another table, nodded at her in recognition. She nodded back. Harold had a milky complexion and a light brown, short afro that looked baby soft. He wore a white polo shirt and blue jeans. Coincidentally, they studied in the library at about the same time usually. After organizing her books and papers on a reading table, Sojourner looked at the list of books for which she needed to search.

In the narrow aisles of the old stacks in the upper levels of the library, Sojourner saw that several stacks were devoted to contemporary African writers. It was early in the fall semester, so the library wasn't crowded. She was virtually alone in this section of the library stacks. In spite of the stuffiness and heat of the stacks, Sojourner was enthusiastic about selecting an African writer's work as the topic of her research paper, and she took her time to select a novel.

Since the age of ten, Sojourner had been interested in African history. Her father, David McIntosh, had introduced her to the topic when he provided her with an African history textbook and encouraged her to read through it. She remembered that her father had just been released from prison, and he visited her for her tenth birthday. David walked into the living room of her mother's small apartment. He was a tall, lean, dark complexioned man. He carried a thick textbook in his hand and presented it to Sojourner. As a ten-year-old, Sojourner read through the chapters in this college-level textbook, with some difficulty; however, she would later become fascinated by what she read in the textbook.

As Sojourner's eyes scanned the bookshelves of the library stacks, one book suddenly caught her eye. The author's name was on the spine of the book, "Joseph Kalisa." Sojourner stopped and stared at the name on the spine of the novel; she thought about the name of the author for a moment. Then she realized that she'd found a novel written by an author with the same name as the tall African attorney at the law firm where she worked, Attorney Joseph Kalisa.

Sojourner grabbed the book and read the title on the front cover. It was a novel entitled Blood for the People, and the author's name was, indeed, Joseph Kalisa. She opened the book, which was old and dusty. The novel was published in 1960. That was thirty years ago, Sojourner thought. Sojourner read the brief biography of the author. It stated that the author had been born in 1920, in Rwanda, and had attended a university in France.

The African attorney that Sojourner saw at work didn't look to be much older than she was. Sojourner was twenty-three years old. Attorney Joseph Kalisa appeared to be in his late twenties or early thirties. Sojourner recalled Joseph's fresh woody scent and his reserved mannerisms.

It was 1990, so the author of this novel would be seventy years old, Sojourner thought. She surmised that this author could be Joseph Kalisa's father, or grandfather.

That evening, Sojourner sat in the Founders Library and

read a chapter from *Blood for the People*.

Blood For the People

Rwanda, 1959

Felix remembered the schoolmaster, a tall, thin, good-looking man in his thirties, who was always neatly dressed in a gray suit and white shirt. The suit was always clean and neat. The schoolmaster's wife was a silent young woman with a svelte figure, always prettily dressed, thought Felix. He had heard that she was one of the King's daughters, but Rwanda had no king anymore. Felix's sons, Alphonse and Charles, attended this school, but today, they would be spared the fate of their classmates. Felix's comrades said that they were doing their part for the "Hutu Revolution," and Felix was called upon to participate in the bloody activities.

A schoolhouse surrounded by palm trees was set on fire. The palm trees, luscious in their greenness, were also ablaze in an orange and yellow conflagration. Screaming young students could be heard in the area surrounding the compound of the school. When the fire was initially set, the schoolmaster had attempted to guide his students out of the building. However, he and his students were beaten by the crowd and forced back into the schoolhouse. Screams of agony could be heard from within the building. The schoolmaster was inside with his students, burning alive.

As flames consumed the building, Felix thought to himself. His father and grandfather had worked for an influential Tutsi family. It seemed to Felix that the Muzungu preferred Tutsi because of their long noses and narrow faces. Many marveled at the distinct height that some of the Tutsi reached. No one can deny the beauty and grace of many of their women. Felix remembered that he had fallen in love with a Tutsi girl, who refused to acknowledge his existence. The young woman was a bronze dream, tall, slim, and graceful. She wasn't a member of the royal family, but she sure behaved as though she were. They all think they're royal, Felix thought. The Hutus can be like royalty, too. Hutus are not just servants and lackeys for Tutsis and Muzungu.

Standing with a group of men who stood around the burning school, Felix saw two adolescent boys run out of the school; their clothes aflame, both were screaming wildly. A man next to Felix laughed at the boys as the fire consumed them. Felix swallowed hard. He suppressed his first instinct, to assist the unfortunate boys. Struggling to mask his sympathy for them, he bit his bottom lip. His own little sons were standing next to him. The boys looked shocked. Smoke rose from the burning school, rising into his nostrils. The heat from the flames burned his face. He could do nothing about it. His comrades would call him a traitor if he showed mercy. The mob around him was chanting at the burning the school.

Felix had plans to rise up through the ranks of this murderous rabble and become the town burgomaster. Felix believed that he had to play the part of the revolutionary to attain that goal.

As the library was about to close, Sojourner closed the book, and prepared to go home. She was captivated by *Blood for the People*.

CHAPTER TWO

Sojourner admired Joseph Kalisa from a distance at the law firm. One evening while working late at Livingston & Richards, she saw him reading in the library at 9:00 p.m. She had observed that he'd been reading and taking notes for hours. Joseph was reading some international law books. Sojourner noticed that he often worked with a group of senior attorneys. It seemed to her that Joseph's perceived foreignness was an asset to him. A few other attorneys greeted him and often included him in their conversations. One Canadian attorney, Jacques Bovary, spoke to Joseph in French. Sojourner noted that Joseph was a part of an elite world of international law attorneys.

That evening, while working late in the library, Sojourner overheard Joseph speaking with another attorney. She was in the international law section of the library, shelving books. Joseph was speaking with Peter Shininsky, a middle-aged partner in the firm.

"What languages are spoken in Rwanda?" Peter said.

Peter was a thickly built man in his late forties, with brown hair, streaked with gray.

"French and Kinyarwanda, mostly," Joseph said.

"How long has it been since you've been home?" Peter said.

"The last time I was in Rwanda was fifteen years ago," Joseph said.

"Do you miss it?"

"Sometimes… Rwanda is very beautiful."

"Oh, yeah. What's it like there?"

"Rwanda is very hilly and green. In some areas, it's tropical."

"Where is it in Africa exactly?"

"It's located in East, Central Africa, surrounded by Zaire, Burundi, Uganda, and Tanzania."

A few feet from Joseph and Peter, who both seemed not to notice her presence, Sojourner shelved books silently. Sojourner liked the sound of Josephs low, but soothing voice. His intricate accent was still a challenge to understand though.

"I'm from the Midwest. Sometimes, I miss my hometown," Peter said.

"Which state in the Midwest?" Joseph said.

"Iowa."

"So you're a long way from home, too. It's not always easy being away from your home, right?"

"Yeah … There are a few things that I miss about the Midwest, but basically I like the D.C. area."

"If one has to be away from home for a long time, this is a good place to be, I think. Here there's an international community, and there are always interesting things going on in D.C," Joseph said.

"Right. You cannot get bored here," Peter said.

Joseph glanced at his silver and gold watch.

"Well, I'd better get back to working on this brief."

"Yeah, I think I'll go home now," Peter said, collecting some papers, as he prepared to leave the library.

Peter stood up and started to leave. Then he turned to Joseph, as if he'd forgotten to say something.

"Hey, Joe, by the way, my wife and I are having a get together next Friday. It's sort of a celebration for the new international cases that we've acquired. We'd be glad if you could join us, especially since you're a part of the international team. Besides, my wife enjoys speaking French with you."

"That's kind of Jane. I'd be delighted to attend, Pete. About what time should I arrive?"

"7:00 p.m. would be good, Joe. Do you still remember the location?"

"I remember that it's north of Georgetown, off Wisconsin Avenue …"

"That's close. Actually, we live in Chevy Chase, off of Wisconsin Avenue. I'll have my secretary provide your secretary with an invitation, which contains some directions. My wife made some invitations for the occasion."

"Your wife is an artist, right?" Joseph said.

"Yes. That's right. You know she was in the Peace Corp for ten years, in Senegal. She taught there. Now she's home full time with our children. Invitations and artwork are a hobby for her."

"I admire artists. I'll be there. Thank you."

"Great. I'll see you then."

Peter then turned and left the library.

Sojourner continued with her various duties in the library. She filed loose leaf service publications and checked in periodicals in the library staff work room area. She shelved some books. Many of the books were heavy, and it was an arduous task. As Sojourner shelved the books, she would occasionally glance at Joseph, who was sitting in the library at a distance from her. His presence took the tedium out of her tasks. Sojourner peeked around the stacks, and she saw that Joseph was reading, leaning back in a black leather chair. She saw Joseph sneeze; even his sneeze was sexy, Sojourner thought.

Sojourner wondered if Joseph had taken much notice of her. Sojourner saw that Joseph had glanced in her direction once, but he quickly continued to read. Maybe he was snobby, like the other attorneys in this firm, she thought. He did not greet her, even with a nod. Joseph Kalisa didn't know her, and, apparently, he was taking no interest in her. Joseph seemed to be immersed in the task before him. Sojourner contemplated Joseph, an African man proving that he could survive and thrive in the American corporate world. As she finished shelving the books, she saw Joseph Kalisa leaving the library. It was 10:30 p.m.

Washington, D.C., October 1990

Joseph Kalisa peered into the mirror over the sink in his bathroom, applying a powdered mixture of hair remover to his face. He stood near his sink, in his underpants. After waiting for the shaving cream to work, Joseph took a shower. Joseph stooped as he entered his shower. His height was often a source of inconvenience, Joseph thought, as he showered. A few of the inconveniences that he noted were pants that were too short, fitting comfortably in a normal car or bed, and being singled out for physical or verbal abuse in his homeland because of his Tutsi ethnicity.

When Joseph emerged from the shower, he dried off and patted aftershave on his face. He then smoothed lotion on his face and body. There was the thin nose and lips that made some of his fellow Rwandans hate him, Joseph thought. In America, people took a second look at him, a dark brown man with sharp facial features.

He thought about his cousin, Michel Gasagamba. Michel had joined a rebel army and rose up through the ranks of the army. Michel had achieved a high military rank and was promoted to the second in command post of the army. Joseph had little contact with his cousin since he left Rwanda, but he admired Michel's bravery. Michel was shot down in battle near the Rwandan border two weeks ago. The rebel army engaged in a battle with the Rwandan army near a forest bordering Rwanda. Heavily outnumbered, the rebel troops lost, with numerous casualties. Michel was one of them.

Joseph put on a bright white V-neck undershirt and briefs and slipped his feet into silk dress socks. He dressed in a grey pinstripe suit, a white dress shirt, and a sky blue satin tie. As he adjusted his tie, he thought of the young library assistant who smiled so innocently at him the other day. He guessed that she was no more than twenty years old. She was a black American woman of exceptional beauty and grace, Joseph thought. He admired her height and slender figure. Her round derriere was also tantalizing. It seemed to him that she had the slow natural elegance of a cow, as his uncle would have said. Growing up in Rwanda, Joseph had often heard his male relatives compare a beautiful woman to a cow. Americans would think that very strange, Joseph thought. However, cow metaphors were commonplace in his homeland. The young library assistant dressed in a classic, preppy style that reminded him of his days at Princeton University.

Was it possible that she liked him, Joseph thought? Was it his imagination, or was she peeking at him while he read in the library? Whenever he passed her in the corridors of the firm, she displayed a shy smile for him. The contrast between her flawless dark chocolate skin, and her white teeth was enchanting, he thought. However, he was too busy for pretty faces right now. Joseph snapped out of his reverie about the young woman in the library. He had an important career to develop. Joseph finished adjusting his tie and buttoned his suit jacket. He was ready for the evening dinner party at Attorney Peter Shininski's home in Chevy Chase.

Joseph left his luxury high-rise apartment on Wisconsin Avenue in Washington, D.C. He entered his black Mercedes-Benz CLK500 Coupe and drove north on Wisconsin Avenue to Peter Shininski's home. He arrived at the dinner party and was greeted at the front door by Nancy Shininski. A petite woman in her late thirties, with reddish hair and pale, freckled skin, Nancy wore a white blouse, with a laced collar, and white slacks. She seemed happy to see Joseph, as she greeted him in French. Nancy led him to the formal living room area, where several attorneys had already arrived.

Peter's home was a spacious six-bedroom Georgian, brick single family home. It was decorated with Victorian furniture and expensive antiques. The dinner party was held to celebrate the acquisition of the Cameroon and South African cases. There were a dozen guests, and most of them were attorneys on the international law team, the others were attorneys from the intellectual property, entertainment law, and medical malpractice committees.

Attorney Betsy McShane greeted Joseph when he entered the formal living room. Joseph was glad to see Betsy. She was an international law attorney who had been with Livingston & Richards for fifteen years. At forty-seven years old, she had a husband and two children, ages seven and five. Betsy was a buxom woman with blue eyes and long blonde hair; she had attended Ivy League universities for both her undergraduate and law school education. She had also studied in France for a year at the Sorbonne.

Betsy was an experienced corporate lawyer, and it seemed that she spared no expense to maintain her physical appearance. Joseph knew about her weekly visits to an upscale beauty salon where she would have her hair and nails done. The salon was not too far from where he lived. Her jewelry was obviously purchased at expensive and exclusive jewelry stores. The same habit applied to Betsy's clothes.

Joseph had met Betsy a year earlier, while he worked as a law clerk at the Superior Court of the District of Columbia. Betsy was having lunch with an old school friend who worked as public defender with the Superior Court. Betsy's friend introduced her to Joseph. Betsy found Joseph very attractive, and she responded with interest. She told him that she loved the elegant way he spoke French.

During a subsequent lunch date, Betsy alerted Joseph to an opening on the international law committee at Livingston & Richards. Joseph applied and was called in for a series of interviews with the firm. During the interview process, Betsy praised Joseph for his excellent grades as an undergraduate and in law school. When Joseph was hired as an international law attorney at Livingston & Richards, Betsy was designated as Joseph's de facto mentor. Unlike his experiences in past jobs, this mentor actually wanted to help him.

While serving as a law clerk to a judge in the Civil Law section of the Superior Court, Joseph was assigned a mentor. The mentor was Andrew Newman, a senior law clerk. Andrew simply introduced Joseph to the staff in the judge's office and showed him where the cafeteria was. That was the extent of his mentoring duties. Joseph was left on his own to navigate the scope of his duties and to figure out where everything in the office and the entire building was. Luckily, he was able to procure information from the ladies in the office and the building. Joseph realized that he could normally get the information he required by displaying a generous smile to a receptive female face.

When the judge asked Andrew if he had provided a thorough orientation for Joseph, Andrew heartily assured the judge that he had done so. Joseph, who sat quietly at his desk at the time, never complained that Andrew was, in fact, useless to him. Instead, Joseph worked twelve hours each day, six days a week, to familiarize himself with all of his duties. It had been that way in most of his jobs. Joseph knew that he had to work harder, put in longer hours and be the epitome of discretion and charm in order to be accepted by his professional colleagues. This was necessary for his success as an attorney.

During Peter's party, Betsy McShane sat by Joseph's side for the entire evening. She wore a pink Carolina Herrara two-piece, wool suit. Her neatly trimmed blonde hair flowed beyond her shoulders. Since she'd studied at the Sorbonne for graduate studies, Betsy was fluent in French. Betsy, Jane, and Joseph conversed in French during the party. The Canadian attorney, Jacques Bovary, also participated in the conversation in French. Sitting in the formal parlor of Peter and Nancy Shininski, they discussed the cases at Livingston & Richards, as well as current events.

After the dinner party, Joseph drove home to his apartment in D.C. Joseph changed into his pajamas and prepared for a good night's sleep. He then received a call from Betsy McShane. Betsy was crying.

"Joseph, I'm sorry to call so late, but I need to speak with you," Betsy said.

"What's wrong, Betsy? Are you all right?"

"Not really. It's my husband. Damn bastard! He's with his mistress, again. I can't take this anymore, Joe. I hate him."

"No, no. Betsy, don't say that. He's your husband, and the father of your children."

"He's spending my money on his mistress. The damn bastard isn't making any money in his own career. I mean, he's a musician, and not a rich one, either. I'm falling apart, Joe."

"You're going to be all right, Betsy. You have a good life. You are an experienced lawyer, and you have two beautiful children."

"Joe. Can I come over, tonight?"

Joseph was silent at first. He sat on his bed rubbing his forehead. Then he spoke.

"All right, Betsy, come on over."

The following day, during the international law committee meeting, Betsy recommended Joseph Kalisa to be the main contact for the Cameroon case. He sat there in the conference room with all the other international committee members. He knew that this was like a promotion for him, since he had been with the law firm for only two months.

CHAPTER THREE

On a sunny and unseasonably warm day in late October of 1990, Sojourner Brown was eating alone on the patio adjacent to the law firm's cafeteria, when Joseph walked by and sat down at a nearby table. He was a splendid sight on a sunny day, Sojourner thought. Joseph started to eat his lunch. He wore a tailored, navy pinstripe suit and a silk yellow tie. Sojourner gathered her courage; then she gazed at Joseph intently. Joseph was reading The Washington Post and eating a pasta dish. He continued to eat his lunch, apparently unaware of Sojourner. Sojourner was ready to give up trying to get Joseph's attention. Then, to Sojourner's surprise, Joseph put his newspaper down and looked in her direction. He greeted her with a nod. She nodded in return and finished her garden salad and orange juice. After finishing her lunch, Sojourner stood up and picked up her cafeteria tray. She disposed of her lunch in a nearby receptacle and started to walk toward the patio exit. Sojourner then stopped suddenly near Joseph's table, where Joseph sat alone, finishing his lunch.

"It's a beautiful day, isn't it?" Sojourner said.

"Yes. Gorgeous," Joseph said, gazing at Sojourner.

His face was smooth and clean-shaven, with skin the color of an expensive dark, heavy wood.

Sojourner thought about her clothes. She wore a royal blue oxford shirt, a black skirt that fell well below her knees, off black stockings, and black, low-heeled pumps. She remembered that Rose had often said that she wore too much black. She smiled, trying to maintain a professional demeanor.

"My name is Sojourner Brown, and I'm a circulations assistant in the library."

Sojourner knew that Joseph was aware that she worked in the library. She had helped him check out books several weeks earlier, and she often walked through the library shelving and searching for books. However, she wanted to refresh his memory.

"Right, I've seen you there many times. It's a pleasure to meet you, Sojourner. That's a beautiful name. I'm Joseph Kalisa, but please call me Joe."

Sojourner thought Joseph's smile was charming; his teeth

were straight. She noticed that Joseph's accent was thick and intricate, but his voice was still soothing.

"Thank you. The name was my father's idea. He wanted to name me Sojourner Truth Brown, but my Mother convinced him to settle for Sojourner Ann Brown."

"Sojourner Truth …," Joseph said, thoughtfully. "…Oh, yes. She was a 19th century black American abolitionist."

Sojourner struggled to understand Joseph's words, but his face made the struggle well worth the effort.

"Yes. That's right," Sojourner said.

She was impressed. Feeling less nervous, she decided to continue.

"Can I ask you a question, Joseph?"

"Of course you can, Sojourner. Please sit down."

Joseph gestured to a chair at his table.

Sojourner complied. She felt a little self-conscious. She knew that, as an attorney, it would not be socially advantageous for him to sit and discuss with library staff. Most of the attorney's at the firm displayed a snobbish demeanor toward the administrative staff. They preferred to speak with only other attorneys. However, Joseph had offered her a seat at his table. He had an urbane manner.

"I was wondering…" Sojourner said.

She stopped speaking because she felt nervous.

"Yes? What were you wondering?" Joseph said.

He sat back in his chair and stared into Sojourner's eyes. Sojourner looked into his dark eyes and was mesmerized by the intensity of his gaze. She redirected her gaze to her hands and continued to speak.

"Well, I'm reading a novel for a class, and the author's name is the same as yours. The novel was published in 1960 …," Sojourner said.

"…My father did write a novel. It's entitled Blood for the People," Joseph said.

"Yes. That's the one," Sojourner said.

She felt excited, but she tried not to appear too excited.

"I'm writing a research paper on it," Sojourner said.

"Where did you find the book?"

"I found it at Howard University, while doing some research for one of my classes."

"What year are you at Howard University?"

"I'm a graduate student there."

"What degree are you working on?"

"I'm working on my Masters."

"Very good," Joseph said, nodding.

Sojourner sat there, feeling like Joseph was mentally sizing her up.

"Would it be possible for me to interview you as one of my references, for my research paper?" Sojourner said.

"Okay… Yes. I would be glad to help you, Sojourner."

"Thank you, Joseph. That's so nice of you. My paper is due next month."

"Then you can call me so we can set up a time to talk, all right?" Joseph said.

He reached into the front inner section of his suit jacket and deftly pulled out his business card. Joseph then offered Sojourner his business card, gracefully held between two long, brown fingers. She noticed his oval cuff links, with an inscription of "JK" on them. His gold and silver watch looked expensive.

"Yes. Thank you. I'll do that," Sojourner said.

Sojourner extended her hand and reached for the card. At that moment, she regretted not splurging on manicures, as her roommate, Rose, often did. Sojourner didn't like very long and highly decorated fingernails, but she supposed she was due for at least more than one clear coat of nail polish.

Sojourner telephoned Joseph a week later.

Joseph's secretary answered.

"Attorney Kalisa's Office, may I help you?"

"Yes, may I speak to Mr. Kalisa, please?" Sojourner said.

"Who should I say is calling?" the secretary said.

"Sojourner Brown."

"Oh … Just a minute. I'll see if Attorney Kalisa is available."

Sojourner surmised from the secretary's tone that the secretary was surprised that Sojourner was calling to speak with Joseph. The secretary may have recognized Sojourner's name as someone who worked in the library.

The secretary returned to the phone and said that she would transfer Sojourner to Attorney Kalisa. Sojourner sensed that the secretary was not pleased.

"Hello, this is Joseph Kalisa."

"Hi Joseph. This is Sojourner. How are you?"

"Hello Sojourner! I'm fine."

"Is there a time, within the next week or so, when we can discuss *Blood for the People*?"

"This weekend, Saturday, would be good for me. We could talk over dinner. Would that be all right, Sojourner?"

"Uh … yeah … okay," Sojourner said. She was surprised.

"There's an excellent restaurant near Georgetown University. The name of the restaurant is Marie Antoinette," Joseph said. His voice was confident and professional.

"That's just fine, Joseph."

"I can pick you up at 7:00 p.m., Sojourner?"

"Yes, that works."

"Can I get your address?"

"It's 2719 Georgia Avenue, apartment 302, in Northwest."

"I'd like to call you, in case I need directions. I'll need your number, too."

Sojourner gave Joseph her phone number and said goodbye. She suddenly felt daunted. This handsome lawyer was showing that he was interested in her. She was flattered, but she was nervous, too.

It was Saturday evening, and Sojourner was dressing in her bedroom.

"Oh, my God. Is that what you're wearing?" Rose said.

Rose had just entered Sojourner's bedroom.

"We're just going to talk about a novel, Rose," Sojourner said.

"Girl, please," Rose said. "You're going to a very expensive restaurant with a good-looking, corporate attorney, whom you like, so it's a date. Okay?" Rose said.

Sojourner had told Rose about Joseph Kalisa, the day she introduced herself to him. She could tell that Rose was curious about her date.

"Okay. So, what's wrong with my suit?" Sojourner said, glancing down at her navy blue suit and pink blouse.

"This is not a job interview, Soj. You look like you are going to your first day at work, teaching college. Let me find something for you to wear, girl."

Then Rose disappeared into her bedroom and re-appeared ten minutes later.

"Now, this is what you should wear, one of these outfits," Rose announced.

Rose had two outfits, each one hanging on a hanger. One outfit consisted of a brown suede mini-skirt and a black cashmere V-neck pullover sweater, and the other was a dark, grape-colored, silk-jersey wrap dress.

"Thanks. Are you sure you don't mind?" Sojourner said.

"Soj, you let me borrow your stuff all the time, so we're cool."

Sojourner knew this was true. Rose had no problem asking to borrow clothes or money. As a matter of fact, Rose was almost always late with her share of the rent, Sojourner thought.

Sojourner selected the grape-colored dress, and Rose handed the dress to Sojourner who stared at it admiringly. The dress wasn't the type she would normally wear.

"It's by Dian von Furstenberg. This will look better on you, since you're skinny," Rose said.

"Not that skinny, I hope," Sojourner said.

"No. Not really. You have good figure, anyway," Rose said.

Sojourner changed her clothes.

Since Rose was a voluptuous young woman, the fit of the

dress was loose on Sojourner. Luckily, it was wrap dress, so Sojourner simply tied the belt more tightly. The dress that was too long for Rose was just right for Sojourner. She wore some silky textured, sheer panty hose, and a pair of high-heeled shoes.

Sojourner brushed her hair. She'd just had a wash and set at the hair salon. Her relaxed hair was loosely curled in a pageboy. She rubbed a small bit of fragrant hair oil in her palms and gently smoothed it over her hair. She applied some raisin-colored lipstick.

While growing up, Sojourner had refused to believe the message that she believed the world sent her daily, that as a dark-skinned black woman she wasn't the standard of beauty. Her father had told her that he thought her complexion was pretty. According to her father, she was like an African princess from long ago, when Africa was great. When Sojourner turned on the TV, she received a different message. She deduced that the world thought otherwise.

Like so many girls, Sojourner's imagination was filled with images of Caucasian women with rosy cheeks and long blonde, or brunette, hair flipping and tossing silky tresses blithely on TV commercials, sitcoms, and movies. Their silky strands of hair billowed in the air. Hair was often a source of longing and envy for Sojourner, as well as other black women whom she knew. Sojourner had to almost burn her scalp with relaxers to simulate this texture, transforming her own tightly curled hair texture.

CHAPTER FOUR

Joseph arrived five minutes early to pick Sojourner up. As Sojourner looked out the window of their small living room, she saw Joseph parking his car in front of their apartment building on Georgia Avenue. Sojourner didn't know that the person in the car was Joseph, until she saw his lean figure emerge from the black Mercedes-Benz. The car was fabulous, but Sojourner had prided herself on not being overly impressed with material luxuries. She wasn't going to start now.

"Damn! Now that is a fly car, girl!" Rose said.

Rose was also peeking through the curtain of their living room window.

"Yes. It's nice," Sojourner said, trying to contain her growing euphoria and nervous tension.

"Hmmm … He's very tall," Rose said, still staring out the window.

Sojourner knew that the lobby door of her apartment building would be locked, so she started to go downstairs to meet Joseph. She looked in the living room closet to get her coat.

"That dress looks good on you, Soj," Rose said.

"Thank you, Rose."

"You should be a model, Soj. You have the body for it."

"Really? I never thought about doing that," Sojourner said, putting on her trench coat. "You do some modeling, Right Rose?

"Yeah. I do some modeling here and there, but I'm too plump for high fashion."

"Okay. See you later," Sojourner said.

"Take that coat off, girl. Let him see you in that dress first," Rose said.

Sojourner sighed.

"Bring him up here, and let's have a look," Rose said.

"This is not a TV show," Sojourner said.

"Soj, it just seems like the polite thing to do."

Sojourner realized that bringing Joseph up to their apartment would be a more polite protocol.

"Well…okay," Sojourner said.

Sojourner descended the stairs slowly.

Joseph was even more handsome outside of the confines of the law firm. Joseph looked up at her through the glass lobby door. He smiled broadly, as Sojourner descended the staircase.

Sojourner opened the lobby door.

"Hi, Joseph! It's so good to see you again. I hope you didn't have trouble finding this place," Sojourner said.

"No, I didn't," Joseph said.

Joseph wore a tan suit, with a bronze, silk shirt. He smiled pleasantly. The scent of his cologne was delicate; it perfumed the air around him. Sojourner liked the fragrance. Joseph's clothes were neat and perfectly fitted on his long, lean body, and his face was baby smooth. They stood close to each other in the small lobby of the apartment building.

"Have you ever been in this neighborhood before?" Sojourner said.

"Yes. I have a cousin who's a resident intern at Howard University Hospital," Joseph said.

Sojourner nodded, staring up at him, virtually mesmerized.

"You look radiant," Joseph said. "That's a lovely dress."

"Oh, thank you. And I must say you are looking quite dashing yourself."

Joseph blushed.

"I'll get my coat," Sojourner said.

She gestured with her hand for Joseph to follow her up the stairs. Rose was standing near the entrance of the apartment. She devoured Joseph with her eyes. She seemed to be waiting to be introduced.

"Joseph, this is Rose. She's my roommate."

"Hi, Joseph. It's nice meeting you," Rose said, smiling up at him, displaying a wide toothy smile.

Rose, who wore blue jeans and a T-shirt, had put on a bit of pale pink lipstick in the few minutes that Sojourner had been out of the apartment.

"Hi Rose, pleased to meet you," Joseph said.

Sojourner picked up her coat, and Joseph gingerly took the coat from her hands and began to assist her with putting the coat on. Sojourner was amazed by Joseph's gentlemanly gesture, and Rose looked on in approval. Joseph opened the door for her, as they exited the apartment. Together, Joseph and Sojourner descended the hall stairs and exited the apartment building.

It was after 7:00 p.m. The night air was cold, so Sojourner buttoned her coat, as she followed Joseph to his car. She was not sure if she trembled from the cold, or the nervousness that she felt inside.

Peeking through their living room curtains, Rose watched as Joseph and Sojourner walked toward the sleek black, Mercedes. Rose often wondered what the deal with Sojourner was. As far as Rose knew, Sojourner had a limited social life, consisting of a small circle of graduate school associates with whom she occasionally studied. There was once a meeting with a handful of her writer friends, who also were graduate students at Howard. During the meetings, they discussed what seemed to be boring topics to Rose, like blank verse, iambic pentameter, and couplets.

Rose had invited Sojourner out a few times, but Sojourner would almost always politely decline. Sojourner had accepted an invitation to go out with Rose once to celebrate Rose's birthday. Rose and a girlfriend of hers, Janelle, were going to a local nightclub. Rose asked Sojourner to join them, and Sojourner went. Rose remembered how difficult it was to convince Sojourner to wear her short black dress. Rose and Janelle finally succeeded in convincing Sojourner to wear the dress, and Sojourner looked ready for the high fashion runways of Europe. Rose thought that Sojourner had the potential to be quite stunning. Nevertheless, Sojourner wore the dress with all the sexiness of a nun.

Sojourner had accompanied Rose and Janelle out to a nightclub, and she was constantly being approached by men at the nightclub. Rose and Janelle watched as Sojourner turned down one offer after another. The offers were dance requests, or offers from men to purchase a drink for her.

Some of the guys in that particular night club were aggressive, and even tacky in their approach. They might just stand next to a woman and start dancing, hoping she would join in. Sojourner was visibly horrified when this happened. Rose and her friend chuckled at Sojourner's reaction. However, there were a few good looking and polished men who also approached Sojourner politely, but they were turned down, too. Finally, Rose spoke.

"What was wrong with that one, Soj?" Rose said. "He was fine, well dressed, and he seemed nice."

"A little to fast for me, Rose," Sojourner's said. "He was touching on my hand, and I don't even know him."

"Hold up. I saw him, and he just tapped your hand, just barely," Janelle said. "Damn, I wanted to bust in and say 'I'll dance with you.'"

Rose remembered what Janelle had said about Sojourner. They were sitting in the living room of Janelle's apartment in Southeast.

"Your roommate…what's her name again?" Janelle said.

"Sojourner," Rose said.

"What kind of name is that? …One of them stuck up names I bet," Janelle said.

"Come on, Janelle. Haven't you heard of Sojourner Truth?" Rose said.

"What? Her Mama named her after Sojourner Truth," Janelle said. She laughed.

"Yep," Rose said.

"Damn…so it's like they named her Harriet Tubman or Rosa Parks," Janelle said.

"She's into black history. She writes about it in her book. The girl wrote a book," Rose said.

"Oh, well, excuse me," Janelle said.

"I call her Soj, anyway, not Sojourner," Rose said.

"She's stuck up, child," Janelle said. "Act like she thinks she better than us."

"She's okay. I mean…she's a bookworm," Rose said.

"…She acts white anyway. Her tall, skinny self, walking around like she's white…black as she is," Janelle said.

"She's cool with me. When I'm late with my rent, she doesn't give me grief," Rose said. "And I'm late a lot."

Rose had lived with Sojourner for thirteen months, and Sojourner had never brought home a date during that time. This seemed odd, since Sojourner was pretty and lady-like. Rose felt a little self-conscious when she would invite her boyfriend over, especially if the boyfriend would occasionally spend the night. It was awkward, making love to her boyfriend with Sojourner in the adjacent bedroom, alone. At one point, she wondered if Sojourner preferred women, but there was no sign of a female paramour either.

It seemed that Sojourner went from no romance at all to a date with Prince Charming, from famine to feast. Rose was skeptical when Sojourner told her Joseph was from Africa. Rose, like most African Americans, had limited interaction with people from Africa. There was an ocean of ignorance between the two groups, who were genetically and historically closely linked. Once an average looking African man had approached her in a night club, and Rose thought that he seemed aggressive and arrogant. He told her she was beautiful less than two minutes after he first saw her and invited her go to another nightclub with him. Rose felt insulted. What did he take her for? What nerve! Then there was the African taxi driver, who apparently was not in the habit of using deodorant, but had the audacity to ask her if she was married.

Joseph had changed her view of African men, in a single ten minute appearance, Rose thought. She realized that African men were just as varied in looks, attitude, and background as men from anywhere else. From what she could tell, Joseph was an aloof man, proud, and a little snobby. Rose got the impression that being flirtatious was beneath Joseph. He'd come to take Sojourner out, and he was focusing his attention on her. He was definitely good-looking, Rose thought. He had smooth, deep brown skin. Also, not many black people had pointy noses like that.

Furthermore, Rose couldn't get over the broad smile on Sojourner's face that evening. She'd never seen Sojourner so vibrant and happy. When Sojourner stood close to Joseph, her wide brown eyes became radiant. Her full lips formed a wide, joyful smile. For Sojourner, Joseph was like a special battery that she'd needed for so long, a cure for a terminal illness, or a panacea for her private sadness. Rose was amazed at what she'd just witnessed, her roommate being brought to life.

CHAPTER FIVE

Joseph opened the door of his car for Sojourner to get into the passenger side of the front seat, and she entered the black Mercedes with studied grace. He waited for her to sit down comfortably; then he closed the door for her. Sojourner was impressed with the good manners that Joseph was displaying. This was how she always wanted to be treated by the man of her dreams. The interior of the car contained the same enticing fragrance as Joseph's cologne. She found the smooth, grey leather seats were comfortable. Joseph entered the driver's seat and closed the door.

"It's convenient that you live so close to campus," Joseph said.

"Yes, it is. That's the main advantage for me," Sojourner said.

"Do you like being a graduate student?"

"Oh, yes. I've always liked the campus environment of intellectual creativity."

"I feel the same way. I enjoyed undergraduate and law school," Joseph said, as he drove south down Georgia Avenue.

As Joseph drove to the restaurant, Sojourner thought about his father's novel. Although she was looking forward to discussing the novel with Joseph, she felt a little nervous. The novel included the recounting of a bloody massacre in Rwanda in 1959.

It was the story of a rift between two ethnic groups in Rwanda, the Hutu and the Tutsi. This split was exacerbated by a colonial system that used the physical differences (one group had a tendency to be a little taller, with thinner noses) between the two groups to further divide them politically. The story was about a respected Tutsi schoolmaster, who is murdered, after the independence of Rwanda.

As she and Joseph entered the Marie Antoinette restaurant, Sojourner felt like she was floating in a dream. It was an elegant restaurant with fresh flower arrangements on the tables, and delicious aromas wafting in the air. The tables were covered with white linen tablecloths, and there were crystal vases with Calla Lilies in them. A painting of Marie Antoinette hung over the mantel of a fireplace, in which a flame blazed and danced. The Queen's beautiful turquoise blue eyes seemed to follow Sojourner as she walked through the restaurant. The dark, hardwood floors were shiny and smooth, and Sojourner could hear the rhythmic sound of their footsteps as they approached their table. She focused on moving gracefully, as she and Joseph followed the hostess to their table.

When they reached their table, Joseph pulled the Louis XVI style chair out for Sojourner to sit down, and he helped her to remove her coat.

After they were seated, a waitress, dressed neatly in a white blouse and cream-colored wool skirt came to take their order. The waitress was a young woman with long, strawberry blonde hair.

"Good Evening, welcome to Marie Antoinette. My name is Nicole. I will be your waitress this evening," the waitress said, smiling cheerfully at Joseph.

"Good Evening," Joseph said. Sojourner said the same.

The waitress gave them the menus, one for the main entrees and one for the beverages. She announced the special of the day.

"The special today is Boeuf bourguignon léger aux légumes. We also have a Potage aux Champignons."

Sojourner and Joseph glanced through the menus.

"Would you like to order anything to drink now? This is our list of beverages and our wine list," Nicole said.

Then she bent over slightly and started showing Joseph the list of wines. Joseph quickly glanced at the list.

Sojourner felt a small wave of jealousy, and she quickly reminded herself to smile and behave maturely.

"Sojourner, please look at the wine list. Is there any wine you would like?" Joseph said, offering the wine list to Sojourner.

Joseph focused his attention on Sojourner. His attention pleased Sojourner, and she smiled triumphantly.

"I think I'll have something sweet. Can you recommend a sweet wine?" Sojourner said to the waitress.

"Oh, yes. White Zinfandel is sweet," Nicole said, smiling at Sojourner faintly.

To Sojourner, it seemed that the waitress's smile for her was different, less welcoming.

"I would suggest that," Nicole said.

"Okay. I'll take that," Sojourner said.

"Sure," the waitress said, flashing a quick, tense smile.

"And what would you like to drink?" Nicole said to Joseph.

The one thousand watt smile reappeared on Nicole's face, as she looked at Joseph.

"I'm interested in your French wines, red wine specifically," Joseph said.

"Oh, yes," Nicole said, searching the wine list. "Here is the list of our vin rouge." Nicole showed the list to Joseph.

He perused the list.

"I'll have the Pinot Noir Louis XVI," Joseph said.

"Okay. Very good. I'll be back with your wine in a

moment."

The waitress collected their wine lists and continued on to wait on another table. Sojourner was glad.

"Are you okay?" Joseph said.

"Yes. Why?" Sojourner said.

"You're rubbing your hands together. Are you cold?" Joseph said, touching her hand lightly.

"I'm fine. This restaurant is very elegant."

"I'm glad you like it... So, how do you like attending Howard University?"

"I have a healthy respect for Howard. I received my Bachelors of Arts from Howard, and I'm there pursuing my Masters."

"It's a good school," Joseph said. "Many famous black Americans have passed through Howard."

"Thank you. It has a long history. I'm glad I selected it, or that I was selected to attend."

"Is this your first year in graduate school?" Joseph said.

"I'm in my second year in graduate school. I have an assistantship."

"It's good that you have an assistantship."

"Yes. I feel fortunate to have some financial support, for my graduate studies."

"And what are you studying?"

"Comparative Literature," Sojourner said. "I'm completing some of my general requirements this semester."

"That's interesting," Joseph said. "So, do you plan to teach or write?"

"Actually, I do write. I've published a book of poetry. I would really love to do more writing, but right now I'm focusing on completing my Masters degree."

"You've published a book of poetry?" Joseph said.

"Yes. It's a small book, with twenty poems and two short stories."

"That's wonderful."

"Thank you."

Sojourner couldn't help but notice Joseph's smooth, brown lips. They might as well have been Godiva chocolates, as she was convinced of their deliciousness.

"I read in the firm's newsletter that you graduated from Princeton. And, that you received your J.D. from Georgetown Law," Sojourner said.

"Yes," Joseph said, smiling, modestly. "That's right."

"That's fabulous. Your parents must be very proud," Sojourner said.

Sojourner noticed that Joseph's smile waned for a moment, and he was silent. Then he spoke.

"I love to learn. Just like you," Joseph said. "What is the topic of your Thesis?"

"It's a comparison of the themes of several poets of the Colonial American period, Phyllis Wheatley, Jupiter Hammond, and Ann Bradstreet, to name a few," Sojourner said.

The waitress returned with their drinks. Then she brought them a basket filled with slices of a hot baguette, with a small silver tray of butter. Again, she returned to take their order. Joseph ordered vegetable chowder with a salad, and Sojourner ordered Saumon au Riesling à la ciboulette, and a salad.

"Do you come here often, Joseph?"

"No. I came here once, with some other attorneys, and a client."

"That painting of Marie Antoinette is exquisite. Isn't it?" Sojourner said.

"Yes. It's an exceptional print," Joseph said.

"She lived during a dangerous time in French history, and I read that she wasn't as selfish and

uncaring as she was characterized to be. She was a strong, creative woman and mother who loved beauty," Sojourner said.

"Economics and politics can breed violence," Joseph said.

"Many people were starving in France at that time."

Sojourner nodded.

"Marie Antoinette and her husband were executed by the revolutionaries, both beheaded," Sojourner said.

The waitress brought the meals, and they started to eat.

"How is your soup?" Sojourner said.

"It's all right," Joseph said.

"Is that all you're eating?" Sojourner said.

"Yes. And salad, too. Actually, the soup is very thick," Joseph said.

"Soup and salad is a healthy combination," Sojourner said.

Joseph nodded.

"Are you a vegetarian?" Sojourner said.

"I suppose I fall into that category, sometimes," Joseph said.

"Oh that's great. I'm slowly trying to go in that direction with my diet. It's hard to give meat up completely," Sojourner said. "Did you have difficulty giving up meat?"

"I've not had to give it up. I grew up that way, for the most part. A long time ago, it used to be the traditional diet of many Tutsi people in Rwanda, but ninety percent eat meat these days. My mother had insisted that I not eat meat though. Sometimes... I do anyway."

"How interesting. Actually, something like that was mentioned in Blood For the People," Sojourner said.

They finished their meal. Sojourner wanted to change the topic. She decided that it was time to ask questions about the novel.

"The novel *Blood for the People* really gives me a sense of what life was like for most people in Rwanda in the 50s and 60s," Sojourner said.

Joseph nodded his head slowly.

"Well... the novel says much about the legacy of colonialism in Africa, Rwanda specifically," Joseph said.

"I was amazed at the extent of the violence. The two groups,

Hutu and Tutsi, shared the same language and land. I read that they'd coexisted for centuries, occasionally intermarrying. So why did this sudden explosion of hatred and violence occur? What is your opinion about the deep-rooted causes of the violence?"

"Conflict in Africa, as on most continents, is age old. It preceded the coming of the Europeans. However, the Atlantic Slave Trade and the subsequent colonization of Africa introduced a new philosophical dynamic in Africa as a whole," Joseph said.

"What kind of philosophical dynamic?" Sojourner said.

"The idea of racially categorizing people, as well as the total dehumanization of a people, was devastating. Africans were routinely dehumanized during colonization. There are many things about colonialism that most people don't know. There was mass forced labor, and even torture... many atrocities, especially in the Great Lakes Region of Africa," Joseph said calmly.

"Yes. There's a lot of ignorance and misinformation about colonialism," Sojourner said. "Some people think it's all about white people going on safaris and having adventures in a beautiful setting. But the racial categorization of people was definitely destructive."

"This concept was emulated by Africans after independence," Joseph said.

"Yes, those are my thoughts exactly. Maybe that explains the extent of the cruelty, that the Rwandans could be so cruel to each other?"

"Well..." Joseph said, thoughtfully. "Some minor physical traits between the two dominant groups in Rwanda were used by the colonialists. It is the old divide and conquer method," Joseph said.

"Yes. That worked so well in Africa," Sojourner said.

"Right, but European colonizers did more than just divide. They encouraged a deep hatred, based on these physical differences, such as height, body type, and facial features. It was a new kind of intra-racial racism within Rwanda," Joseph said.

"Oh, that's sick," Sojourner said. "Both groups are African people. All were being oppressed."

"Yes. That's true," Joseph said, drinking his wine elegantly.

"What do you think of the protagonist in the novel?" Sojourner asked.

"The protagonist of the novel was a Rwandan man, who was educated in France. He had lived in Europe for years before going back to Rwanda, so he could see beyond the pettiness of Hutu and Tutsi divisions. He had Pan-African ideas. The colonial masters didn't like him, and neither did his fellow Rwandans, specifically Hutu people," Joseph said.

"Right... There is a scene in the novel when the schoolmaster tells his wife about his experiences in Europe," Sojourner said. "The schoolmaster's wife is afraid that their Hutu neighbors are going to kill them, and she wants to go to France. But the husband doesn't want to go to France. He said that he didn't feel comfortable there as an African man. Unlike many Africans, he saw himself as an African man, not just a Rwandan, or a Tutsi," Sojourner said.

"That's an important theme in the novel. The inability of Rwandans to see beyond ethnic divisions, to see that much of the exploitation was done by the European colonizers," Joseph said.

"I agree," Sojourner said.

Joseph finished his wine.

"Can I ask if you can make any comment on your father's personality? I mean, the novel is complex, so I wondered about the author's personality, and as his son, I suppose you might have some comment," Sojourner said.

"You ask about my father?" Joseph said.

"Yes. The novel is so poignant that I wondered about the author's personality, in relation to this novel, of course," Sojourner said.

Joseph seemed to be thinking about her question. He was

silent momentarily. His countenance changed from confident and pleasant to reserved and guarded.

"I'm not prepared to discuss at length about my father, at the moment," Joseph said.

"Oh… Okay," Sojourner said.

Sojourner hoped that she didn't offend Joseph, but she also was a little disappointed. She stared at Joseph's handsome face. He looked back at her. He wasn't smiling anymore.

"My father died in the 70s… It's not easy for me to discuss about him," Joseph said.

He looked uncomfortable, but Sojourner continued.

"Oh, I'm sorry, Joseph. Was he ill?"

She knew that she risked making this lovely man angry with her, but curiosity pushed her on.

"My father was murdered," Joseph said, sighing a little. "There was another massacre in 1973, after the one you read about in the novel. My father, who was a university professor, was killed."

"My God, Joseph, that's horrible… My mother died when I was a teenager," Sojourner said, staring at the Calla Lilly in the clear crystal vase in the center of the table.

"Really? Then I, too, am sorry to hear that," Joseph said.

"Thank you, Joseph."

"Was she ill?" Joseph said.

Sojourner licked her lips as he stared into his eyes. It was Joseph's turn to hear her confession, but she was too ashamed to tell him the truth.

"My mother died of cancer," Sojourner said.

Joseph had a solemn expression on his face, the color of dark chocolate.

There was a long moment of silence between them. Then Joseph spoke.

"Where are you from Sojourner? You don't seem like you're from this area."

"No, I'm not from D.C. I'm from Rockwell, New Jersey," Sojourner said.

"Is that near Atlantic City?"

"Yes, it is. It's about fifteen minutes, by car, from Atlantic City," Sojourner said.

"Have you been to the casinos?"

"Oh, yes. I've been there, but only a few times. I don't gamble a lot."

"It would be interesting to visit there, I suppose," Joseph said, smiling again.

Sojourner said nothing.

"Please order dessert, Sojourner," Joseph said. "Let me call the waitress to bring the dessert menu."

"No, thank you, Joseph," Sojourner said.

Joseph looked disappointed.

"The meal was very delicious, and I'm so full," Sojourner said.

Sojourner couldn't bear the disappointed look on Joseph's face. She did enjoy the meal, and most of all, Joseph's company. Sojourner knew that Joseph had a very good reason for not wanting to discuss his father.

Joseph asked for the check, and paid for the meal.

As they left the restaurant, Joseph said that he would like to take her to a nearby nightclub. However, Sojourner said that she wanted to go home, so he drove her home. He insisted on walking Sojourner to her apartment door.

"Sojourner, I've enjoyed your company. You're a lovely young lady," Joseph said.

"I've enjoyed this evening, too, Joseph. Thank you."

Sojourner and Joseph stood facing each other in the apartment hallway.

"I think that it's wonderful that you've read my father's novel. It's been a long time since anyone has mentioned his writings to me. Very few people in the U.S., or anywhere, have ever heard of my father's book, only scholars of francophone noir literature. I didn't know there were any English translations of the novel," Joseph said.

"Then I was lucky to find one," Sojourner said. She looked

up into his eyes, and she quickly looked away. She was afraid of her feelings.

Joseph held out his hand and looked into Sojourner's eyes. Sojourner felt like she was falling into a trance. Before she realized it, she placed her hand in his. Joseph held her hand; his hand was very smooth. Sojourner felt a warm sense of physical pleasure flow through her entire body, as she stood there in the corridor of the apartment building with Joseph.

"Sojourner, I'd like very much to kiss you good night. May I?"

Sojourner thought about it for a moment, but she didn't answer.

"Only on the cheek, Sojourner," Joseph whispered, smiling playfully. Sojourner assented with a nod.

Joseph planted a gentle kiss on Sojourner's cheek, right under her eye. Just like she had imagined, his lips were smooth and his breath was fragrant, like peppermints.

CHAPTER SIX

One late afternoon a few days later, Sojourner arrived home, after going grocery shopping. The familiar heavy-set, homeless man sat on her steps.

"Ann," the man said.

"I don't know you. Don't call me," Sojourner said.

"I'm David, baby, your…" the man said.

"Leave me alone, David," Sojourner said, quickly walking up the concrete steps outside of her apartment building.

"I'm your father, Ann," the man said.

"What?" Sojourner said.

Sojourner was just about to enter the apartment building lobby. When she heard this new information, she turned around and stared at the man for a moment. Yes… It was him, her father. Those wide dark eyes used to be surrounded with long eyelashes. She couldn't believe how corpulent he was. The last time she saw him, he was a lean man. Grimy and old, his clothes smelled badly. Fourteen years ago, David McIntosh was a handsome, clean shaven ebony man.

"How did you get here, Davey?" Sojourner said to her father.

As a child, Sojourner had routinely called her father Davey, which was his nickname.

"My Mom told me you were still in D.C… I wanted to see you, Ann" her father said.

"Where are you staying?" Sojourner said.

"At the Angel of Mercy shelter," her father said.

"I have a roommate, and I don't have room for you, Davey."

She held her grocery bags and didn't move any closer to her father.

"I understand, baby," David said. "Come and see me at the shelter though."

"Okay," Sojourner said. "Where is it?"

"It's on 14th and S Street," David said.

Sojourner nodded and stared at her father…stunned by his transformation. It had been fourteen years since she'd seen him.

"Ann… You have a few dollars?" her father said.

Sojourner reached into the pocket of her coat. She pulled out a twenty dollar bill, and offered it to her father. Then she offered him the grocery bags that she held. He accepted the money and the bags of groceries with a sad expression on his face. Then she let herself into her building with her key to the lobby door.

In the first floor lobby of her apartment building, she checked her mailbox. There was a letter with Joseph Kalisa's name in the return address. Sojourner was excited, but she still thought about her father. She looked through the glass doors and saw her father walking to the nearest bus stop. Should she run after him and try to be more helpful? He could sleep on the sofa, but what would Rose think? Sojourner thought about the last time she saw him. She was ten years old.

Sitting at her dining room table, she read the letter from

Joseph Kalisa.

Dear Sojourner,

I cannot describe to you how much I enjoyed your company.

I should have been more helpful in providing you with all of the information that you wanted for your research paper, in reference to my father's novel. I did agree beforehand to help you with your analysis of the novel.

As I briefly stated, my father was murdered in 1973. That's not to mention other members of my family who were murdered, but I digress. It's difficult for me to talk about my father.

I must confess one of the reasons that I agreed to discuss my father's book with you. From the first time I saw you standing behind the counter in the library I have been impressed with your beauty and gracefulness. You have the look of an African princess of yore. However, I did not deem it appropriate to show any outward sign of my attraction to you, and I had no intention of approaching you.

When you approached me on the patio that day, I was elated. Then, you informed me that you had read my father's book. My father's book has been out of print for three decades, so I knew that you had to be a serious scholar to find and be interested in it.

If you would permit me, I would like to invite you out again.

Yours truly,
Joseph Kalisa

Sojourner folded the letter. She smiled to herself, flattered that Joseph had taken the time to write her. She went to her bedroom and placed the letter in her drawer.

Sojourner awoke at 6:00 a.m. the following morning and prepared for another day in academia. Sojourner washed and dressed. She wore a pink polo shirt, a navy blue sweater, and navy blue pleated slacks. She slipped into knee highs and her penny loafer shoes. Then she glanced at her watch. It was time for her to go to class and administer an exam on behalf of Dr. Julia Harris, who was out sick. Sojourner left her apartment and walked south down Georgia Avenue. She entered the campus ground, passing the School of Business and Crampton Auditorium. She then passed Frederick Douglass Hall, and crossed the quadrangle of the main campus. It was a cloudy and cool November morning. The campus was a buzz with activity, as usual.

That evening Sojourner was scheduled to work at Livingston & Richards. As Sojourner started to shelve the books, she saw Joseph reading in one of the private reading rooms. The door was closed, but Sojourner could see him through the glass window of the door. His back was to the door. Joseph was engrossed in what he was reading. He did not look up, as Sojourner passed the room, while shelving books. He wasn't aware of Sojourner's presence, and she didn't want to disturb him. So Sojourner made an effort to pass quietly.

When Sojourner finished shelving books on the first level of the library, she decided to go greet Joseph, before going downstairs to shelve books on the lower level of the library.

As Sojourner approached the room where Joseph had been reading earlier, she heard a woman's voice. The woman was speaking in a whisper, so Sojourner couldn't hear exactly what the woman was saying. Sojourner picked up a book from a table and pretended to be shelving a book and scanning the library shelves. As Sojourner got closer to the reading room, she could hear the conversation between Joseph and the woman.

"Peter is having another dinner party. Did you know?" the woman said, whispering.

"Yes. I know about it. He invited me last week," Joseph said, whispering back.

"I really enjoyed the last one," she said.

Sojourner moved close enough to get a glimpse of the woman, all the while pretending to be shelving books. Sojourner recognized her as Betsy McShane, an attorney in the firm. Betsy wore a light blue, knit Chanel dress and cardigan ensemble, and navy blue high heels. A diamond tennis bracelet dangled from her wrist, and her nails were painted red. She stood in the doorway, blocking Joseph's view. Sojourner could only see her back.

"I'm not sure if I can attend this time. The Cameroon case

needs my attention," Joseph said softly.

"Oh, come on, Joe. It's just a few hours. Are you going to just forget about me?" Betsy McShane said.

Sojourner heard no reply from Joseph.

"I need to see you again, Joe," Betsy said.

Sojourner turned around and walked away.

CHAPTER SEVEN

One of Sojourner's duties as the library's circulation assistant was to retrieve overdue books from the offices of the attorneys. Sojourner checked her list, and she saw that Joseph had two international law books checked out and overdue.

She walked through the hallway of the law firm, on her way to Joseph's office. Noticing that her penny loafers made no sound as she walked over the shiny hardwood floors of the hall, she was relieved. A young man, Jamal, who worked in the mailroom was walking in the opposite direction of Sojourner. Jamal was stocky with a Jerry Curl hairstyle. He was pushing a metal cart filled with mail to be delivered to various offices in the law firm.

"How you, Miss Lady?" Jamal said.

"Hi Jamal, I'm fine," Sojourner said.

"True," Jamal said.

She walked up to Joseph's office. His secretary was away from her desk at the time, so Sojourner passed the secretary's desk and walked straight to his office.

"Hi Joseph," Sojourner said, knocking gently on the door of his office.

Joseph looked up and smiled. His office was a good size, with a window view of the Post Office Pavillon's clock tower. He looked stately, sitting at his large cherry wood desk. He wore a dark grey suit and a champagne colored tie. He was writing on a yellow legal pad.

"Hello Sojourner. How are you?" Joseph said.

"Fine, thank you. I just came to get the books you checked out."

"Oh, yes. Here they are."

Joseph picked up the books from his desk and walked over towards Sojourner. He handed her the books. Sojourner glanced quickly at his desk, looking for photos or anything else that would indicate a significant other. There were none. She wondered if Joseph was still involved with Betsy McShane.

"Okay, thanks," Sojourner said, holding the books. "Joseph, thank you for the letter you sent me."

Joseph started to speak to Sojourner, but at that moment, his secretary approached them. So he remained silent for a moment.

Sojourner was a little startled by the sudden appearance of the secretary.

"Attorney McShane is on the line, Mr. Kalisa," the secretary said. She was an older woman with blue eyes and neatly styled white hair.

"Let me know when you are ready for me to transfer her over to you, Mr. Kalisa," the secretary said, with a feigned grin, and returned to her desk.

"I'll be going now," Sojourner said. She turned to leave.

"Sojourner, how did you do on your research paper?"

"I think I did well, but the papers haven't been graded yet."

"Excellent. I have to take this call now. But I really would like to make up for that somehow."

"Don't worry about that, Joseph. You really did help me a lot. I understand that you didn't want to talk about your father."

"I want us to go out again, Sojourner."

"Are you going to the company party?" Sojourner said.

"Yes."

"Well, then we'll see each other there."

"All right. I look forward to seeing you at the party then," Joseph said, picking up the phone.

As she walked through the corridors of the law firm,

Sojourner glanced at her list of checked out books. She stopped and read the next name on the list. It was that of Attorney Paul St. James. Sojourner walked to Attorney St. James's office, which was on the same floor as Joseph's office. Coincidentally, his secretary was also away from her desk at the moment, so Sojourner ventured to knock on the door to request a checked out book. She tapped lightly on the door.

Paul St. James was an African American man in his late thirties. He was a short, honey-toned man with close cropped, curly hair. He was wearing a royal blue dress shirt, and beige pants with suspenders.

Sojourner noticed that on his desk was a photo of a blond woman wearing a wedding gown.

"Is my secretary not at her desk?" Attorney St. James said, with a stoic expression on his face.

"No, Mr. St. James, she isn't. I'm sorry to disturb you, but I've come to retrieve some overdue books. That's all," Sojourner said.

She held her head high.

"It's the loose leaf Tax -- " Sojourner said.

"Yes, I know. It's there," St. James said.

Paul St. James didn't move from his chair; he just pointed to his bookshelf.

Sojourner walked over to the shelf and scanned the books.

Attorney St. James grew impatient, and he stood up to retrieve the book himself. He walked over to the bookshelf and knelt down to get the book, which was located on the very bottom shelf. He stood up and handed the book to Sojourner. As Paul St. James stood near her, Sojourner noticed that she towered over him, looking at the top of his head. She was not even wearing high-heels, Sojourner thought. She then thanked Attorney St. James and quickly left his office.

The firm's holiday party was in mid December 1990. Rose had talked Sojourner into purchasing an elegant dress, a black strapless, satin gown that originally cost $600. It had been reduced to $60. The Holiday gala was going to be a formal gala, and Sojourner wanted to be dressed appropriately.

She was excited about the opportunity to see Joseph dressed in a tuxedo. Sojourner hadn't dated anyone since her college boyfriend Donnell Walker had disappointed her. She had endeavored to be a dedicated student, but she realized that Donnell's commitment to school was weak. She remembered that not long after matriculating at Howard, Donnell became more interested in going to parties and dating the wide variety of pretty girls who decorated the campus. He misused his freedom from his strict family, and his grades plummeted. Sojourner had called Donnell once, late at night, and another girl had answered his phone.

When Sojourner later found out that Donnell's G.P.A. had gone down so low that he didn't qualify for his student financial aid, she decided that their relationship was definitely over. Donnell would eventually drop out of college. He telephoned Sojourner and wrote her a letter explaining that he still wanted her to be his girlfriend, but she'd lost interest in him. He'd paid her so little attention before that his late apologies didn't impress her. Sojourner focused on her studies and her future. She abandoned the dating scene all together. Sojourner felt that her college education was a privilege that she had to live up to, and she completed her Bachelor of Arts and graduated with distinction.

After successfully completing her first year in graduate school, Sojourner applied for a graduate assistantship. It was awarded to her. Despite the prestige of being a graduate assistant, the annual stipend was low.

Rose was watching TV when Sojourner entered the living room of their apartment.

"You look sensational, Soj," Rose said.

"Thanks, Rose. So what are you up to tonight?" Sojourner

said, out of politeness.

"Jamarr and I are going to the movies."

"What are you going to see?"

"The Godfather Part III."

"Okay. See you later," Sojourner said.

"I hope that you aren't gonna wear that beat up coat," Rose said.

"My coat is not beat up. Thank you. Anyway, I'm wearing a shawl."

"Oh, excuse me, Miss Thing," Rose said, smiling.

"You and Joe would make a cute couple, you know," Rose said.

"Really?" Sojourner said.

"Yeah. You're both tall and skinny," she laughed.

"Oh! Thanks a lot," Sojourner said, feigning indignation.

"Anyway, he's not really skinny, Rose. He's lean, but not skinny."

"Relax. I'm just kidding. Joseph's very attractive, and he's successful. You're so lucky."

"I hope that I'll be lucky. I really do," Sojourner said.

"Is Joseph going to pick you up tonight?"

"No. I'm going to the company party," Sojourner said.

Rose looked at Sojourner suspiciously.

"You plan on seeing him there, right?" Rose said.

"Yes," Sojourner said, as if she were confessing.

Sojourner peered out the window and saw that her taxi had arrived.

"My taxi is here. See you later, Rose," Sojourner said.

"Buy Iman," Rose said, referring to the famous high fashion model.

"I wish," Sojourner said, walking to the front door.

Sojourner put on her shawl and left the apartment. As she descended the steps of her apartment building, Sojourner saw her father, Davey, sitting on the steps outside. She stopped momentarily. Then she proceeded down the staircase and opened the lobby door slowly. Davey looked up at her admiringly.

"Look at my beautiful girl. You look magnificent," her father said.

"I'm on my way out, Davey," Sojourner said, passing him.

"You said you would visit me," her father said. He was attempting to stand up now.

"Don't bother getting up. My cab is here," Sojourner said, walking away from him.

Sojourner walked towards the taxi that was waiting for her.

"Why are you treating me like this, dammit," her father said. He started to follow her.

"Leave me alone," Sojourner said, turning around and facing him.

"I'm your father, Ann."

"Never around though…" Sojourner said softly.

"I spent a lot of time in prison, Ann," her father said. "I wanted to be with your mother, but…"

"She's dead because of you," Sojourner said.

"That's not my fault, Ann. You know that."

Sojourner looked at the ground.

"Let me have a few dollars, and I'll take the bus back to New Jersey," her father said.

Reaching into her little black satin purse, Sojourner retrieved two twenty dollar bills. She held it out at arms length. Her father lumbered towards her and gently grasped the money. Sojourner then entered the taxi that was waiting for her.

CHAPTER EIGHT

Sojourner felt like a lonely diva, as she entered the luxurious lobby of The Willard Intercontinental Hotel in D.C. The décor was grand.

The library staff members were supposed to meet in the lobby at 7:00 p.m. It was 6:55 p.m., and Sojourner saw no one she knew. Feeling conspicuous, she walked to the front desk and asked where the holiday party for Livingston & Richards was located. The clerk, an elderly gentleman smiled at Sojourner and gave her directions. Sojourner decided to sit in the posh lobby and wait another ten minutes before going straight to the party.

Carol entered the lobby, and Sojourner stood up carefully to get Carol's attention. Carol was a short, heavy set woman in her thirties, with hazel eyes," When she saw Sojourner, she smiled broadly.

"Oh, look at you, Missy," Carol said, as she touched Sojourner's hand. "You look so beautiful, my dear."

"Hi Carol! Thank you. You look ravishing, too, darling," Sojourner said, feigning an Eva Gabor accent.

"Well, thank you. You'd make an excellent Essence cover model," Carol said.

Sojourner smiled.

"Annie said she would be here," Sojourner said.

"Well…let's just go to the party then. We'll keep an eye out for the others. They can meet us in the ballroom," Carol said.

After checking in their coats, Sojourner and Carol collected their name tags and entered the ballroom to attend the Livingston & Richards Holiday Party. The ballroom contained a few dozen elegantly decorated tables. The room was also decorated with fake white columns, and life-size pictures of angels, all prepared for this occasion.

There were too many people in the ballroom to spot Joseph immediately. Sojourner reminded herself to be patient.

As Carol and Sojourner walked across the ballroom, looking for a place to sit, Sojourner saw Joseph sitting at a table with several other attorneys, two middle-aged men, and one elderly attorney. The elderly attorney was talking to Joseph. Joseph nodded, listening to him. There were also two women attorneys seated at his table, and one of them was Betsy McShane. All the men wore tuxedos.

Sojourner deliberately slowed her pace, pretending to look for a vacant table. She glanced quickly in Joseph's direction.

Joseph did not seem to notice her, so Sojourner continued to walk with Carol. They found a vacant table and sat down.

"This ballroom is so elegant," Sojourner said.

"Yeah, they go all out for the Christmas party," Carol said.

The main stage contained a live jazz band, playing contemporary jazz tunes. Sojourner liked it. On the other side of the room, near the banquet area, a string quartet played classical music. The buffet included a large variety of high quality dishes and appetizers. There were different types of seafood, meat, cheese, and vegetable platters, a bewildering variety of desserts. There was also a special ice cream section. Sojourner was glad that she would go home full, since the refrigerator in her apartment was just about empty.

"Well, it's self service, so we might as well eat," Carol said.

"Okay, sure," Sojourner said.

As they stood, they saw Annie walking in their direction. The Head librarian, Ms. Mahoney, was with her. Miss Mahoney, a stocky, middle-aged woman, who walked like a soldier.

"Hi ladies, we were just getting ready to go serve ourselves," Sojourner said.

"Well, you just go ahead then," Miss Mahoney said. "Enjoy yourself, dear." She grinned coldly.

"Yeah, you two go ahead," Annie said, echoing Miss Mahoney.

Carol and Sojourner perused the buffet. Everything looked spectacular so it was hard to decide. They made their plates and sat down to eat. The food was delicious, and Sojourner ate heartily. Carol and Sojourner talked about what was going on in the library, and Carol asked Sojourner about school.

The CEO of the law firm made a speech about the progress that the law firm had made to date, the new clients and cases acquired. Announcements were made about some attorneys who had just become partners. Then there were some employee awards distributed.

After the formal speeches were over, the jazz band started

playing more contemporary music, and the employees were invited to dance. Sojourner sat at the table with the other library staff members who had shown up and watched the revelers. It was fun to watch the employees dancing. The atmosphere was a stark contrast to the stoic and business-like atmosphere that normally dominated the law firm. People who were usually uptight and unfriendly were softened by the abundance of food, alcohol, and music.

"There's that attorney you like," Carol said, whispering.

Sojourner was surprised to see Joseph walking in the direction of her table. He looked around, as if he were searching for something.

"Do you need help, Mr. Kalisa," Miss Mahoney said.

"Thank you. I thought the beverage section was in this area," Joseph said.

"Actually, it's on the other side," Miss Mahoney said.

Miss Mahoney always turned on her charm for the attorneys, although she was gruff with the library staff.

Joseph nodded and smiled. Sojourner thought that the tuxedo emphasized his height. The bowtie around his neck seem to draw attention to his angular face.

"Good evening ladies," Joseph said to them. "This is an excellent party, isn't it?"

Everyone nodded their heads in approval and said yes.

The band played a song Sojourner liked, and she tapped her foot under the table. Sojourner wanted to speak, but the social circumstances prevented her from doing so. She was just a library assistant, and Joseph was an attorney.

Then Attorney Betsy McShane walked up to Joseph and spoke to him.

Sojourner saw Betsy talking to Joseph, but the music prevented her from hearing what she said.

Betsy wore a mauve Valentino style silk dress with spaghetti straps; her big breasts were pushed up. Her blond hair was styled in an elegant French chignon; she wore red lipstick and high heeled shoes. As she and Joseph talked, Betsy smiled coquettishly up into Joseph's face. She gestured toward the dance floor. Joseph shrugged his shoulders, good-naturedly.

Sojourner felt envious and disappointed, and she struggled not to let it show. Carol smiled, as if she knew how Sojourner felt. Sojourner's focus was on Joseph and Betsy McShane. Betsy was smiling broadly, as she danced. As Joseph danced, his elegance and calmness contrasted Betsy's giddy, offbeat dance movements.

"Anyone for ice cream?" Annie said.

Miss Mahoney shook her head.

"I'll have some," Sojourner said.

Sojourner was glad for the chance to get away from the table. She glanced back at the dance floor, tilting her head to get a better view of Joseph and Betsy. Then Sojourner noticed a short man, with curly, black hair moving in front of her. She looked down and saw that the man was Attorney Paul St. James. Attorney St. James looked her up and down and winked. Sojourner stood up straight and folded her arms across her chest. She had not forgotten the condescending expressions that she had endured from Attorney St. James during normal business hours. Heading for the opposite end of the ice cream section, Sojourner walked away from St. James.

Looking over the various ice cream flavors, she listened to the band playing. The music had changed to Abba's "Dancing Queen." Then Sojourner felt a presence behind her, and she turned around. Joseph was standing directly behind Sojourner.

"Miss Sojourner Brown," Joseph said, reading her name tag.

"Attorney Joseph Kalisa," Sojourner said, also reading Joseph's tag.

Sojourner put a teaspoon of the chocolate ice cream in her mouth, as she gazed into his deep brown eyes.

"So, you like ice cream, do you?" Joseph said.

"Yes. The double chocolate is excellent," Sojourner said.

"Well, I was hoping to have the honor of a dance with you

this evening," Joseph said.

"Really? You seemed to be having a good time, with Attorney McShane," Sojourner said.

Joseph smiled and took a step closer to her.

"I've been waiting to dance with you for weeks now," Joseph said.

"Joseph, I'd be delighted to dance with you," Sojourner said, putting her bowl of ice-cream down on the nearest table.

Without realizing it at the moment, Sojourner left Annie at the ice cream buffet.

As they danced, Sojourner felt like a real dancing queen. Joseph's movements were elegant, but reserved. He looked at her steadily as they danced. She moved freely to the rhythm of the song, feeling a sense of joy. When the song ended, Joseph walked her back to her table. She thought only of him the entire evening.

CHAPTER NINE

A small photograph of her mother, Nora Lee Brown, was on her dresser drawer. Sojourner stared at the photo of her Mother. Nora Lee was dressed in a pink pantsuit. The pants were bell-bottom cut, and the jacket was waist-length. She wore a matching hat, stylishly tilted on her head. Sojourner imagined her mother strutting into a nigh club. This was what Nora Lee liked, the glamorous life filled with high fashion and dreams, Sojourner thought.

After dressing, Sojourner left her apartment. She descended the stairs of the apartment building, and she noticed her father was sitting on the steps. He called to her softly.

"Ann …" her father said.

"I thought you were taking the bus back to Jersey, Davey," Sojourner said.

Sojourner stopped and crossed her arms.

"I need to explain something before I go."

"I have to meet my advisor, Davey."

"But...Please hear me out."

"Not right now. I gotta go, Davey."

Sojourner walked away. She walked fast, not uttering a sound. She thought about her father's request. Maybe she should have listened to what he had to say, thought Sojourner, as she walked across Howard's main campus quadrangle, passing Frederick Douglass Hall. She looked up and gazed at the Founder's Library. Sojourner felt fortunate to be there, where some of America's best-known African Americans had attended and taught. She envisioned Howard as the home of W.E.B. Dubois's "talented tenth." She aspired to be a part of that group.

It was a cold December day, and the main campus was crowded and busy with activity. This was the time for finals, and Christmas vacation preparations. Students were walking in all directions, crossing the quadrangle on the hilltop.

Sojourner walked to Alain Lock Hall and went to the second floor, where the English Department Office was located. She picked up her mail before going to the graduate assistants' office. After picking up her mail from the department's mailbox, Sojourner proceeded to her cubicle in the graduate students' office. She took off her coat and hung it up on a rack near her cubicle and opened her navy blue canvas tote bag. The bag contained a stack of papers bound together by a rubber band. These were undergraduate multiple-choice exams that Sojourner had marked and graded, per Dr. Harris's instructions. Sojourner was scheduled to meet with Dr. Harris at 7:30 a.m., before her 8:00 a.m. class.

Sojourner's phone rang, and she answered it.

"Hi, Dr. Harris. Yes, I've finished grading the grammar tests. I can bring them over now," Sojourner said.

With the tests in hand, Sojourner walked over to Dr. Harris's office, which was right down the hall.

Dr. Julia Harris was an English professor, who'd taught at Howard for twenty years. She had a very pale complexion and sky blue eyes. If it weren't for her long sandy blond dread locks, she could have been easily mistaken for a white woman. Sojourner thought it was interesting that some lighter toned black women often used their hair to assert their blackness. Proving their blackness had become important to them.

Sojourner had observed many lighter toned black women had grown up being teased by their family members and neighbors, called "high yella" and "red bone." They were most often outnumbered in the black community, and not always affectionately regarded. In the segregated black community, officially and de facto, the privileged professions were once dominated by light-skinned black people, making them the object of envy.

As a child, Sojourner's best friend was a beige complexioned girl with golden brown hair and matching eyes. Her name was Antonia, and she lived with her grandmother, who was very poor. As Antonia's friend, Sojourner observed that Antonia was often the target of many brown girls' resentment and envy. Antonia was bullied regularly. She was teased for looking "white" by the same girls who pleaded with their mothers to straighten their hair. These were the same girls who said Sojourner was too dark. This envy was often disguised as superiority, since Antonia was most often sloppily dressed and alone. Sojourner could relate to Antonia's sense of isolation.

On the other hand, Sojourner remembered feeling the pangs of envy toward her friend, Antonia, as they approached adolescence. As a teenager, Antonia realized that her lighter skin tone and golden hair could easily win her the attention of boys. Then Sojourner was deeply irritated that the boys preferred Antonia's light skin to her dark complexion.

After grading papers and tutoring undergraduate students in the Center for Academic Reinforcement, Sojourner spent the afternoon working on her dissertation in the Founders Library. She was getting sleepy and hungry, so she decided to go home and make herself a sandwich.

As she approached her apartment building, she saw her

father was still sitting on the steps of her apartment. He looked half asleep, with sweat pouring down his face. As she approached the steps, he slumped over and lost consciousness. Sojourner stared down at the unconscious man. She called to him.

"Davey? Are you okay?" Sojourner said.

"I don't think he is," a passerby said.

The passerby was an elderly woman, who stopped and looked down at her father with compassion.

Coincidentally, Rose was exiting the building at that moment.

"Hey, Rose, call an ambulance! This man's sick," Sojourner said.

Rose went back to the apartment to call the ambulance, and Sojourner kneeled down to take a better look at her father. She silently admitted that she should have treated him better this morning.

Davey was still unconscious when the ambulance arrived. The medical technicians went to work on him. Sojourner watched.

"Do you know this man, Miss?" the medical technician said, as he and his crew loaded Davey into the ambulance.

"… he's…a family member," Sojourner said.

"Would you like to accompany him to the hospital?"

"Yes. I would."

Sojourner accompanied Davey to Howard University Hospital, two blocks south of the main campus, on Georgia Avenue. She provided information to the hospital registration attendant.

The nurse said that Mr. McIntosh had passed out from exhaustion and that he had very high blood pressure. He had been diagnosed with hypertension. An hour later, a nurse met Sojourner in the waiting room. Sojourner approached her father slowly, as he lay in the hospital bed, looking up at the ceiling. He noticed her approaching and smiled weakly.

"Hi, Ann," Davey said.

"Hi Davey. How you feeling now?" Sojourner said. She was standing next to the hospital bed where her father lay.

"I'm alive, but I still feel dead," Davey said.

"After you get some rest, you need to go back to Jersey. I'll call Grandma, Davey," Sojourner said.

"No. I'll go back to the shelter, for now," Davey said. "Don't bother."

"Why?" Sojourner said, staring at him incredulously. "Anyway, I spoke with the nurse, and I told her you're a Vietnam veteran. She said that there's a special program for veterans, so you can stay here for a week."

"Ann …" Davey said. "Thank you for coming with me to the hospital."

"I'm your daughter," Sojourner said.

"Sit down for a minute, baby," Davey said.

"Okay," Sojourner said, sighing a little.

"I was in prison, when Nora died. By the time I found out she died, the funeral was over. I did what I could for her, but I was just a kid, you know. I just turned seventeen when you were born. At eighteen, I went to Vietnam. That was a nightmare… Your Mom waited for me to return from Vietnam, but she didn't wait for me, when I went to prison. When I wasn't struggling to stay alive, I did a lot of reading in prison. Educated myself on the truth about black history, the lost greatness of African people."

"Yeah… I remember the birthday present you gave me for my tenth birthday…a huge college-level African history textbook," Sojourner said, laughing softly. "But I was so glad to see you, Davey."

Sojourner saw her father smile.

"When I was in prison, Nora had a relationship with a big time drug dealer. She moved in with him and took you. Then, she had Langston. I heard he beat her pretty bad, put her in the hospital a few times. She started using dope, riding that white horse. That was the greatest mistake of her life."

Sojourner sat in a chair next to the bed, nodding her head.

"Tell me what happened the day she died?" Davey said. He turned and stared at Sojourner.

"We were living with Earl, her boyfriend. He worked as a maintenance man in a resort hotel. Mom's habit had gotten really bad the last few weeks before she died. We lived in an apartment in Rockwell. Earl went to work, and Mom was in the bathroom when Langston and I went to school. When we came home, the ambulance was there and so were police cars. There was commotion, neighbors staring at us..." Sojourner said.

She closed her eyes and bit her bottom lip. Then she continued.

"They took her body out, covered with a sheet. Langston and I were standing there."

Sojourner noticed that her father was listening to her intently.

"Aunt Mae came to get us. I overheard her tell uncle Jobe that Mom had taken a bath after shootin' up, and then passed out. That's how she drowned, right in the bathtub." Sojourner said.

"I'm sorry baby," Davey said. "I was back in the joint. I wrote you many letters after your Mother died, but you didn't write me back."

"I didn't get any letters, Davey," Sojourner said, surprised.

"Oh... Damn that Mae!" her father said.

"You sent letters, really?" Sojourner said.

"Yes. And when Nora died, I sent some money, too. Did your Aunt tell you that?"

"No. She didn't."

Davey closed his eyes and shook his head. Then he re-opened his eyes and sighed.

"I see you're doing well, right?" Davey said.

"I'm fine," Sojourner said.

Sojourner stood up.

"I have to go now, Davey. I'll come and visit you tomorrow."

"Ann... I'm proud of you, baby."

"Thanks, Davey," Sojourner said, as she left the hospital room.

CHAPTER TEN

Sojourner sat down, and watched reruns of The Cosby Show with Rose. This was her favorite TV show, but Rose preferred Dynasty. Rose asked her about what had transpired with the homeless man, and Sojourner gave her the highlights. However, Sojourner didn't tell Rose that the "homeless man" was her father. As they watched TV, the phone rang, and Sojourner answered it. It was Joseph.

"Hello, Sojourner! How are you this evening?" Joseph said.

"I'm fine. Thank you, Joseph."

"How was your day in school?"

"Good," Sojourner said.

"Anything interesting going on in academia today?" Joseph said.

"Let's see. I graded some exams for my advisor and tutored some students," Sojourner said.

"Okay... Very good," Joseph said.

"But the most interesting part of my day today was a man collapsing on our doorstep," Sojourner said.

"Really?" Joseph said.

"Yeah," Sojourner said.

"What did you do?"

"We called the ambulance for him, and they took him to the hospital," Sojourner said.

Sojourner didn't share any other information with Joseph about the incident.

"So, what are you doing now?" Joseph said.

"I'm just watching TV. How about you?" Sojourner said.

"I'm working on a brief."

"That sounds interesting."

"You think so?"

"Yes, I do," Sojourner said.

Sojourner sat on the sofa with her feet propped on their little coffee table. She wore a gray flannel pajama set and Bugs Bunny slippers.

"May I take you out this weekend? There's a new night club in Adams Morgan. I hear that they play some good African music. My friend runs it, so he plays Rwandan music, too. Have you ever heard Rwandan music, Sojourner?"

"No. I don't think I ever have heard Rwandan music," Sojourner said, wiggling her feet.

"Well, I'd like to invite you out so that you can hear it."

"All right. That sounds like fun."

It was Saturday night, and Sojourner sat on her sofa, waiting for Joseph. She felt the same mixture of euphoria and nervous tension that she felt the first time she went out with him.

The phone on the coffee table rang, and Sojourner answered it. It was her Aunt Mae.

"Hi Aunt Mae," Sojourner said.

"How you doing, Ann?"

"I'm fine, Aunt Mae."

"How's your Masters coming along?"

"I'm working on it. How's the family in Rockwell?"

Aunt Mae didn't make long distance phone calls for nothing, so Sojourner knew there was some news coming.

"Well, everything's just about the same here, except that your brother's in jail," Aunt Mae said calmly.

So that was the news, Langston was in trouble.

"Oh, no. What happened?" Sojourner said.

"Buying drugs...," Aunt Mae said. "I don't want to disturb your studies, but he's being held on a five thousand dollar bond, and I don't have anything close to that."

"Oh, my God. Neither do I, but we need to do something," Sojourner said.

"He goes to pre-trial in two weeks. I visited him today,"

Aunt Mae said.

"How is he?" Sojourner said.

"He's okay, but he looks depressed. He asked about you."

"I need to visit him, too. You know Auntie, I got some news of my own," Sojourner said.

"Oh, yeah. What is it?" Aunt Mae said.

"Davey's here," Sojourner said.

"Get outta here!" Aunt Mae said. "He's in your apartment?"

"No…he was staying in a shelter, but…" Sojourner said.

"What's that fool doing down there in D.C.?" Aunt Mae said.

"He had a passed out, and he's in the hospital, Aunt Mae," Sojourner said.

"What's wrong with him?" Aunt Mae said.

"Exhaustion…hypertension," Sojourner said.

Sojourner thought about what Davey said about the letters and the money he had sent to her when her mother died. Why didn't Aunt Mae tell her, Sojourner thought? She dared not mention this right now.

"That's too bad, but how'd he find himself down there, anyway?" Aunt Mae said.

"I'll talk to you about it, when I get there, Aunt Mae. I'll take a bus to Rockwell tomorrow."

"Okay. I'll see you when you get here."

As Sojourner put the telephone receiver down, she heard a car door close outside. She looked out the window and saw Joseph walking up to the apartment building. Biting her nails, she hurried to the hall bathroom. There, she brushed her hair and added more lip gloss. A mild tickling sensation invaded her stomach. Silently, she convinced herself to be calm; then she descended the staircase and let Joseph into the apartment building. When she opened the lobby door, Joseph walked in and greeted her.

"Hello, Sojourner," Joseph said. "You look stunning."

Sojourner looked at Joseph and forgot all her problems.

CHAPTER ELEVEN

Adams Morgan was a sort of bohemian area in D.C., with lots of immigrants from all over the world, and yuppies. Previously run-down, it was being architecturally and economically renovated and revived. It contained a plethora of restaurants and nightclubs.

Joseph pulled up to the nightclub called the "Sub-Sahara Room" and parked. There were well-dressed Africans standing outside the building. Some were about to enter, and others were talking causally. The women and men both wore evening attire.

The gate fee was $10 per person for the Sub-Sahara Room. A disco light twirled at the center of the nightclub, as African music played. The place wasn't crowded, since it was only about 10:00 p.m. The nightclub patrons sat at various tables. There were two palm trees on either side of the entrance. The room was decorated with various African motifs. There were large vintage black and white photos of young African warriors, which hung on the walls of the nightclub. The young warriors held long spears, and they wore a kind of ceremonial headdress. They seemed to be unusually tall, as well as thin. Some of the men had narrow facial features, similar to Joseph's. In the photos, they carried themselves with a mixture of haughtiness and bravado that Sojourner admired.

Joseph reached down and held Sojourner's hand.

"Come. Let's find a seat, my dear," Joseph said softly.

They sat down at a table near the dance floor and ordered drinks. Joseph ordered a beer, and Sojourner ordered a Pina Colada. A short, muscular man emerged from behind the bar area and approached. He greeted Joseph in what seemed to Sojourner to be their native language.

"*Gira Inka*, Joe," the man said.

"*Muraho*, John," Joseph said.

"Good Evening, *Mademoiselle*," the man said to Sojourner, nodding politely.

"Hi," Sojourner said.

"John, this is my dear friend, Sojourner," Joseph said.

Sojourner smiled and nodded at John.

"Sojourner, this is John Uwayezu. We were neighbors in Rwanda."

A tall man behind the bar appeared to be beckoning to John, so he touched Joseph's shoulder and excused himself. He went back to the bar area.

Sojourner tried to ask Joseph about his work at the law firm, but her voice was drowned out by the loud, upbeat music. The nightclub slowly filled up. People flowed in, and the music got louder.

Soon all of the tables were filled, and people started to dance. Sojourner had finished her Pina Colada, and dancing seemed like a good idea. She tapped her finger on the table, enjoying the music. Joseph noticed.

"Shall we dance?" Joseph said.

"Yes. Let's dance," Sojourner replied, cheerfully.

The songs were not familiar, but she liked the beat of the music. She moved to the rhythm of the music, and felt like she was in another exciting world.

Sojourner felt safe in Joseph's company. She danced freely. Balancing herself on high-heels was a feat for her, since she normally wore flats and casual attire. Being on the tall side for a woman, Sojourner enjoyed Joseph's height.

Then the DJ played Whitney Houston's "All the Man That I Need.". Joseph gently held Sojourner's hands, and then he slowly, gently embraced her. They slow danced to the rhythm of the music. Joseph gently pressed her against his chest. Sojourner rested her head on his chest.

Sojourner felt naturally drawn to Joseph. She was aroused, and that frightened her. She hadn't had sex in four years. She'd had intercourse with only one other man in her life, Donnell, and that relationship had ended. Sojourner intentionally avoided relationships with men and dating. Painful disappointments were to be avoided. She wanted to do nothing but focus on obtaining her masters, and publishing her second book. However, she was willing to take a chance with Joseph.

After dancing, Sojourner and Joseph sat down, and Joseph ordered more drinks. Two women approached their table. One was over six feet tall, with a voluptuous build, and the other woman was a slender woman of medium height. Both women were focusing their attention on Joseph.

"*Bonsoir*, Joseph. *Ça va?*" the tall woman said.

"*Je vais bien, Merci*, Theodetta," Joseph said.

Joseph stood up and embraced the tall woman quickly and respectfully. He acknowledged her companion with a brief nod.

"*Où avez-vous été ? Je vous ai téléphoné la semaine dernière*," the tall woman said.

"Theodetta, let me introduce you to my friend, Sojourner Brown. Sojourner, this is Theodetta Mukanyonga, and her friend, Annette. Theodetta is my cousin," Joseph said.

"Pleased to meet you, Theodetta," Sojourner said.

"Hello," Theodetta said.

Sojourner extended her hand, and they shook hands.

The two women stood there, as if waiting to be asked to join Joseph and Sojourner. John returned and nodded respectfully at Theodetta. Then he led her and her companion to some seats in another part of the night club. Sojourner was relieved to see the women move on.

"She's very tall, like you," Sojourner said.

Joseph smiled.

"Does your cousin also live in the area?"

"Yes," Joseph said.

"What does she do?"

"She's a resident intern, soon to be a doctor."

"Is she the person you told me about before?"

"Yes."

Joseph sipped his drink and told Sojourner that one of the songs was a Rwandan song.

To Sojourner the song sounded like lots of very rhythmic drumming and chanting, like African warriors preparing for an important ceremony, or war.

A couple approached their table and greeted Joseph.

"*Bonsoir, mon frère*," the man said.

"*Bonsoir, Francois. Ça va?*" Joseph said.

"*Je vais bien. Merci. Mais, je travaille trop*," the man said.

"*Naturellement. C'est l'Amérique et le travail est bon*," Joseph said.

"Francois, I would like you to meet my dear friend, Sojourner," Joseph said.

"Hi Sojourner. What a pretty name," Francois said.

"Thank you," Sojourner said.

"This is Edith," Francois said, gesturing to the woman with him.

Edith smiled, and uttered a quick, "Hi."

"We'll go and find some seats. See you all, later," Francois said.

Then they moved on to another part of the nightclub.

"Is your friend, Francois, also from Rwanda, too?"

Sojourner noticed that Francois' accent was different from Joseph's.

"Oh, no. Francois is from Cameroon," Joseph said.

"He said that he works a lot," Sojourner said.

"Yes, he did say that," Joseph said.

He stared more intensely at Sojourner.

"*Parlez-vous français, Madamoiselle?*" Joseph said, winking playfully at Sojourner.

"Oui. Un peu, tres peu. I took some French classes as a part of my language requirement as an undergrad," Sojourner said.

"How did you meet Francois, since he's from Cameroon?" Sojourner said.

"I attended the University of Yaounde, which is in

Cameroon," Joseph said.

"Oh…And what does Francois do now?" Sojourner said.

"Francois is a scientist," Joseph said.

"He's a close friend?" Sojourner said.

"Yes. He's like a brother to me," Joseph said.

Sojourner grew pensive. Sojourner felt guilty for enjoying herself in a bohemian nightclub, while her brother was in jail in New Jersey and her father was in the hospital, only a few miles away. She glanced at her watch. Joseph noticed.

"You can sleep late tomorrow, right?" Joseph said.

"Well, not really," Sojourner said.

She looked down at the table for a moment.

"I have to go to New Jersey tomorrow."

"Really? Is everything all right?"

"Well … my brother … he's umm … sick," Sojourner said.

"I'm sorry about that. Is there anything that I can do?"

"No, thank you."

"I could drive you to New Jersey," Joseph said.

"No. You have to work on Monday, right?"

"But tomorrow is Sunday, and this sounds like an emergency."

"I'll be all right. I need to go home."

"Yes, of course."

Joseph paid the check for the drinks, and they stood up to leave. As usual, he quickly picked up Sojourner's coat from the back of her chair and helped her to put it on. As Joseph and Sojourner headed for the door, Joseph's friend, Francois, approached them, this time, without his female companion.

"I'm having a little dinner at my place next Saturday. Make sure you're there, and please bring your beautiful lady, too."

"That sounds good. Right, my dear?" Joseph said, looking at Sojourner.

Sojourner smiled, but said nothing.

Joseph and Sojourner entered the car, and he drove her back to her apartment. As they entered the building, Joseph again requested a good night kiss. Sojourner assented, and Joseph kissed her on her lips. As he kissed her, he embraced her. She could taste the beer in his mouth. Sojourner almost shuddered from the intense arousal that was swirling in her body. Then she opened her apartment door and waved at Joseph. He waved back and turned and descended the staircase. Sojourner closed her eyes and smiled, as Joseph exited the apartment building.

As she sat on her bed alone that evening, Sojourner thought about how much she'd enjoyed herself. She remembered the black and white photographs on the wall of the night club. Those photos reminded her of some photos that she'd first seen in the textbook that her father had given her when she was ten years old.

Fourteen years ago, Sojourner was sitting on the carpeted floor of the small apartment where she lived with her mother and her brother. She read through the textbook her father had given her. The book was entitled Through African Eyes.

At first Sojourner would just flip through the pages of the textbook, staring at the old black and white photographs of African people and reading the captions under the pictures. The people reminded her of many of the people in her family, as well as some family friends and neighbors. The people looked normal to her, except for their clothing, and the rural background. As she read the book, one of the photos that she found interesting was captioned "Ruandan Royal Family ca. 1898." It was a picture of a group of black people who were posing in a dignified manner. One woman was identified as a queen mother in the picture, and she was a very beautiful older woman.

At ten years old, Sojourner began to entertain the notion that her face contained some unacknowledged beauty. These people seemed more dignified than most of the people, black or white, that she had encountered. Until she saw this picture, Sojourner didn't appreciate her dark skin tone; she had wished to look more like the girls and women who paraded themselves across the TV set.

As a girl, she looked at the photographs in the textbook. The next photo was of a group of African warriors. They stood together smiling, a group of young men holding spears. There was a great bravado in their attitudes, and their heads were held high. Even as a child, she knew it was rare to see black men who looked so free and happy. The young men were lanky and tall. Sojourner could tell that they were tall because of the way they towered over a white man, who was looking on in the background. In spite of their leanness, their brown bodies seemed strong. The caption read, "Watutsi warriors, ca. 1894."

Sojourner would always remember the faces of these warriors. At fifteen years old, inspired by these images of African people, Sojourner wrote a poem about them for one of her high school classes. She remembered her poem.

Watutsi Warriors

The Watutsi warrior stood, with a spear in his hand,
With the grace of a woman, but the strength of a man.
In ceremonial regalia, he dances.
With a smile on his face, he prances.
The Watutsi warrior is thin and tall,
From my imagination he will never fall
From his wooden pedestal.
He is more than a sculpture in a museum.
He represents an ancient black people,
Flesh, blood, and beauty.
To write this poem is my duty.

CHAPTER TWELVE

The next morning Sojourner took a Greyhound bus to Rockwell, New Jersey. It was a four hour trip. Sojourner then took local bus transportation to her Aunt Mae's apartment complex, which was adjacent to the Black Horse Pike highway. Sojourner walked toward the front entrance and knocked on the door. She stood there waiting. The lobby door was locked. Her aunt's apartment was on the first floor, so Sojourner decided to tap on the apartment window. Her ten-year-old cousin, Mimi, peeked through the curtains and smiled. Mimi emerged from the apartment and greeted Sojourner.

"Hey, Ann," Mimi said.

"Hi Mimi," Sojourner said. She hugged her cousin and entered the apartment.

"Mom's at work now. She just got a new job at Resorts."

"Oh, good for Aunt Mae," Sojourner said.

Sojourner had decided not to ask her Aunt Mae about the letters her father said that he had sent. There would be another time for that.

She visited her brother in jail at the Rockwell Detention Center the same afternoon. Langston was led out of his cell to the visitor's section. Langston wore an orange jumper with numbers in bold print.

He sat down and spoke through the glass window that separated them.

"What happened, Little Man?" Sojourner said.

Little Man was Langston's nickname. He had earned it as a toddler because of the way he walked, with a cool stride.

"It wasn't my fault, Ann," Langston said. "I was hanging out with my boy, Tiny. He knows this drug dealer, but I don't have nothing to do with that. Tiny copped a bag, and I was just there. The police busted the dealer and Tiny. Then they arrested me, too," Langston said.

"I'll have to talk to the attorney about this," Sojourner said.

"I have a public defender," Langston said. "His name is John Baker."

"I'll give him a call. What's his number," Sojourner said.

Langston gave her the number.

Sojourner thought about Langston. He used to be a mild-manner person who did well in school, excelling in math and science. But he changed, after their mother died. He became a bully, always fighting and getting suspended from school. Hanging out at the gym all the time with men who were much older than he was, he grew muscular and adopted a tough attitude. Langston then dropped out of high school and started job hopping. His mind was not settled.

Sojourner tried to reach the public defender, but she could not. She finally left a message for him to contact her in D.C. After leaving the detention center, Sojourner visited her Grandmother at a senior citizens home in Atlantic City.

"Hi Grandma! How've you been?"

"I'm okay, Ann. My eyes were bothering me, last week though," Grandma said.

"Really, I didn't know that, Grandma," Sojourner said.

"Langston drove me to the doctors last week. He helped me to pay for a new pair of glasses, too. Medicaid didn't pay for the whole bill," Grandma said.

"Oh, did he really? Good for Langston," Sojourner said, remembering that Langston did not have a car. She kept that to herself.

"Yes. He means well, God knows," her Grandmother said.

Sojourner was thinking of a way to gently tell her that Langston had been arrested, when her Grandmother spoke.

"He's in trouble?" Grandmom said.

Sojourner was relieved that her Grandmother already knew.

"Who told you about it, Grandma?" Sojourner said.

"The Lord told me," Grandma said.

Sojourner wasn't skeptical. She had experienced Grandma's uncanny ability.

"He said that he didn't do anything, was just at the wrong place at the wrong time. So he says," Sojourner said.

"Well, I'm nobody's judge. I'm just praying he gets his life together, and lives right," Grandma said.

"I don't know what to do. I don't have much money to help with legal fees. I took a bus to get here," Sojourner said.

"Do the best you can, Ann. That's all. Help him as much as

you can. Then leave it in the Lord's hands," Grandma said.

"I have more news, Grandma," Sojourner said.

"What is it, Ann?" Grandma said.

"Davey's in D.C." Sojourner said.

Her grandmother nodded.

"A few months ago, he visited me and asked for your address, Ann. I thought he just wanted to write you a letter, but then he said he was going to go see you," Grandma said. "I told him to leave you be for now, 'til he gets himself cleaned up."

"He's in the hospital now, Grandma," Sojourner said.

"Oh Lord, what happened?" Grandma said.

"I saw him walking down the street near Howard, and I didn't recognize him at first. I mean, he changed so much. He was heavy, and he had a thick beard and dirty looking hair. His clothes looked like they hadn't been washed in weeks. Grandma, I live in a small apartment I share with a roommate so I didn't have a place for him to stay. I gave him some money to catch the bus back to New Jersey."

"Oh, God, my son! I dreamed he was lying on the ground," Grandma said. She closed her eyes and shook her head.

Sojourner thought about how Davey actually was lying on the ground, but she didn't tell her Grandmother that. Secretly, she felt ashamed of the way she had treated her father.

"So why is he in the hospital?" Grandma said, regaining her calmness.

"Exhaustion and hypertension," Sojourner said. "He'll be there for a few more days."

"I'm calling Jess now. Ann, tell your father that he can stay with your Aunt Jess when he comes back to Atlantic City. Jess'll make room for her brother."

Sojourner made some tea for both of them, while her Grandmother called her Aunt Jess. Then they sat quietly in her Grandmother's small apartment, sipping hot tea. Among the old photos, there was a picture of Sojourner's father. It was a high school photo. Her father looked handsome and lean. Sojourner saw that she had inherited his height and dark complexion.

CHAPTER THIRTEEN

One day Rose's boyfriend, Jamarr, visited. He sat in the living room waiting for Rose to get dressed. Sojourner was on her way out to go to the Graduate Office. She walked into the living room, and nodded at Jamarr perfunctorily. She figured it would be impolite to completely ignore him. Jamarr was a thickly built young man who wore an oversized black T-Shirt, with a picture of Ice Cube on it. Sojourner thought that Jamarr looked a bit like Ice Cube himself.

"Hey, Sojourner," Jamarr said, greeting her. "What's up?"

"Oh, the usual," Sojourner said, as she opened the closet to retrieve her coat.

"Studying hard, uh?"

"Yes, I am," Sojourner said. She quickly glanced at Jamarr on her way to the front door.

"But it doesn't look like your eating much," Jamarr said.

"What?"

"You're thin, girl," Jamarr said, smiling.

Sojourner looked at him for a moment, annoyed.

Jamarr winked and blew a kiss her way. Sojourner quickly turned her head and left the apartment. She was disgusted. What did Rose see in him? Rose had told her that Jamarr had connections in the music industry. Nevertheless, Sojourner thought that he was a jerk, flirting with her with his girlfriend in the next room. Was Jamarr just a typical man? She wondered about this. Jamarr wasn't trustworthy; that was obvious. Sojourner was glad that she'd been celibate for the last four years. That was why she had been able to focus and get things done, Sojourner thought. She had vowed to stay away from romantic relationships, but there she was falling in love with a man whom she knew little about, other than that he was a handsome, corporate attorney who was born in

Rwanda.

After her morning classes, Sojourner went to the Center for Academic Reinforcement, located behind Locke Hall on the main campus of Howard. Her assistantship required that she spend ten hours a week tutoring in this center. She participated in a federal program administered by Howard. The purpose was to help a group of "at risk" inner city girls to improve their writing skills.

Two of the girls in the group seemed more interested in observing the latest fashions at Howard than completing the grammar worksheets that Sojourner encouraged them to complete during their tutoring sessions. Sienna Jackson was one of these girls. She was a chubby fourteen year-old with skin the color of ebony itself. Sienna's loneliness was palpable, and she seemed to relish the attention that Sojourner gave her. She was always diligent in completing her assignments. However, Sienna had missed several classes. Sojourner had not seen her for weeks, and she informed the program director.

Before leaving the graduate assistant office, Sojourner called with Langston's public defender to explain Langston's version of what had happened. The attorney said that he would take what she said into account in order to defend Langston.

Sojourner then went to the hospital to visit her father and convey her Grandmother's message to him. The hospital receptionist informed Sojourner that David McIntosh had checked out of the hospital earlier that afternoon. The veteran's insurance coverage had run out. She should have come sooner, Sojourner thought. The next thing to do was to track Davey down at the shelter where he had stayed before. Sojourner figured he was likely to be there.

Sojourner took a taxi to the Angel of Mercy shelter in D.C. She entered the shelter and walked up to the front desk, where an indifferent looking, middle-age woman sat. The woman was the shelter coordinator. Sojourner asked to see Mr. David McIntosh, and the coordinator pointed to the other side of the room. It was a large room filled with people and cots, an old, stale-smelling gymnasium that had been converted to a shelter.

As Sojourner passed by, she felt the stares of men, women, and children. She knew about their discomfort, anxiety, and humiliation. At twelve years old, she had experienced what it was like to have no home to call her own.

Sojourner found her father.

"Hi Davey," Sojourner said, as she stood near the cot on which her father sat.

"Hey Ann, how you doing baby?" her father said.

"Why didn't you call me, Davey? I left my number on the table next to your bed in the hospital."

"I didn't want to bother you, Ann."

"Listen, we got to get out of here. I visited Grandma and told her you were sick."

"What you do that for? She just gonna be worrying now. I'll be all right. I still have the money you gave me, and I'm going back home."

"Fine. Then let's put you on the bus now. Grandma said you can stay with Aunt Jess."

"Jess?"

"Yep. Grandma said that Jess is making room for you to come stay with her. Let's go."

"All right, but I gotta pick up some medication first. The doctor said I have to get it right away."

"Then we'll have to stop at a pharmacy," Sojourner said, sighing.

"Naw. He said I have to get it from this clinic. Otherwise it's gonna be too expensive."

"Where's the clinic?"

"In the same hospital at Howard. It's an outpatient clinic," her father said. "The clinic was closed when I checked out of the hospital."

Sojourner decided that together they would take a taxi to the clinic. How awkward she would look, with a sloppy, homeless man, Sojourner thought. But this man was her father, who encouraged her to read history books. She told her father to go to the bathroom and get washed and dressed. He shrugged and said that he had already washed. Sojourner frowned. So why did he smell so musty?

As Sojourner and Davey walked through the shelter, Sojourner saw Sienna Jackson, the middle school student that she had tutored at Howard. Sienna sat on a cot, next to a sleeping woman. The sleeping woman looked emaciated. Sienna looked up at Sojourner sadly; then she managed a weak smile. Sojourner walked up to her and spoke.

"Hi Sienna, I've miss seeing you at the center," Sojourner said.

"I wanted to come, but my Mom and me had to come here. She's sick, and I gotta look after her," Sienna said.

"I'm sorry she's sick," Sojourner said.

"Miss Sojourner, who's that with you?" Sienna said, staring at Sojourner's father.

"I'm helping Mr. McIntosh," Sojourner said, displaying a tight smile. "Taking him to the clinic."

"Are you one of the volunteers?" Sienna said.

"Yes…," Sojourner said. "Here's my number Sienna. Call me, if you need to," Sojourner said, writing her number on the back of a blank piece of paper that she had pulled from her purse.

"Okay. Bye Miss Sojourner," Sienna said, accepting the paper.

Sojourner and her father exited the shelter.

They stood at the curb of the street. Several taxis passed them by without stopping. Sojourner then told her father to sit down on a nearby bus stop bench. She stood alone near the curb and gestured for the next taxi, which promptly stopped for her. She then gestured for her father to follow her. The taxi driver had a look of surprise on his face as Sojourner approached the vehicle with Davey. His eyes shifted from Sojourner to Davey and then back to Sojourner.

"Hi Sir, I'm a volunteer, helping this veteran to get to a clinic. Can you take us to Howard University Hospital?"

"Sure. Get in," the taxi driver said.

When they arrived at the clinic, Sojourner walked her father to the waiting room area. She saw the curious eyes staring at them. Sojourner was dressed in a light blue, striped oxford shirt and khaki pants. She wore classic boat shoes. Yet, she was walking into the clinic with an overweight derelict, with dirty looking tan pants and a coat that was so small that he could not button it.

Sojourner motioned for Davey to sit down and went to register him at the clinic. The receptionist asked Sojourner a series of questions about Davey.

"What is your relationship to the patient?" the clerk said.

"I'm a graduate student at Howard, and I volunteered to take Mr. McIntosh to visit the clinic," Sojourner said.

"That's nice," said the clerk, staring over at Davey, who was sitting in the waiting area with a vacant look on his face.

Then Sojourner saw Theodetta, walking by in a white hospital coat. Theodetta saw her, too. She stopped and spoke with Sojourner, who was collecting some forms for Davey.

"How are you?" Theodetta said, stopping to speak to Sojourner.

"Oh, Hi. You're Theodetta, Joseph's cousin, right?" Sojourner said.

"Yes. And you are Joseph's friend?" Theodetta said.

"Yes." Sojourner glanced over at her father, who was starting to slump in his chair.

"I saw you come in with the older man," Theodetta said. "Do you know him?"

"I volunteered at the Angel of Mercy shelter. I was asked to assist him in getting to the clinic," Sojourner said. She felt nervous, tired of all the lies she told.

With one hand, Sojourner smoothed back her hair, which

was combed back into a neat bun.

"That's so kind of you," Theodetta said. "He looks really sick."

Sojourner looked at Davey again, and his eyes were now about to close. She rushed over to her father and spoke to him, but he did not respond. Theodetta came over and looked at him.

"I think he's passing out. I'll call the orderly," Theodetta said.

"Thanks," Sojourner said. Then she spoke to her father.

"Davey? What's wrong?"

His face seemed to contort right in front of her eyes. One side seemed to swell, while the other side seemed to shrink. Sojourner felt scared, and she called the receptionist. The receptionist coldly announced that a doctor from the emergency room unit had been paged; then she continued to check in the next patient.

Theodetta rushed in with the emergency room doctor.

"They'll take him to ER now," Theodetta said.

Sojourner watched as the orderlies lifted her father onto the gurney and rolled him into ER.

"I'm at the end of my shift, but I can help out the ER team and let you know how he's doing."

"Okay. Thank you," Sojourner said.

Sojourner pressed her fingers to her mouth, trying to control her emotions in front of Theodetta.

She went to the Emergency Room waiting area. Thirty minutes later, Theodetta came out and spoke with Sojourner.

"The homeless man had a stroke," Theodetta said. "He hasn't yet regained full consciousness, and he is being admitted. The clerk will need your help to complete the paperwork. They will need the name of the shelter where he stays."

"I'll provide the information. Thank you," Sojourner said.

"How sweet of you to volunteer to help the homeless," Theodetta said.

Sojourner swallowed hard and forced a smile.

"Well, my shift is over," Theodetta said.

They exchanged goodbyes, and Theodetta left the waiting room.

Sojourner filled out the paperwork to admit her father into the hospital once again, noting his Vietnam veteran status. A nurse informed her that her father was in the Intensive Care Unit. She asked if she could see him and she said no. Only close family members could stay with him. Then Sojourner sighed and whispered to the nurse.

"He's my father."

The nurse stared back at her with a surprised expression.

Sojourner sat with her father for an hour, watching him sleep in the hospital bed. Then she left the hospital and walked home. She called her Grandmother to explain what had happened.

That evening, as she lay in bed, Sojourner remembered her own homeless experience. At twelve years old, Sojourner, her mother, and her brother had been homeless for five months. For the first month, they lived in a shelter. Then they were moved to a local welfare motel.

Once while living in a roadside welfare motel, Sojourner was befriended by a teenager, Rickie, who lived with his mother and two younger siblings in an adjacent hotel room. Rickie was a muscular fifteen year-old. He would visit Sojourner and her brother in their hotel room, and share his candy with them. Sojourner and her brother went often to Rickie's mother's room to play with him and his younger siblings. Rickie taught Sojourner to play checkers, which she liked. His favorite game was Monopoly, and they would play the game together with the other children.

One evening, they were playing in Rickie's mother's room. His mother had gone out that evening and left him to watch his siblings. Sojourner's mother had also gone out that evening, leaving Sojourner alone in the motel room with her brother. She and her little brother visited Rickie as usual. There, they watched TV and played games. The teenager made sandwiches for them all. Everyone fell asleep watching an adult movie that Sojourner knew they were not supposed to watch. Sojourner also fell asleep on the bed with the rest of the children.

She did not feel Rickie lifting the other sleeping children to a separate bed in the dark room. Nor did she feel him exposing her nipples. But she did feel him as he gingerly removed her shorts and underwear and hovered over her body. Her eyes opened as he attempted to spread her legs. She gasped, and Rickie covered her mouth with his hand. The boy was heavy as he mounted Sojourner, and she struggled beneath him to free herself. She bit his hand, and he winced, moving his hand. Then she screamed, waking the other children up. The lights came on. The other children laughed and pointed at Rickie, who was naked and fully erect. Sojourner got up from the bed and ran into the bathroom. She locked the bathroom door and stood there trembling.

CHAPTER FOURTEEN

Joseph phoned Sojourner the following day.

"Francois is having a dinner party this weekend. He invited us. Remember?" Joseph said.

"Oh, yeah. I do," Sojourner said. "Time flies, seems like yesterday."

"You can come right?" Joseph said.

"Yes. I can come," Sojourner said.

Sojourner sat on her sofa. At her feet was a duffle bag with some toiletries and new clothes that she had purchased to take to her father in the hospital.

"I'm glad you can come… So how's school?" Joseph said.

"Fine."

"So everything's in order for you to earn your Masters in May?"

"I'm working on it everyday," Sojourner said.

"I'll pick you tomorrow at about 8:00 p.m. How's that?"

"That's good... Um, I saw Theodetta at the Hospital yesterday," Sojourner said.

"Oh, yes. Theodetta phoned me about that," Joseph said. "So you volunteer at a homeless shelter?"

"Not all the time. I was just helping out. My church has an outreach program for that shelter," Sojourner said.

Sojourner bit her lip and shook her head, as she held the phone receiver to her ear. She remembered that her church did indeed have a sign up sheet for members to volunteer at a local shelter. However, she didn't participate in it.

"That's a kind thing to do," Joseph said. "Very Christian."

Sojourner thought to herself. What would he think if he knew the truth?

Joseph and Sojourner were the first guests to arrive at the party. Joseph brought several bottles of French wine for the host. The home was a three-bedroom apartment, which Francois shared with his sister, Christine, and another roommate. The apartment was located on 16th Street in D.C. Christine emerged from her bedroom with a red, satin strapless dress. Upon seeing Joseph, she brandished a coquettish smile. She sat next to him on the sofa and greeted him. Then she hugged him, speaking in French all the while. Christine also wore faux-jeweled, high-heel shoes, with an ankle bracelet. Her perfume blasted the air around her. She conversed with Joseph, as if Sojourner were not there. When she finally paused, Joseph introduced her to Sojourner, who sat next to him.

"Christine, I would like for you to meet my dear friend, Sojourner," Joseph said. "Sojourner is a graduate assistant at Howard University."

Christine nodded at Sojourner. Joseph then continued the introduction.

"Sojourner, Christine is Francois's sister. I knew them both in Cameroon. Christine's family was kind to me."

Sojourner smiled and nodded to Christine.

"Ma mère vous a adore, Joseph," Christine said, reverting back to French.

"Est-elle Rwandese?" Christine said.

"Sojourner is from New Jersey," Joseph said.

"Est-elle noire Américaine?" Christine said.

Sojourner understood the question; those few French classes from her undergraduate language requirement had finally paid off. She decided to indirectly answer it by making a seemingly unrelated comment.

"That was so good of your family to look out for Joseph while he was in Cameroon."

Christine looked surprised. Therefore, Sojourner supposed that Christine now realized that she was a "*noire Américaine.*"

Christine then got up and went to the kitchen to retrieve some large aluminum pans of food.

A few hours after Joseph and Sojourner arrived at the party, the apartment was crowded with guests, and the cases of beer that were stacked in the kitchen were being steadily emptied. The dining room table contained a wide assortment of Cameroonian cuisine, which Joseph described to Sojourner. The room was thick with the aroma of African food. Joseph described each dish to Sojourner as they helped themselves, along with the crowd of other visitors. The fare included fried ripe plaintains, whole roasted blue fish, and a spicy rice dish called Jolloff rice, with mixed vegetables and tomato sauce. Then there was oxtail stew, boiled plantains, a spinach dish called *Ndole*, fried African style donut holes called Puff Puff, Egusi Pudding, and much more.

"When did you attend the university in Cameroon?" Sojourner said.

Sojourner had to raise her voice to be heard over the music and chatter in the apartment.

"I attended Yaounde University in the late 1970s. I spent two years in Cameroon, before coming to the U.S."

The music played loudly and the guests, a crowd of Cameroonians about the same age as Joseph and Sojourner, danced enthusiastically. Joseph said that the music was called Makossa. Sojourner's first impression was that it sounded like Salsa or Caribbean Calypso music, with African drums mixed in. She remembered that the Sub-Sahara Room played mostly this type of music.

Joseph and Sojourner danced together through several songs. Then they sat down on the sofa, had drinks, and chatted with the other guests. The apartment grew hot and stuffy, as the guests poured in. Sojourner noticed that Joseph had finished four beers in the four hours that they'd been at the party. When she commented on this, Joseph said that he was being conservative because he still had so much work to complete that weekend. As they sat on the sofa talking and straining to hear each other over the music, Christine reappeared. She approached them shaking her hips and holding her arms out. Joseph smiled, but he didn't move. So Christine stood there, dancing in front of Joseph.

"*Mon frere, allez-vous danser avec moi? Veuillez venir*" Christine said.

"Is it okay with you, Sojourner?"

Sojourner wanted to say no, but she saw Joseph's friend, Francois, smiling at his sister's attempts to persuade Joseph to dance.

"Well, you're just dancing, go ahead," Sojourner said.

Sojourner appreciated that Joseph was respectful enough to ask. He did not immediately get up and gyrate with Christine. That had happened to Sojourner once with her college boyfriend, Donnell. They were at a party at Howard, five years ago. Sojourner went to the restroom, and when she returned Donnell was busy dancing with another girl, the girl was light complexioned, with long blondish hair.

Francois' apartment seemed to get even hotter. Sojourner felt like punching Christine in the neck, as she watched her dance with Joseph. Christine rotated her wide hips and rear end rapidly, while bending her knees and moving closer to Joseph. Finally, the song ended, and Joseph sat down next to Sojourner.

As Joseph and Sojourner left Francois's apartment, Joseph invited Sojourner to his apartment.

"Did you enjoy this party, Sojourner?" Joseph said.

"Oh, yeah. It was fun. Thank you for inviting me to come with you."

"I thank you for agreeing to come with me," Joseph said. "I like being with you, Sojourner. You're sweet and pretty."

She looked up into Joseph's dark eyes. For the first time, Sojourner detected raw lust in him. The night air was cold, so Joseph put his arm around Sojourner's shoulders and drew her closer as they walked down 16th street to his parked car.

"Do you like tea, Sojourner?"

"Yes. I do."

"My mother sent me some tea from Rwanda. I would like to give you some."

"Tea from Rwanda ... That sounds unique," Sojourner said. "But it's so late right now."

"Ma chère, I think you are shivering. I live close by. You can have a hot cup of Rwandan tea, and I will take you home."

A hot cup of tea on a cold night did sound really comforting, Sojourner thought. A hot cup of Rwandan tea with Joseph Kalisa sounded even better.

"Okay. Joseph," Sojourner said. "But I don't want to stay too late."

They arrived at his high-rise apartment building on Wisconsin Avenue. The lobby of the building had pale blue, marble floors that were so smooth that Sojourner had to be extra careful not to slip and fall. Sojourner was also visually drawn to the two large paintings of Louis XVI and his queen, Marie Antoinette, looking magnificently regal in their eighteenth century attire. The cream colored walls were trimmed in a gold-toned paint. There was a Christmas tree in the lobby, tall and well-decorated. The matronly desk clerk wore a pale blue suit jacket with gold trim, with Le Petit Trianon Apartments on her lapel.

Joseph lived on the third floor in a two-bedroom apartment. His apartment was neat and clean, decorated in earth tones, with a dark brown leather sofa set, a thick tan colored carpet, and ebony sculptured coffee and end tables.

On the wall in Joseph's living room hung a series of black and white photographs of his family in Rwanda. Sojourner stood in the living room, admiring the photos. One photo was a family photo of Joseph, his father, mother, and sister. In this picture, he was a little boy and his sister was a little girl in their mother's arms. The couple, a lean, attractive Rwandan couple, stood in front of a modest home in Rwanda. There was another picture of his father with a man that Joseph identified as the King of Rwanda.

A pretty young woman was the center of attention in the last of the black and white photos. According to Joseph, it was dated 1955. The young woman, dressed in what seemed to be traditional Rwanda regalia, was being carried in what Joseph described as a Tipoy. The tipoy was an elaborate, huge basket for transporting people. The young woman in the tipoy was Joseph's mother.

Sojourner was delighted with the delicious cup of Rwandan tea that Joseph had made for her. They sat on the sofa in his living room and watched CNN. The news anchor reported on the details of a coalition led by Chancellor Helmut Kohl which won the first free all-German elections since 1932. Then there was a story about an engineering marvel, the Channel Tunnel. Workers from the United Kingdom and France had met 40 meters beneath the English Channel seabed, establishing the first ground connection between the United Kingdom and the mainland of Europe since the last ice age.

Sojourner asked him questions about Francois and Christine.

"Why did you go to Cameroon to study, Joe?"

"After my father was killed, my mother was afraid I would also be killed, too. So she sent me to Cameroon with a friend of my father."

"Who was this 'friend'?"

"He taught at the National University with my father, but after my father's death, he decided to go back to Cameroon. My mother persuaded him to take me with him."

"And you went to school there?

"Yes."

"That's where you met Francois and Christine?"

"Yes. I met their parents through my father's friend."

"Christine seems to like you a lot," Sojourner said.

Joseph said nothing. He just smiled and gazed at the TV.

"So did you guys date, you and Christine?" Sojourner said.

"We liked each other years ago, but we're just friends. She's married and has three daughters."

"Oh, is she?" Sojourner said. She was relieved to hear that.

As they sat on the sofa, Joseph placed his arm around Sojourner's shoulder, gingerly. She was tired, so she leaned up against his shoulder. Joseph began to slowly caress Sojourner's hair, rubbing her scalp. Almost falling asleep, she slumped a little towards his chest. She felt him gently lifting her head, kissing her cheek, her eyelids, and her lips.

At first, Sojourner kept her mouth closed, allowing Joseph to plant delicate kisses on her lips. A delicious wave of arousal flowed through her, and she opened her mouth to receive his gently probing tongue.

Joseph slowly unbuttoned Sojourner's blouse, and they both stared at her brassiere. The brassiere was a recent addition to her wardrobe; it was a purple lace bra, so sheer that it was like wearing no bra at all. The purple color blended well with Sojourner's skin tone. He hesitated, looking into her eyes, as if to ask for permission. She smiled, bestowing it. His long fingers reached for her brassiere, and she sat still, anticipating his touch.

Then, suddenly, Joseph's telephone rang. A quick flash of annoyance appeared and disappeared on his face. On the fourth ring, Joseph reluctantly answered the phone on the cocktail table.

Sojourner felt like she was being yanked from a delicious haze. She slowly started to button up her blouse.

Joseph uttered monosyllabic responses. He spoke in his native language, Kinyarwanda. The person on the phone obviously had a lot to say, since he was on the phone for a few minutes. Sojourner strained to hear the voice emanating from the phone, while she pretended not to be interested. She was putting on her shoes and checking her watch. It was four in the morning. From what she could hear of the voice on the phone, it seemed to be a woman. Sojourner was perturbed, to say the least.

Joseph apologized after he got off the phone, and he insisted that the woman was his cousin, Theodetta, calling to tell him about a problem that she had with her landlord. Sojourner was skeptical. She politely asked Joseph to take her home. Joseph pleaded with her and explained that she should not take offense at the phone call.

"I'm sorry about that," Joseph said. "My cousin, she is having a problem with her landlord."

"It's almost morning time," Sojourner said.

"Please… Relax, Sojourner. You don't have to rush home."

"I want to go home now," Sojourner said.

"Yes, of course. Then, I'll take you home now."

The following day, Sojourner saw Joseph reading in the law library late one evening with Betsy McShane. Betsy was sitting next to Joseph, flipping back her blonde hair. She wore a cream-colored wool Chanel suit and tan pumps. Betsy crossed her legs, and the stockings made her big legs look smooth. Betsy smiled at Joseph. The red lipstick shimmered on her thin lips. Sojourner passed by, pushing a library cart filled with loose leaf services that needed to be filed. Betsy ignored Sojourner. However, Joseph made eye contact with Sojourner. Feeling a delicious tickle in her stomach, she nevertheless remained stoic on the outside. Sojourner attempted to smile, but she aborted the attempt when she realized that Joseph had redirected his attention to Betsy. Sojourner tightened her full lips and pushed the heavy library cart into the workroom area in the rear of the library. He didn't even speak to her, Sojourner thought. Joseph had taken her on several dates, and he couldn't even say hello. Sojourner felt insulted. Was he so wrapped up in that middle-aged vixen that he couldn't acknowledge her presence? A solitary tear traveled down her face.

Sojourner had fallen asleep in Founders Library one evening, only to be awakened by a light tap on her shoulder. She looked up and there was Harold, smiling down at her. He informed her that the lights in the library were starting to flicker on and off, signaling that it was about to close. She gathered her books. Harold asked Sojourner if he could give her a ride home. She said that she lived nearby, so she would be all right. He said that it was getting dark out and that he'd be glad to give her a ride. So Sojourner accepted a ride home.

During the ride home, Harold invited her out to the movies. She declined his offer, saying that she had to work on the evening he had suggested.

The following day, Sojourner saw Joseph and Betsy having lunch together in the cafeteria at work. Again, it seemed like Betsy was doing all the talking. Joseph's eyes discreetly followed Sojourner, but Sojourner decided not to eat in the cafeteria. After paying the cashier, she returned to the library workroom to eat her lunch at her desk.

Joseph called her on Christmas Day.

"Merry Christmas, Sojourner," Joseph said.

"Joseph. It's so good to hear from you," Sojourner said.

"I wanted to wish you a happy holiday," Joseph said.

"Thank you. Merry Christmas to you, too," Sojourner said.

"What are you doing for Christmas?" Joseph said.

"Nothing really... I mean I'll go to church today. Do you have something in mind? "No... Actually, I'm traveling tomorrow. I'm packing some things now," Joseph said.

"You're traveling alone?" Sojourner said.

"No. I'll be with some other attorneys from the firm," Joseph said.

"Like Betsy McShane?" Sojourner said.

"...And Peter Shininsky," Joseph said.

"How long will you be away?"

"Three days," Joseph said.

"Call me when you get back."

"Of course."

"Okay. Enjoy your trip," Sojourner said.

"Thanks. Merry Christmas...Take care," Joseph said.

Weeks passed with no call from Joseph, and Sojourner felt disappointed.

The next time she saw Harold in the Founders Library, Harold repeated his offer of a movie and dinner. This time, Sojourner accepted his offer. "Dances with Wolves", starring Kevin Costner, was just released, so she suggested that movie.

CHAPTER FIFTEEN

Sojourner was getting dressed for her date with Harold. Rose and her girlfriend, Janelle, were conversing in the living room. Sojourner listened to their conversation as she dressed. It seemed like every other word that came out of Janelle's mouth was "Nigga," Sojourner thought. Sojourner detested the word, and she could hardly stomach to hear other people utter it. Why were so many black people okay with that word? She could not get herself to speak the "N" word comfortably. She had heard some of her peers and a few of her family members use the word, but she still felt uncomfortable with it. To her the word meant degradation for people of African descent.   Dignity was something that Black people had struggled and died to maintain, so why throw it away with the use of one word? Whenever she would voice her opinion about the "N" word, she would often get a justification for the use of the word. Sojourner remembered what she had heard her father say about the word when she was a child; he said it was "a part of the slave mentality."

Nevertheless, Sojourner envied Rose's friendship with Janelle, since she had no close friendships. Most of the time, she was fine with this situation. Women could be so catty, and men were untrustworthy, Sojourner thought. Maybe it was best to be alone. Sojourner finished dressing.

Harold picked Sojourner up from her apartment in a champagne colored Cadillac.   When he arrived at her apartment building, he tapped on the glass door of the lobby. Sojourner walked down the stairs to open the door for him. As she descended the stairs, she saw Harold standing there placidly.   He stared up at her blankly.   Harold wore a navy blue polo shirt and beige slacks, with a brown leather jacket. Sojourner perceived no enthusiasm on Harold's part, as he watched her descend the stairs.   When she opened the door, Harold did smile, but his smile didn't light up the world the way Joseph's did. His smile was a quick, perfunctory smile. Harold's smile did not have the generosity of Joseph's smile, which lingered and pierced through her loneliness.

He walked Sojourner to his car and opened the car door for her to enter the passenger side. But he did not wait for her to enter his car and close the door for her, as Joseph had done. She closed the door herself. Sojourner felt like, for Harold, she was just another Saturday night date. She glanced at her watch as they drove to the movies, hoping the movie would be more exciting than Harold's company.

She sat silently on the velour seats of the car, which he mentioned belonged to his father. Harold did most of the talking, about his engineering aspirations and his father's connections with Howard University. He talked about his assistantship in the School of Engineering. His assistantship was sponsored by a government grant that his advisor, a professor in the School of Engineering, had received. A part of the grant involved the programming and maintenance of one of the mainframe computers in the computer laboratory of the Engineering building. Harold said that he helped out with the operations of the computer lab.

Sojourner listened as Harold told her that his father and his grandfather had gone to Howard. He was proud to be a "third generation Howardite." His father owned an engineering firm in D.C., and Harold planned to work there one day. He eventually wanted to be his father's partner. Sojourner barely managed to squeeze in a few words like "that's interesting" and "impressive." He drove to the movie theatre, content with the sound of his own voice. Sojourner noticed that her silence didn't seem to bother Harold.

After Harold and Sojourner saw the movie, Harold didn't have much to say about it. Sojourner told Harold what she liked about the movie, as they exited the theater. She liked the cinematography and the historical background of the movie. Harold nodded. Then he stared at her clothes and commented on the sophistication of her apparel. Harold said that he really liked her dress and her shoes.

Harold took Sojourner to the Georgia Avenue Diner, two blocks from her apartment. As Harold and Sojourner entered the restaurant, Sojourner noted Harold did open the door for her. However, he did not pull out her chair, and he did not help her to take off her coat, as Joseph had done. The specialty at the restaurant was soul food. Harold smiled and told Sojourner that she could order anything she wanted. She felt awkward by that remark. Sojourner reasoned that since Harold had invited her out to the movies and then to a restaurant, she should be able to order what she wanted. Why did he make it sound like it was such big a treat for her?

Sojourner ordered the fish and chips, and Harold ordered a rack of barbecue ribs, with collard greens, macaroni and cheese, and corn bread. As she ate, Sojourner caught Harold, staring at her. Harold commented that Sojourner had a "pretty skin." Sojourner felt like an expensive, imported candy bar in a greedy man's hands.

She finished her meal and asked Harold some questions about where his family was from. Harold said that his family was from Washington, D.C. He'd grown up in a house off Rock Creek Park. However, Harold didn't ask her where she was from, and this annoyed Sojourner.

When she finished her meal, Harold asked her if she had enjoyed the meal. Actually, she did enjoy the food. Her grandmother had cooked such foods when she was a child, and the food brought back memories of family get-togethers. Nevertheless, Sojourner resented this question. Why can't Harold be patient and allow her to volunteer that information? Moreover, Sojourner felt a chill because Harold had selected a table near the entrance. Each time the door opened, a cold breeze entered the restaurant. She rubbed her hands together and trembled a little, but Harold didn't seem to be aware of her discomfort. He just gazed at her and smiled approvingly.

As they exited the restaurant, a short man, wearing a trench coat, jeans, and tennis shoes, approached them. Sojourner noticed him first.

"My brother, do you have some extra change?" the man said. "I'm trying to take the bus home."

Harold didn't respond to the man. He continued to walk toward his car, gesturing to Sojourner to follow him. Instead, she stopped and handed the man a one dollar bill. The man smiled and spoke.

"Thank you, my sister," the man said.

Harold waited for her near his car.

"You didn't have to give him anything," Harold said.

"Maybe he really did need change for the bus," Sojourner said.

"That Nigga stands in front of this place everyday, begging," Harold said.

There was that word she hated, Sojourner thought. She was annoyed.

In the car, Harold asked Sojourner to come home with him to listen to some music. He'd just purchased Ice Cube's AmeriKKKa's Most Wanted cassette. He told Sojourner that he was living with his parents, just while he was in graduate school. His parents had gone out to a dinner party given by his father's old fraternity friend. Sojourner declined this offer. Who the heck did this joker think he was, she thought?

Harold walked Sojourner to the front door of her apartment building, and Sojourner said good night to him. She noticed his baby soft-looking, short, light brown afro. Harold seemed to want to say something to Sojourner, but he did not. Going the extra mile to reach Sojourner's heart did not seem to be a part of Harold's initial plan. Sojourner reasoned that Harold thought winning her affection was more challenging than he had originally anticipated. Before she opened the door, Harold said that he would call Sojourner the following day. Sojourner thanked him for the movie and dinner.

The phone rang at 9:00 a.m. on the following morning, and Harold was on the line.

"Hi Sojourner."

"Hi Harold."

"So, what are you doing today?" Harold said.

"I think I'll go to church today," Sojourner said.

"That's nice. You go every Sunday?"

"No, but I really should."

"I haven't been to church in a while, either."

There was a silence on the phone.

"I had a nice time last night," Harold said, breaking the silence.

Again, silence followed.

Sojourner relented and spoke.

"Thank you for inviting me out, Harold. I enjoyed the movie."

"Was the restaurant okay? I got the feeling the restaurant didn't impress you," Harold said.

"It was okay, Harold."

"My stipend doesn't pay enough for much more," Harold said, suddenly realizing that Sojourner was indeed, unimpressed.

"I understand. I'm a graduate assistant, too, with rent to pay," Sojourner said. Holding the phone to her ear, she sat up in bed.

Sojourner wished that she could tell Harold that it was not so much the quality of the restaurant, but the quality of his behavior that didn't impress her.

"Okay. I'll try to do better on our next date," Harold said.

"Our next date? Are you asking me for another date, Harold?"

"Yes, Sojourner, I am."

"Well … let me think about it."

"All right," Harold said, also playfully. "I'll give you two minutes."

"Just two minutes to think it over?"

"Yep."

"Okay, then… No."

"Oh, come on, Sojourner. Give a brother a break," Harold said.

Sojourner chuckled.

"I'm busy actually," Sojourner said.

"Okay... Now you want to make a brother beg, right?"

Sojourner smiled to herself.

On their second date, Sojourner sat in the living room waiting for Harold to pick her up from her apartment. Rose was surprised.

"You're on a roll, Soj," Rose said. "We were roommates for more than a year, and Joseph was the first man you'd brought to our apartment. Two months later, you're on your second date with this high yellow big brain."

"He's a graduate student, like me. By chance, we study about the same time in the library, most days. He asked me out, so I decided to accept his invitation. It's not a romance at all," Sojourner said.

"You looked more cheerful when you were dating Joseph," Rose said.

"Yep... Felt like a brand new woman," Sojourner said.

"What about Joseph, anyway?" Rose said.

"I think he's busy at the office," Sojourner said.

Silently, Sojourner yearned for Joseph's presence.

"Did y'all have a fight?" Rose said.

"I hear someone tapping on the lobby door," Sojourner said, slowly getting up from the sofa.

Sojourner descended the staircase of the lobby. She saw Harold standing outside. He smiled politely, as she opened the door.

"Hey Sojourner," Harold said.

"Hi Harold," Sojourner said.

They stood in the lobby face to face. He looked at her quickly, a glance that skims the surface only.

"You look good," Harold said, putting his hands in his khaki pockets.

"Thanks. I'm ready," Sojourner said.

The name of the club was the Boardroom 2000, and it was located on the Waterfront in Southwest D.C. The music was contemporary R and B and pop music, with some rap thrown in. The crowd consisted of young urban professionals of all backgrounds, but mostly African American.

Sojourner was dressed in a black cocktail dress and black high-heel pumps. Harold and Sojourner had entered the nightclub at 9:30 p.m., before it was too crowded. They seated themselves at a table near the dance floor, and Harold ordered drinks. He ordered a beer, and Sojourner ordered a Pina Colada. Harold told Sojourner that he heard that several local NBA and NFL basketball players frequented the Boardroom 2000. She hoped that Harold would not start rambling about basketball or football. She had been exposed to these sports as a child. The local playground in several of her childhood neighborhoods contained a well-used basketball court, where teenagers and adult men would play vigorous games. Old Black and white movies and cartoons were the entertainment of preference in her mother's home. She grew up in the home of a single Mom who had no interest in sports.

Harold asked Sojourner to dance, and they both moved toward the dance floor. As they danced, Harold danced close to Sojourner. He kept touching her waist and hips with his hands. This annoyed Sojourner, and she gently guided his hands away from her body.

As he drove her home, Harold mentioned that his parents would be sleeping, and they would not mind if he brought her home for a while. They could listen to some soft music in the basement. Harold said that there was a fireplace there, as well as a new stereo set. Sojourner shook her head and said that she didn't want to go to his place. She wanted to go home and get some sleep.

When they reached her apartment building, Harold walked Sojourner to the front entrance of the building. Sojourner said goodnight to Harold and used her key to open the glass lobby door. Harold was silent for a moment; then he asked

Sojourner if he could use her bathroom. He really had to go, he said, smiling. It was all the beer he drank at the nightclub, Harold explained. Sojourner agreed.

When they entered her apartment, Rose and her boyfriend, Jamarr, were sitting on the sofa watching a movie. Sojourner greeted them and then pointed out the bathroom location to Harold. He went into the bathroom.

There was a love scene on the TV screen, and Sojourner felt awkward. The movie featured a naked couple in bed kissing passionately. Sojourner hung up her coat and went to their small dining room area. Seeing her mail on the table, she sat down and started to open it. Sojourner heard moans coming from the TV set, a sex scene began on the TV screen. She should change the channel, for goodness sakes, Sojourner thought. When Sojourner looked up, she saw Harold standing in the living room gazing at the TV screen. He looked like he was going to start to drool. Sojourner knew it was time for Harold to go home before he got any ideas.

That evening, as Sojourner lay alone in her bed, she thought of Joseph Kalisa. Her pride had prevented her from telephoning him. If he wanted to speak with her, then he should call, Sojourner thought. She knew that Rose and Jamarr were together in Rose's bedroom. The sound of their love making drifted into her room, even though her door was closed and locked.

A few days later, Sojourner was coming from the McDonald's on Georgia Avenue across the street from the main campus of Howard. She was walking back to Founders Library, after taking a lunch break. Taking a short cut through a parking lot adjacent to the School of Engineering and the School of Architecture, she saw Harold walking with another student, holding hands. Harold glanced at Sojourner and froze in his tracks; he then waved. Sojourner waved back at him, nonchalantly. She continued walking. When he saw her in the library that afternoon Harold explained to Sojourner that the girl he was walking with was his ex-girlfriend. He said that he was just trying to be polite to her. Sojourner shrugged and stated that it was none of her business, since they were not romantically involved.

Harold telephoned Sojourner that evening and asked her out again, and she declined. She said that she needed to concentrate on completing her dissertation. He pleaded with her that he was really sorry about his ex-girlfriend, but they weren't involved anymore. Sojourner stood her ground, saying that she was busy.

She was tired of Harold's attempts to reconnect with her after she'd sighted him, holding hands with an undergraduate student. The girl looked to be no more than eighteen years old, Sojourner thought.

CHAPTER SIXTEEN

Sojourner was worried sick about what to do with her father. How long could she keep this secret to herself, without bursting? Her aloneness was by choice, but it was a tough choice. It meant bearing burdens without the benefit of a shoulder to lean on. She was studying at the dining room table when Rose entered their apartment.

"Hey, Soj," Rose said.

"Hi Rose," Sojourner said.

"Dang, girl, you look depressed. We gotta get Joseph back up in this place," Rose said, playfully.

Sojourner pretended to read.

"Come on, Soj. Talk to me. You're always quiet, but not depressed. What's wrong, girl?"

Sojourner looked at Rose. She wondered if she could trust her. They'd shared an apartment for more than a year, without any serious problems, other than Rose's tendency to be late with her share of the rent.

"My father is sick in the hospital," Sojourner said.

"What happened?"

"He had a stroke."

"I'm sorry to hear that, Soj. Are you going to New Jersey?"

"He's here in D.C."

"But I thought all your family was in New Jersey."

"They are. He came to D.C. to visit me, but he had a stroke while he was here."

"What? You didn't say anything about your Dad being in town, Soj. We've been roommates for a while now. You could have at least mentioned it."

"It wasn't your normal visit, Rose. My father sort of showed up…out of no where. I hadn't seen him in fourteen years."

"Seriously? He just showed up like that?" Rose said.

"Yeah. And passed out…right on our doorstep downstairs."

Sojourner made eye contact with Rose. She could see that Rose remembered the incident.

"What! That was your Dad?"

"Yep," Sojourner said.

"Oh, my God, Soj."

"He's been in and out of the hospital since. I've been doing what I can for him. Howard Hospital is discharging him. I don't think he's strong enough to travel yet. He needs some follow up care before I take him back to New Jersey."

Rose listened; then she sat down at the dining room table with Sojourner.

"How about the VA Medical Center, Soj? There's one in D.C. Jamarr's Dad's a veteran. His dad had a heart attack, and he stayed there for a month."

"Thank you, Rose," Sojourner said. "I'll try that."

Sojourner looked up the phone number and address to the VA Medical Center in D.C. in the big yellow phone book in their small kitchen. She called them and explained her father's situation. She purchased some clothes for her father, a pair of khaki pants, a navy blue turtle neck sweater, and a coat. Then she met him at the hospital. Before leaving the hospital, he had washed and combed his hair, so he looked presentable. He was looking more like the man who brought her the African history book when she was a child, Sojourner thought.

CHAPTER SEVENTEEN

Washington, D.C. January 1991

One Friday night, Francois telephoned Joseph and invited him out for some drinks at the Sub-Sahara Room nightclub. When Joseph arrived, Christine happened to be there with her brother, Francois, and some other Cameroonians. Christine asked Joseph to dance with her, and he did. He was there for two hours, and he was about to leave when two of his Rwandan friends, Ibrahim Kabaija and Moses Gasana, showed up. They invited him to join them for a drink in a corner table in the nightclub.

"Gira Inka," Joseph said, greeting Ibrahim and Moses.

The men nodded graciously. One of them spoke.

"Are you thinking about joining the troops?" Ibrahim said.

"No. I'm with this law firm now. It's one of the best in D.C., and the pay is excellent. I'm not giving this up."

"I understand…but still we can't turn our back on our people," Moses said.

"I'm not turning my back on them. I sent six thousand dollars for the cause, and I support my mother back home, too. I'm doing my duty."

"Madame Kalisa is a princess. You're an heir to the Rwandan royal family. It's high stakes for you," Ibrahim said.

"Gentlemen, it's getting late. I've some business to attend to for the firm. Ijora Ryiza," Joseph said, getting up from the table.

Joseph went back to the table where Francois and company were sitting.

"I'll see you later, Francois," Joseph said.

"Going so soon, Joe?" Francois said.

"Yes. I've some urgent things to do at the office tomorrow."

"Joe, drop me off on your way home. I have to get up for work early. You can drop me off on your way home," Christine said.

Christine was standing up and adjusting her gold toned handbag on her shoulder, apparently not entertaining the possibility of a rejection. She had her hands on her shapely hips, her gold sequined dress shimmering.

During the car ride, Joseph listened as Christine complained to him.

"Joe, why haven't you returned my phone calls? I left messages," Christine said.

"Christine, I've been busy. I apologize," Joseph said.

"My family was good to you in Cameroon. Remember when your money was running low in Cameroon?" Christine said.

"Yes. Your father paid me to tutor your brother," Joseph said.

"And you used to spend the weekends with us," Christine said.

"Right. I did," Joseph said.

"Anyway, I'm happy to hear that you are doing so well in D.C.," Christine said.

"Thanks," Joseph said.

"Joe, I want to see your place," Christine said.

"All right, Christine."

Christine complimented him on the elegance of the location and the apartment itself. She walked around the apartment, admiring the furniture and artwork.

"Joe, Remember when you got sick in the dormitory?"

Christine said. She was sitting comfortably on Joseph's living room sofa.

"Yes. I could barely stand. Madame Mbang brought me pepper soup," Joseph said.

"That's right. When I told my mother that you were sick, she insisted on going to check on you in the dormitory. She brought you pepper soup."

"Madame Mbang…a very kind lady," Joseph said.

He gazed at the TV, watching the CNN news channel.

"My mother adored you, Joe. She said you were the perfect gentlemen, and so good-looking," Christine said.

"How is your husband, Julius?" Joseph said.

Joseph leaned back on the sofa and folded his arms.

"My husband… You wouldn't believe what he did. I'm so angry," Christine said.

"Francois told me that his business wasn't doing well, but that's all," Joseph said.

He stared at her.

"We married a year after you left Cameroon…Julius was okay at first," Christine said. "He wanted to impress my father, who was a minister at the time. When my father lost his position as Minister of Special Construction Projects, my family had to move out of the ministerial mansion and back into our old house. Julius stopped being generous, ignoring me and our daughters. I got an administrative position with the Cameroon government. The pay was low, but I was glad to have something of my own. Then my husband brought that village girl into our home. She was about sixteen years old, with only a primary school education. I had graduated from Yaounde University. I threw her out, and he got angry with me. So he kept her in a small house that he purchased, on the other side of Douala. Soon the girl was pregnant."

Joseph sat back on the sofa, listening to Christine's story.

"When she birthed his first son, he wanted me to be as happy as he was. He started telling me all that rubbish about me trying to get along with her, saying that I was his first wife, and I would always be his number one wife. Crazy fool! I should have expected it, since his father had two wives. Then he started losing money; his business was not doing well. Soon I was paying household expenses, and he started borrowing money from me. Money became really tight, and the second wife, who did not work, was pregnant with their second child. I wasn't going to be the one to support that household, so I asked Julius to allow me to come to the U.S. to go back to school."

"So how are your children doing?" Joseph said.

"They are well. My daughters are in a private school in Douala," Christine said. "I send them money to pay for their schooling, since Julius can't afford their tuition on his own."

"I see...," Joseph said.

"Remember the first time we made love, Joe?" Christine said.

"Yes. We were celebrating the end of the school year. Francois and some other students went to a local alimentation to have some soda and dance. You and I found private place..."

"I loved the way you kissed me, Joe."

"In the darkness of night, with music blasting from a nearby nightclub, we did it. Right there, on our knees. So sweet," Joseph said, smiling at the thought.

Christine snuggled up to Joseph on the sofa. She rubbed his leg. Joseph yawned and looked at his watch. He kissed her perfunctorily. Joseph helped Christine to remove her dress; then he removed his own clothing. On her hands and knees, with Joseph kneeling behind her, Christine moaned with delight, as they had sex on the plush carpet of his living room floor. When they finished, Joseph then got up from the floor and went to the bathroom. Upon exiting his master bathroom, Joseph was surprised to see Christine sleeping naked on his bed. He sighed and lay down on the other side of the bed. Within minutes, he was asleep.

At three in the morning, Christine woke Joseph up. He looked at her, as she kissed his lips. She had showered and dressed. She told him she had to go to work.

Joseph drove her to an upscale nursing home, not far from where he lived.

"Joe, I looked in your refrigerator, and it looks empty. You could really use a good, home-cooked meal. I want to come over and cook for you," Christine said.

"You don't have to do that, Christine. I'm all right, really," Joseph said.

"It's no problem, Joe. I really want to…I'll come over next weekend."

"No… I'm busy next weekend, Christine. Thank you for offering."

Joseph returned home and took a shower. Glad to have his bed to himself again, he reset his alarm clock for twelve noon to make up for his lost sleep. Six hours later, Joseph's sleep was interrupted again. The phone rang, and it was Betsy McShane. She was crying on the phone, and she explained to him that her husband was up to his usual adulterous antics. The husband had disappeared for the weekend, after withdrawing several hundred dollars from their joint bank account. Betsy told Joseph that she'd be over as soon as she talked to her nanny. She needed to inform the nanny that she had to go out. Betsy said that she needed a shoulder to lean on. Joseph took another long, hot shower and brushed his teeth; then he changed his bed sheets. Betsy was on her way over.

When Joseph opened the door to let Betsy into his apartment, he saw that Betsy's eyes were red, from crying. She was carrying a large, expensive duffle bag. Joseph sliced a French baguette and placed a cup of hot Rwandan tea in front of her on the coffee table in the living room.

"You know, Joe, when I first met Tim, I was so impressed. He had thick dark hair, sky blue eyes, and a body like Adonis. He composed songs for me…we went on romantic vacations," Betsy said.

"Sounds good," Joseph said.

"I was forty years old when I married Tim...tired of the dating game... He was five years younger and had his own local band...but he wasn't making much money."

At one point, Joseph had fallen asleep on the sofa, as Betsy continued her monologue. He awoke when he heard her calling his name. Betsy asked Joseph if he'd gotten much sleep last night, and Joseph said no. Joseph told her that he'd been spending some time helping his cousin to relocate to a new apartment. He said that he did not get home until four in the morning. As Joseph said this, he remembered how he carefully put the used sheets in the washing machine near his kitchen. He then added detergent and bleach. Opening his linen closet, he took fresh, clean sheets from his linen closet. Carefully, he had made his bed, so that it looked fresh and inviting. He knew that he could not tell her the truth, that, nine hours ago, he was having sex with an old college girlfriend.

Betsy apologized for the inconvenience of coming over on short notice, but she said that she was beginning to feel a little better, just being in his company. Joseph changed the subject and started talking about the Cameroon case at Livingston and Richards. Joseph didn't want to miss the opportunity to express his desire to take on this case.

She leaned up against Joseph on the sofa, and they watched TV together. Joseph was watching CNN news, when he felt Betsy's hand rub his thigh lightly. They kissed. Joseph watched as Betsy began to unbutton her blouse, allowing him to see her large breasts. They hung a little, but she still looked good for her age, Joseph thought. She grabbed her duffle bag and followed Joseph to his bedroom. Betsy went into Joseph's master bathroom with her duffle bag. Joseph undressed and lay in bed, naked, waiting for Betsy to emerge from his bathroom.

Wearing only a black lace thong, Betsy emerged from the bathroom. Joseph watched Betsy walk over to the bed where he lay, propped up against some pillows. She sat on the bed next to him and brushed the hairs on his chest with her red fingernails. Then she kissed his mouth, searching for his tongue. Joseph closed his eyes and felt her warm hands massaging his erection. Joseph saw Betsy's pale, voluptuous body hover over him; the scent of expensive perfume wafted around him. Joseph reached for her pinkish breasts and massaged them gently. Betsy moaned and licked her lips, as Joseph carefully removed her thong. Positioning herself over Joseph's pelvis, Betsy allowed him to enter her. She was on top of Joseph with her legs wide apart, enjoying their union. It culminated in a frenzy of movement with Joseph atop Betsy.

When Joseph awoke Saturday afternoon, Betsy had left. There was a note on the dining room table. It said that she had to go home because her daughter had a cold. Joseph was relieved that Betsy was gone, and that he would have the rest of the day to spend the way he pleased.

Joseph got up out of bed and went to his bathroom; there he took another shower. After dressing in jeans and a T-shirt, he did some house chores. These included dusting off the old photos that he'd hung on his living room wall. These were the black and white photographs of his family in Rwanda.

He stared at the photos of his father hanging on the wall. A tall, thin, serious looking man in his early thirties stood in front of the National University in Rwanda. It seemed to Joseph that his father was staring back at him. He had to make his father proud, Joseph thought. He remembered a conversation he had with his father, shortly before his father was murdered. They were sitting in the parlor of his parents' home in Kigali, Rwanda.

"You are very capable of succeeding in the career of your choice, but don't forget who you are, my son," his father said.

"What do you mean father?" Joseph said.

"You are a Rwandan man. We have a critical problem in Rwandan, with divisions between our people, Hutus and Tutsi. We are Tutsi, and we live in under the threat of violence. Be vigilant, my son. For your mother, your sister...yourself."

"I'll work hard...help with the family responsibilities," Joseph said.

There was another old black and white photo of his parents on his living room wall. His mother was holding his sister in her arms. Joseph was a small boy, standing near his father, his hand almost grabbing one his father's long legs. The young, neatly dressed Rwandan family was standing in front of a home in the background. Joseph wanted to speak with his mother, so he telephoned his brother-in-law in Kigali, Rwanda.

His sister, Teresa Uwimana, was married to Laurent, a man of Hutu ancestry. Laurent was a high ranking government official in Kigali, the capital of Rwanda. As such, he had a telephone in his home. Very few Rwandans had a telephone in their home.

Joseph spoke with his mother, who spent most of her time with Teresa and Laurent.

"Hello Mother," Joseph said.

"My son, how are you?"

"I'm well, Mother."

"Who has been cooking for you, my son?"

"I'm cooking for myself, Mother."

"Oh, my son, you are a big man in America. It's past time for you to have a wife. If you were here I would have found you the very best wife, one to cook for you and keep your home well organized. You'd have many children by now."

"There is still time for that mother."

"I know a very pretty and proper girl from a good Tutsi clan, a real umwaari. She applied for the National University, but they rejected her application. I'm sure it's just because she is a Tutsi girl. Oh, if you could meet her... I wish I could see you again, Joseph. It's been so long, my son."

"I would like to visit, Mother," Joseph said.

"No, my son. That would be very dangerous. Tutsi, rich and poor, have been killed mysteriously. There's so much discrimination and intimidation of Tutsi. Don't come back yet, my son. Please don't. Please. Not now."

"I'm still supporting our forces. Perhaps they can influence the policies there..." Joseph said.

"We shall continue to pray to Imaana, my son. Remember to pray my son."

"Yes, Mother…I will."

"How is Theodetta?"

"She's all right. Her medical studies are going well."

"Is she married?" his mother said.

"Not yet, Mother."

CHAPTER EIGHTEEN

One Saturday morning in mid January 1991, Joseph telephoned Sojourner.

"Hello Sojourner, how have you been?"

"Hi Joe, I'm a little sick, actually."

"Oh, really … What happened?"

"I have the flu."

"Oh, no. You know, I was concerned because I haven't seen you in the library in a few days. You sound tired."

"Well … I think I have a fever, right now," Sojourner said.

"I'm coming now, ma chère," Joseph said.

"You don't have to, Joseph."

"No, please, I want to. I'll be there within the hour."

"Okay."

Joseph showered and dressed. He selected coal grey slacks and a light grey turtleneck sweater.

He arrived forty-five minutes later at Sojourner's apartment.

"It's good to see you, Sojourner," Joseph said, as he entered the lobby of the apartment building.

"I'm glad to see you, too, Joseph," Sojourner said.

Sojourner wore a tan peasant dress and bunny rabbit slippers.

Joseph appraised her discreetly.   She was exceptionally beautiful, Joseph thought. He embraced her in the lobby, and he felt her yield to him momentarily.

They both ascended the stairs and entered Sojourner's apartment. She asked him to have a seat on the sofa, and he did.

"Can I get you something to drink," Sojourner said.

"Sojourner, you're sick. I want to do something for you."

Sojourner sat next to him on the sofa and coughed. Then she sneezed and wiped her nose with a napkin.

"Have you eaten today?" Joseph said.

"Yeah, I had some soup," Sojourner said.

"Fresh soup?"

"Oh, no. Canned."

"Sojourner, you need some fresh food."

Joseph touched her hand.

"You are very warm."

Sojourner was silent.

"Have you been hiding from me, Sojourner?"

"Maybe," Sojourner said.

Joseph noticed her mischievous smile.

"Why?" Joseph said.

"Well … Because I think you are involved in another relationship," Sojourner said.

"Okay. I understand now. Is it because my cousin called me early in the morning, the evening we were together?"

"Yes. That was part of it. I didn't believe she was your cousin."

"She is my cousin, Sojourner. It was Theodetta who called me that night, and she is my cousin," Joseph said, triumphantly.

Sojourner sighed and rubbed her forehead.

Joseph gently touched her hand.

"She is the same woman that I introduced you to at the

night club, the intern you met at the hospital," Joseph said.

Sojourner nodded slowly.

"That night, she was having some problems with her landlord, and she called me for advice," Joseph said.

"Okay, then. What about Attorney McShane?" Sojourner said.

"Attorney McShane is my colleague, Sojourner," Joseph said, smiling wryly. "She's married with two children, and she's fifteen years older than I am."

Joseph thought that Sojourner still looked skeptical.

"Sojourner, my work often requires that I socialize with my colleagues outside of the office, at dinner parties and other events. Relationships that develop as a result of this, could be misconstrued," Joseph said.

"I suppose," Sojourner said.

"How is your dissertation going?" Joseph said. He wanted to change the subject.

"It's going well. Thanks. I've finished my first draft."

"Congratulations!"

"Thank you. But I still have a ton of work to do."

"Is this your book?" Joseph said, picking up a paperback book on the coffee table.

"Yes," Sojourner said.

"Hmm…let's see. 'Flowers of Songhay.' That's an interesting title," Joseph said.

"Is this a reference to the ancient African Kingdom of Songhay?"

"Yes. It is," Sojourner said.

He skimmed through the pages of the book.

Joseph read one of the poems aloud.

Warriors of Yore

Warriors of yore with sturdy brown bodies filled with bravado,
Prancing, dancing warriors who protected our great grandmothers,
Where are you now? Were you just a dream? Legends…?
Warriors of yore with mahogany hues showing your teeth

When you smiled,
Styling, beguiling warriors with the elegance of women, yet you
*   protected our mothers,*
Did you die in Africa, the Jim Crow South, or the riots of Watts?
Warriors of yore with your torsos rippling with muscles from hundred
*   mile hikes in the Savannah,*
Yet you never entered a gym.
Backs and minds rippling with the scars,
Of physical and mental pain,
You are transformed into so many forms.
Warriors of yore, come back to us who loved you
With hurting hearts.
Tell the world of our beauty.
Stand up again, and again,
Undeterred by the visible and invisible kicks.
Warriors of yore, you are transformed into so many forms.
Rise.

"This is magnificent, " Joseph said, when he finished the poem.

"Thank you, Joseph," Sojourner said.

"This reminds me of some Rwandan royal court poetry," Joseph said.

"There's a connection…I was thinking about the majesty of the ancient African warrior, at his best, in contrast to some negative stereotypes of black men," Sojourner said.

She stood up and went to her kitchen.

"I'm making some tea, Joseph. Can I make some for you, too?"

"All right."

"This is like a Rwandan praise poem," Joseph said to himself, as he read the poems. And that's what he thought of Sojourner at that moment, as he sat on her sofa. This pretty, statuesque, woman, with an almost frail beauty, had published a book of poetry. She was supporting herself on a small stipend and a part time job in a library.

"Sojourner, I have a recipe that can cure a cold," Joseph said.

"Really? What is it?" Sojourner said.

"It's pepper soup," Joseph said.

"So ... I guess it's very hot?" Sojourner said.

"Traditionally, yes," Joseph said. "You don't like spicy food?" Joseph said.

"Spicy is okay. I use hot sauce sometimes, like on fried Cat Fish, or fried chicken," Sojourner said.

"Oh, okay. That's Soul Food, right?" Joseph said.

"Yeah, sort of," Sojourner said.

"I can make the soup for you, and I won't put too much pepper in it," Joseph said.

"Joseph, you'd do that for me?" Sojourner said.

"Of course, my Princess," Joseph said.

"Princess?"

"Remember my letter? I said you are like an African Princess in ancient times."

"Okay. That works for me," Sojourner said, obviously flattered.

"Let me see. I have to go to the office today, but I can make it for you tomorrow."

"I don't want to inconvenience you, Joseph."

"Let me do something special for you," Joseph said.

"Well, okay, if you insist."

"I do," Joseph said.

CHAPTER NINETEEN

After leaving Sojourner's apartment, Joseph went to the office to do some work in the law library. When he finished, he went home and retrieved the voice messages left on his answering machine. He sat on his brown leather sofa, listening to his messages. He had one message from Peter Shininski, one from Theodetta, one from Betsy, and three from Christine Mbang.

Christine Mbang's voice messages indicated that she wanted to come over the following weekend. Joseph was apprehensive.

He did not wish to encourage another get together, no matter how delicious it would be.

The following morning, Joseph went shopping at an international market where he could find the ingredients he needed to prepare the pepper soup for Sojourner. He purchased fresh garlic, ginger, and hot peppers. Then he purchased some potatoes and carrots. Normally, some beef or goat meat would be added, but Joseph normally tried to avoid eating meat. This was one way to honor his father, a man who adhered to the old tradition.

Joseph prepared the soup in his apartment. He peeled and sliced garlic and ginger. Then he ground them up in the blender, along with hot peppers. He peeled and sliced his potatoes and carrots. This was his version of Pepper Soup. Joseph smiled when he thought of what his mother would say if she saw him cooking for a woman. A man from his country did not cook for himself, traditionally. Either his mother, or his wife, would cook for him. However, he had been away from Rwanda for fifteen years. When he finished the soup, he phoned Sojourner. Joseph told Sojourner that he'd prepared the pepper soup for her, among other dishes, like fried ripe plantains. He told Sojourner that he wanted her to have lunch at his place, and that he'd pick her up right away. She seemed delighted.

He picked Sojourner up from her apartment in the early afternoon, and he drove her back to his apartment. They had lunch together and discussed Sojourner's dissertation topic, her love of writing, and life in D.C.

Sojourner and Joseph sat on the sofa watching TV. The news coverage was on the Gulf War, Operation Desert Storm. She seemed reticent, but he liked that. It was a refreshing relief from the experienced professional women, whom he had dated within the last few years. Some, like Betsy, were older women whose sexual inhibitions had long disintegrated. Generous salaries and the hedonism of urban life had emboldened them.

"Joseph, I'd better go home, so you can get some work done. Thank you so much for the excellent meal. The food was delicious," Sojourner said. "Next time, I'll cook for you."

"All right, then Princess," Joseph said. "I can't wait to taste your food."

Sojourner was shelving books in the library of the law firm one day, and she saw Joseph walk by. When Sojourner saw Joseph walk by, she thought that maybe he didn't see her, since he didn't stop. She continued to shelve books, feeling annoyed. As she turned, she bumped into Joseph Kalisa's chest. He was standing right next to her in the library stacks. Joseph winked, and she winked back. He looked wonderful in his crisp white dress shirt, with a gray paisley print tie.

She breathed in the gentle fragrance that surrounded him. Joseph had just had his hair cut, and Sojourner thought the boyishness of his face was adorable.

"What are you doing for lunch?" Joseph said, in a whispered tone.

Joseph was reading from a book and speaking to her at the same time. Sojourner whispered back; she also pretended that she was shelving books as she stood next to him.

"I brought a sandwich and a salad for lunch," Sojourner said.

"All right, then can we go out for an early dinner?" Joseph said.

"Okay," Sojourner said, enjoying the whispering.

"How about 6:30 p.m.?" Joseph said.

"That'll work," Sojourner said. "Where should we meet?"

"I will meet you in the lobby. Is that okay with you?" Joseph said.

"It's okay."

At 6:30 p.m. Sojourner and Joseph met in the lobby. They had lunch in a restaurant in the Post Office Pavilion and chatted. Joseph drove Sojourner home and went back to work at the law firm.

Joseph surprised Sojourner with a bouquet of flowers for Valentine's Day. The bouquet arrived at her apartment while she was on campus. Luckily, Rose was home to sign for them.

Sojourner entered her apartment and went to the small kitchen area.

"Go ahead and open them, girl. What you staring at them for?" Rose said.

Sojourner slowly opened the little white envelope attached to the flowers.

"Child, please! You know those flowers are from Joseph," Rose said.

"Of course, they are," Sojourner said. She was smiling as she read the note from Joseph.

That evening, Sojourner telephoned Joseph and thanked him. Sojourner felt guilty that she hadn't sent him a gift or a card. Joseph reminded her of her offer to prepare dinner for him. Sojourner said she would be delighted to make dinner for him, but she admitted that her cooking skills were limited. Joseph promised to help Sojourner prepare the dinner, as long as they could be together.

CHAPTER TWENTY

The following week, Sojourner was preparing angel hair pasta with Alfredo sauce, jumbo shrimp, and broccoli, in Joseph's kitchen. The only dishes Sojourner could cook were sandwiches and spaghetti with sauce and meatballs. She was nervous about cooking for Joseph, and she asked Rose for ideas on what she could cook for him. Rose showed Sojourner how to make the Angel Hair Pasta dish. She also suggested that Sojourner should make a garden salad and garlic bread to compliment the meal. Once the meal was prepared, Joseph showed Sojourner where his cutlery and plates were kept.

Sojourner set the table, and Joseph brought out a bottle of French Merlot and two elegant wineglasses.

Sojourner wore a long, brown skirt that fell just above her slender ankles and a V-neck beige pullover sweater which outlined her delicate torso and long neck. Joseph was in his living room, looking through his collection of cassettes. He told Sojourner that he wanted to listen to some Rwandan music.

Joseph and Sojourner watched a CNN report of an IRA bombing at both Paddington station and Victoria station in London.

They finished the bottle of wine together; then they turned the TV down and listened to what Joseph described as Rwanda royal court music. To Sojourner it sounded like the playing of a string instrument accompanied by a man rapping in his native language. She stood up and danced gracefully to the sound of the Rwandan music that filled the living room. Joseph applauded, and Sojourner then wiggled her lithe body in front of Joseph as he sat on the sofa. Joseph stood up and took off his shirt and slacks, revealing crisp, white underpants and a sleeveless undershirt. He stood there like an African warrior. His long, lean body was actually muscular and sturdy. He danced with grace and pretending to be wielding a spear. Then he reached for Sojourner's narrow waist. Sojourner allowed him to grab her and pull her close. He cupped her face in his hands and kissed her lips delicately, allowing his hands to slowly descend from her face, to her neck, shoulders, and breasts. Sojourner closed her eyes, feeling intense pleasure and yearning. Joseph then picked her up as if she were as light as a baby and carried Sojourner into his bedroom.

Joseph carried Sojourner into the darkness of his bedroom. Sojourner was impressed with his physical strength. His bed was perfectly made, and the room had a fresh scent. He gently placed her on his bed. The thick white sheets were crisp and cool against Sojourner's skin. Joseph gently massaged her neck and back, and he unbuttoned her blouse and un-strapped her bra. In the darkness, he found her mouth, and the sweetness there. He patiently undressed her. Then, kneeling over her, Joseph sucked her breasts and parted her legs. As he allowed his hand to descend into her private valley, Sojourner's legs began to relax.

Sojourner's eyes were adjusting to the darkness of Joseph's bedroom. She saw him remove his underpants. Reaching out for him, with a great thirst for his touch, she let her hand touch his chest, stomach, and abdomen. She pulled her hand back quickly when she touched his erection, but he grasped her hand firmly and forced her to touch it. Sojourner closed her legs for a moment. The uncontrollable moistness emanating from her secret place intimidated her. She could feel that Joseph was ready to experience what was hidden between her closed thighs, as he spread her legs again. A tickling sensation moved up her inner thighs, and his fingers lightly brushed the hairs of her private area.

Sojourner's momentary resistance was replaced by quiet eagerness, as Joseph slowly lowered himself down on her. She felt each contour of him as he entered her. Reaching down, she rubbed his baby soft buttocks. Joseph filled her up, and the gracefulness of his movement was a marvel to Sojourner. Each movement elicited a grateful groan from her. With Joseph deep into her, their movements were rhythmic. Clinging to a wave of intense pleasure, she wrapped her legs around Joseph's torso. It seemed that they fused, glided, exploded, and melted, all at once.

The following morning, Sojourner awoke in a sweet haze of love and affection, her head resting on the hairs of Joseph's chest. Both were wrapped in stark white sheets, their bodies bare and relaxed. Sojourner played with the hairs on Joseph's chest, feeling both peaceful and joyful. Joseph wrapped his arm around her shoulders, as he lay beside her. He gently rubbed her dark nipples, until they pointed to the ceiling.

CHAPTER TWENTY-ONE

The following week, Sojourner called Joseph to tell him about a special art exhibit at the National African Art Museum. It was an exhibit of sculptures of Watutsi warriors and other aspects of the ancient royal family of Rwanda. Sojourner thought that Joseph would like to see the exhibit, since he himself was a Tutsi man whose mother was of royal heritage.

Joseph seemed pleased to hear from Sojourner, and he agreed that they should see the new exhibit. He said that would be a perfect reason for them to spend some time together.

The weather was sunny and slightly warm. Sojourner wore a sun dress that was hand picked for her by Rose. It was a pale orange cotton dress with thin shoulder straps. Sojourner was pleased with the wide approving smile that she received from Joseph. He held her hand, as they walked together.

In the National Museum of African Art, Sojourner and Joseph perused the Rwandan Exhibit, admiring the old vintage photographs of Rwandan royalty. Joseph was a little amused that photographs of some of his family members were actually on display in a Museum. One of the items on display was a royal tipoy. There was a brass plaque underneath of the display, indicated that the tipoy had been donated to the Museum by the Belgium government. Sojourner and Joseph walked about the museum, holding hands.

A few days later, Sojourner was standing in the living room of her apartment. Her father was sitting on her sofa. Luckily, Rose wasn't home, Sojourner thought. She had gone home to visit her mother. Rose was two months late with her share of the rent anyway, Sojourner thought. If she doesn't like it, she can move out. Her grandmother had asked her to bring her father home, and Sojourner intended to do that. Funds were low though, since Sojourner had to pay the entire rent amount by herself for the last two months. Her bills were piling up, with her purchasing new clothes for her father.

As for Joseph, Sojourner wondered if he really cared for her. It sure felt like it when they made love, she thought. Picking up the receiver, she dialed Joseph's number.

"Hi Joseph," Sojourner said.

"Hello my Princess," Joseph said. "How are you?"

"I'm fine... How are you?"

"Glorious, when I hear your voice," Joseph said.

"Joseph..." Sojourner said, hesitantly.

"Yes."

"I have a favor to ask," Sojourner said.

"Okay, go head, Princess."

"My father is here...and I was wondering if you could..."

"Wonderful, I would be honored to meet him," Joseph said.

"That's so nice of you, Joseph. Well, it's a long story, but my father is just getting out of the hospital."

"Really? You didn't tell me that he was sick. And he's in the area?"

"The man who collapsed on my doorstep...that was my father. My father came to D.C. to visit me, and I didn't expect him. I didn't want to talk about it at the time. He's been in and out of the hospital since. He was at Howard Hospital."

"I'm sorry to hear that, Princess. You should have told me. I could have visited him in the hospital."

"I'm sorry, Joseph," Sojourner said. "I know this all sounds so crazy."

"Don't worry about it, Princess. Would you like for me to come over?" Joseph said.

"Yes," Sojourner said.

"All right, I'm on my way, Princess," Joseph said.

Sojourner smiled as she put the receiver down.

Joseph arrived an hour later. Sojourner introduced Joseph to her father who was sitting on the sofa, watching TV.

"I am honored to meet you, Sir," Joseph said. He stood in the living room.

"It's good to meet you, too," Davey said. Despite his frail health, he eyed Joseph, from head to foot.

Then he slowly stood up from the sofa and offered his hand to Joseph.

"Thank you, Sir," Joseph said, shaking his hand.

"Joseph, I have to take my father home, since he's sick. I was wondering if you could help me, since I don't have a car."

"Ann, I don't need a handout," Davey said.

"Sir, I would be honored to drive you and Sojourner to New Jersey," Joseph said. "I have to work tomorrow, but I can take you there on Saturday."

"Thank you, Joseph. You're a life saver," Sojourner said.

Sojourner noticed that her father's eyes quickly shifted from her to Joseph.

"Well, that is nice of you," her father said.

CHAPTER TWENTY-TWO

The following Saturday Joseph drove Sojourner and her father back to New Jersey. Sojourner had telephoned her Aunt Mae, and her grandmother, to inform them of their pending arrival. She explained that Joseph wanted to meet her family while they were in town. Sojourner's Aunt Mae invited them to spend the night at her apartment. Sojourner had suggested that Joseph wanted them to stay at a casino hotel in the area, but her aunt insisted that they stay with her for at least one night.

Sojourner thought about Joseph's suggestion. He wanted to bring his Rwandan friend, Moses, with him. He wanted Moses to act as a family member, since his family was back in Rwanda.

Sojourner explained that her Aunt Mae had invited them to spend the night with her and that her aunt's apartment was very small. However, the aunt had insisted that they spend the night with her. So Joseph did not bring Moses along.

Joseph drove Sojourner and her father to New Jersey. Sojourner was apprehensive about taking Joseph home with her. There was no "home" to go to, Sojourner thought, as they drove north on I-95. Her mother had died, and her father had no home of his own. She looked in the rear view mirror, and saw father, staring out the window, blankly. Then Sojourner looked at Joseph. He seemed cheerful.

"Are you comfortable Sir?" Joseph said. Sojourner saw Joseph glance at Davey through the rear-view mirror.

"I'm okay, my man," Davey said.

They stopped at restaurant after crossing the Delaware Memorial Bridge. It was an old fashioned, family styled restaurant with small booths. The three of them squeezed into the booth. Sojourner worried that Joseph was not entirely comfortable, due to his long legs.

They ordered their food.

"Where you from, my man?" her father said.

"I'm from Rwanda, Sir."

Davey nodded.

"That's deep in the heart of Africa, right?"

"Yes, it is in the heart of Africa," Joseph said.

"Lots of turmoil in that region... Them Europeans really did a number on you all. Got ya killing each other," Davey said.

"You have a valid point, Sir. But at some point, we have to take responsibility for our own actions, too," Joseph said.

Davey nodded.

"You a Watutsi?" Davey said.

Sojourner saw a look of surprise appear and quickly disappear from Joseph's face.

"Yes. I am," Joseph said.

"Davey...Let's finish our meal. It's getting late," Sojourner said to her father.

"Thanks for the meal, my man," Davey said.

"You're welcome, Sir," Joseph said.

Joseph paid for the meal and they continued to Rockwell, New Jersey.

They took Sojourner's father to her Aunt Jess's home in Atlantic City. There, Joseph was introduced to her father's sister, Jessica, better known as Aunt Jess. Sojourner and Joseph sat in the cozy apartment. Aunt Jess offered Joseph and Sojourner slices of freshly baked sweet potato pie and tall glasses of milk. They ate the pie and finished the milk.

Aunt Jess was a retired school teacher who was obsessed with neatness and good manners. Her living room was decorated with cream colored French Provincial furniture. A painting of Jesus praying was on one side of the wall, and a photo of Martin Luther King, Jr. was on the opposite wall. The coffee and end tables had clean lace doilies and small vases with silk flowers. Several little crystal bowls, with peppermint candy in them, were on the tables. Before leaving, Sojourner hugged her father. She asked him if he needed anything, and he replied that he did not. His only request was that Sojourner call him when she returned to D.C. Joseph shook her father's hand and discreetly placed a thick roll of bills in his hands. Sojourner would have missed this action, if she hadn't turned just in time to see her father stare dumbfounded at the folded dollars held together by an expensive looking money clip. They left.

Shortly afterwards, Sojourner and Joseph arrived at the small apartment of her Aunt Mae, her mother's sister. Sojourner introduced Joseph.

"Hello Mrs. Brown. I'm please to meet you," Joseph said.

"Well, it's nice to meet you, too, Joseph," said Aunt Mae, staring up at Joseph.

Sojourner noticed her Aunt Mae was not smiling, but she wasn't frowning either. Aunt Mae rarely hid her feelings,

Sojourner thought Aunt Mae was a woman who was struggling to pay her rent and to stay off welfare. Her behavior was not pretentious. She would smoke KOOLS cigarettes and drink Gin, while cursing out her boyfriend for being a jerk. However, Sojourner's Aunt didn't speak too much when in Joseph's presence. He was shown great respect.

Her cousin, Mimi, was ten years old. She stared at Joseph's tall and lean frame, and she listened with keen interest when he spoke. It seemed that she wasn't so much interested in what Joseph had to say as she was in how he was saying it. Joseph was a novelty to her.

"Ann told me that you're a lawyer," Aunt Mae said, staring.

"Yes, Mrs. Brown. I'm an attorney at the law firm where I was so fortunate to have met Sojourner," Joseph said, smiling graciously.

"How long have you been there?" Aunt Mae said.

"I have been with Livingston & Richards for eight months now," Joseph said.

"Where you from?" Aunt Mae said, leaning back on the sofa.

"I'm from Rwanda," Joseph said, sitting proudly on the sofa.

"That in Africa?" Aunt Mae said.

"Yes, Mrs. Brown, it's a country in Africa," Joseph said.

"Sojourner tells me that you went to Princeton. Now that's a fine school, right here in New Jersey," Aunt Mae said.

"Yes. That's right. I graduated from Princeton," Joseph said.

Aunt Mae nodded approvingly. A smile gradually formed on her face.

"Joseph received his law degree at Georgetown Law Center," Sojourner said.

Sojourner was smiling triumphantly.

"Ann, get Joseph something cool to drink. It's as hot as the devil in this apartment," Aunt Mae said.

Aunt Mae's small one-bedroom apartment had one thing to its credit. It was clean. The furniture was old and outdated, but the apartment had a sort of seventies chic to it. The dark blue was a shag carpet. It was a chore to clean, but it was considered stylish in the 1970s. Her aunt would often rent a carpet cleaner from the A&P; then she would scrub through the thick carpet. It would take two days to dry completely. The velour sofa and loveseat were also old, but perfect for lounging and watching TV reruns and cartoons.

Sojourner returned with a tall glass of Kool-Aid. That was the only beverage in the refrigerator, other than a gallon of milk. She carefully handed the glass to Joseph.

Joseph sipped the drink gracefully.

Mimi continued to openly stare at Joseph, as if he were a marvelous museum item. She seemed to be fascinated by the combination of his height, manner of speaking, and elegance.

"This is my daughter, Mimi," Aunt Mae said.

"Mimi, go and get Mr. Joseph some peanuts and put them on a plate," Aunt Mae said.

Mimi glanced at her mother with surprise and went to the kitchen. She returned with a plate filled with peanuts, and placed them before Joseph on the cocktail table; then she sat on the loveseat and continued to stare.

"What grade are you in, Mimi?" Joseph said.

"Fifth," Mimi said.

Mimi was surprised by this sudden attention, and she pretended to watch TV. There was an old episode of the Flintstones on, one of Sojourner's personal childhood favorites.

"Are you enjoying school?" Joseph said.

It seemed Joseph was trying to be friendly to the girl who had stared at him as if he were a statue.

"No," Mimi said, flatly.

"I made some beef stew. Please have something to eat," Aunt Mae said.

"I'm not hungry. Thank you, Ms. Brown," Joseph said.

"Joseph's probably tired," Sojourner said.

"Well, I fixed up the bedroom, so if Joseph is tired, he can go and relax," Aunt Mae said.

Sojourner then turned to Joseph and spoke.

"Joseph, you should be tired after the long drive here, especially since you worked today. Why don't you get some rest?"

Joseph looked a little embarrassed, but then he smiled.

"All right then," Joseph said.

Sojourner showed Joseph to the bedroom, which was the only one in her aunt's one-bedroom apartment. As they entered, Sojourner secretly hoped that the room would be as neat as possible. It was clean. She could smell the cleanliness of the bed sheets and the blanket; actually, it was the scent of detergent and bleach. Everything had been dusted and swept. Sojourner tried to gauge Joseph's reaction. Joseph returned her gaze and smiled. Then he reached for Sojourner's neck and caressed it with his smooth fingers. Sojourner smiled and left him alone in the bedroom.

That night Aunt Mae and Sojourner slept on the sofa bed, while Mimi slept on a pullout cot.

"Aunt Mae, Davey said he had written me some letters after my Mom passed away," Sojourner said.

They were both sitting on the sofa bed in their pajamas. Mimi was sleeping on the cot next to the sofa.

"He did?" Aunt Mae said, looking sleepy. Sojourner smelled a hint of Alcohol on Aunt Mae's breath.

"Yes. Is it true? Did he send me letters?" Sojourner said.

"One or two, yeah, I think," Aunt Mae said, softly.

"Did he send money?"

"If you call $50 money, yeah," Aunt Mae said.

"Aunt Mae, why didn't you tell me Davey was sending me letters and money?" Sojourner said.

"I misplaced the letters. And for the money, I was busy making all the funeral arrangements for your mother when she died. I had four children to raise, Ann, you, Langston, and two of my own children. How was I supposed to keep up with everything?"

"My father writes me letters and you don't even show them to me, Aunt Mae? For years, I thought he didn't care anything about me," Sojourner said.

"He didn't do all that much. Anyway, did you know that he dumped me, for your Mom? Then he got your Mom pregnant," Aunt Mae said. "Sending letters, with some chump change in them…"

"When I saw him in D.C., I was so angry with him. I treated him mean, 'cause I thought he had abandoned me. Some of that is your fault, Aunt Mae," Sojourner said.

"Oh, hell no," Aunt Mae said.

"It's not my fault your Daddy was a drug addict and a convict," Aunt Mae said.

"I don't have to take this. I could be in a luxurious hotel right now, but I chose to stay here with you, Aunt Mae," Sojourner said. She got out of the sofa bed and stood up.

"Oh, really, Miss High Class. All these degrees is making you forgetful, Ann. You've forgotten where you came from. I'm the one who finished raising you after your Mom passed. Dammit, is it my fault that your Mom was a drug addict who lived beyond her means. Walking around like a fashion model, without a place to live. Is that my fault too?" Aunt Mae said.

"Don't talk about my mother like that!" Sojourner said. She caught herself before she started to shout.

"She was my sister, and I was the one who took care of you after she died, not Davey."

Sojourner thought about the extra Welfare money that her aunt probably received for taking in her sister's children, but she did not say that to her aunt. That would have been grounds for a loud altercation that could have become physical.

"Forget it. Just forget it, Aunt Mae," Sojourner said.

"Okay…Forgotten," Aunt Mae said. Then she lay down and slept.

As Sojourner slept that night, Sojourner dreamt of her mother, Nora Lee. She couldn't see Nora Lee's face, only her shadow. They were watching an old movie with Joan Crawford and Bette Davis. Her mother was often more like an older sister than a mother. Although Sojourner missed that relationship, the thought of her mother also made her angry.

Sojourner took a shower and dressed in the bathroom. She wore navy blue pleated slacks, a pink oxford shirt, and a maroon wool vest. Sojourner slipped into knee highs and penny loafers. She styled her hair in a neat bun and placed faux pearl studded earrings in her ears. After applying some lip gloss, she exited the bathroom and went to the bedroom where Joseph had spent the night. She knocked on the door.

"Yes. You can come in," Joseph said.

Joseph was sitting on the bed looking in his overnight bag.

"So, you are an early bird, uh?" Sojourner said.

"Yes, I am. I would like to take a shower," Joseph said.

"Sure. Let me show you to the bathroom," Sojourner said.

Joseph picked up his bag, and followed.

Aunt Mae had prepared an old-fashioned breakfast for them, consisting of scrambled eggs, grits, sausage, and coffee. This was like a holiday treat. Mimi and Sojourner were impressed. Aunt Mae must have liked Joseph because she rarely made breakfast. Breakfast normally consisted of a bowl of Corn Flakes with milk.

"Ms. Brown, this is delicious," Joseph said, flashing a smile. Joseph ate the eggs and grits, but politely declined the sausage.

"Thank you," Aunt Mae said.

She was apparently flattered.

"I'd like for you to meet my Grandmother," Sojourner said. "She lives in a Senior Citizens home in Atlantic City."

"Okay. That would be good," Joseph said.

"Say Hi to Mrs. McIntosh for me, Ann," Aunt Mae said.

Before they left her aunt's house, Joseph presented Aunt Mae with the bottle of expensive wine that he'd brought. Then Joseph said to her aunt that he wanted to bring an elder member of his family with him, but he could not, since his family was back in Rwanda. Aunt Mae told Joseph that she was glad to meet him. She then hugged him and grinned.

CHAPTER TWENTY-THREE

Joseph and Sojourner drove to Atlantic City via the Black Horse Pike highway. It was there that her Grandma Cecilia lived, at the Seaside Homestead. From the outside, it looked like an old, high rise apartment building.

Sojourner's father's mother lived on the 10th floor. She introduced her to Joseph, and her grandmother smiled. Joseph hugged her gently and told her that he was pleased to meet her. Her grandmother thanked Sojourner and Joseph for bringing her father back to Atlantic City. Grandma Cecilia said that she had called Aunt Jess and had spoken with Davey. Sojourner offered to buy her grandmother some groceries, and her grandmother accepted. Then she and Joseph went out and bought some groceries for her grandmother at a local grocery store.

While grocery shopping, they met Sojourner's uncle, Jobe Brown. Jobe, a man in his mid forties, was rarely sober. His twenty year dependence on alcohol had dulled his senses and consumed his life, making steady employment and relationships with women almost impossible to maintain. Uncle Jobe spotted Sojourner first, as she walked up the aisle in the grocery store. His latest job was as an assistant janitor at a local supermarket.

"Ann!" Uncle Jobe said. "Is that you, baby?"

Sojourner turned around, immediately recognizing her mother's brother, Jobe.

"Hi, Uncle Jobe," Sojourner said.

"Lord have mercy! I knew it was you, Ann, when I saw that pretty dark face of yours," Uncle Jobe said.

Uncle Jobe quickly hugged Sojourner. The scent of liquor

was imbedded on his person. Uncle Jobe wore a dingy janitor's uniform. He stared at Joseph, looking him up and down.

Sojourner bit her lip and breathed in deeply. She feigned a smile, trying to hide her embarrassment.

"Joseph, this is my Uncle Jobe," Sojourner said.

"I'm pleased to meet you, Sir," Joseph said.

"Yeah, me, too, man," Uncle Jobe said.

"How is school, Baby?" Uncle Jobe said. "You still working on your Ph.D?

"Actually, I'm working on my Master of Arts degree, Uncle Jobe," Sojourner said.

"Joseph, dear, could you get some tea from aisle number two please?"

She wanted to redirect Joseph's attention away from her shabby looking uncle.

"All right," Joseph said. He walked toward aisle number two.

"So what you got there, baby? He looks like an African prince, or somebody like that," Uncle Jobe said.

"I didn't see the tea, Princess," Joseph said, as he returned.

"I'll get it, dear," Sojourner said. She moved quickly toward aisle number two.

"That's my pretty niece," Uncle Jobe said. "She's smart, too."

"Yes, I know," Joseph said.

"Say, man, you got twenty dollars?" Uncle Jobe said.

"Oh, yes, of course," Joseph said.

Joseph reached into his wallet and pulled out forty dollars.

"Bless you, man. I appreciate it," Uncle Jobe said, grinning.

"No problem," Joseph said, winking at Uncle Jobe.

"You a cool cat, man," Uncle Jobe said, putting the money in his pocket.

Sojourner returned with the tea and glanced at her uncle suspiciously.

"Well, we have to go now, Uncle Jobe. We have to take these groceries to Grandma McIntosh," Sojourner said. "Take care of yourself."

"Yeah… You, too, baby. Say Hi to Ms. McIntosh for me," Uncle Jobe said. "And it was nice meeting Mr. Joseph here, too."

Uncle Jobe waved happily.

Sojourner and Joseph left the grocery store and entered Joseph's car.

"Joseph, did my uncle ask you for money?" Sojourner said.

Joseph was silent.

"Did he?" Sojourner said.

"Yes, but it's okay, Princess," Joseph said, cheerfully.

"He's a damn bum," Sojourner muttered to herself.

"What'd you say, Princess?"

"Oh, nothing, Baby Love."

They then took the groceries back to Sojourner's Grandmother.

It was a sunny afternoon in Atlantic City, as Joseph and Sojourner walked on the boardwalk in Atlantic City. The Boardwalk was filled with tourists and local residents, walking the ten miles of wooden planks. Joseph seemed to enjoy the environment, looking around with subtle, but keen interest. It was late March, and the weather was still cold and windy, so the beach was empty. The brownish gray ocean was alive as the waves raced toward the shore. Sojourner breathed in the briny scent of the Atlantic Ocean.

Joseph and Sojourner toured several of these casinos. Within each Casino was the clamor of the crowded casino floor, where the main action took place. The entrance to the casino floor was guarded by security personnel, one of whom had stopped Sojourner and Joseph before they entered the casino. The guard wanted to see their identification, proving that they were indeed over twenty-one years of age. They both smiled, since Sojourner was twenty-four and Joseph was thirty-three.

After entering the casino, they surveyed the atmosphere, observing that there were a bewildering number of customers playing slot machines, Black Jack, Craps, Roulette, and other popular casino games. The casinos all seemed to be similar in the general atmosphere. The sound of thousands of coins pouring into and out of slot machines filled the air, as well as the odor of cigarettes, liquor, and perfume.

It had gotten dark outside, so Joseph and Sojourner rested in a casino restaurant/lounge. They sat down, and an attractive waitress approached their table to take their order. They ordered dinner and drinks.

"When am I going to meet your brother, Sojourner?" Joseph said.

"He's out of town, this weekend, visiting his girlfriend," Sojourner said.

This was a lie. She did not know where her brother was. He and Aunt Mae didn't get along well, so he had left there weeks ago. Langston didn't tell anyone where he was staying.

"Next time, then," Joseph said, sipping his glass of wine.

"Are you working on any interesting cases?" Sojourner said, changing the subject.

"Yes, I am," Joseph said.

"Which one?" Sojourner said.

"One of them involves a large, multinational fruit company and some government officials in Cameroon," Joseph said.

"Really? What's their issue?" Sojourner said.

"Actually, it's confidential," Joseph said.

"You don't trust me?" Sojourner said.

"Of course, my Princess," Joseph said. "It's just that I'm not supposed to discuss these cases, you know."

"I understand."

"……Well…., I'll just give you a brief overview of one case," Joseph said.

Joseph made few brief comments about the Cameroon case. Sojourner was glad to have avoided the subject of her brother.

That evening, Joseph and Sojourner checked into an elegant beach side hotel. They changed into some evening attire and went to a nightclub within. The crowd was older and affluent. Here, inebriation was repressed behind the glazed eyes and relaxed legs of middle-aged men, and the multi-carat diamond rings of their spouses, many of whom had deep tans and heavy mascara.

Joseph and Sojourner returned to their hotel room, relaxed from a combination of expensive wines and some light dancing. Sojourner entered the bathroom and took a shower. She couldn't resist the urge to take a hot shower, and lather herself up with soap. A long, hot shower was a luxury. In the apartment that she shared with Rose, the hot water lasted about three minutes, and it turned cold. She had gotten into the habit of lathering herself up, and then rinsing herself off with the precious hot water.

She donned a white satin, negligee that she had recently purchased. She felt a nervous anticipation, but she believed Joseph would ease her fears.

Sojourner exited the bathroom slowly. Joseph was reclined on a king-sized bed, watching CNN. Joseph liked watching the news and reading the paper, as much as Sojourner liked reading Wuthering Heights, or Percy Bysshe Shelly's poems. Joseph wore the brown, silk pajama set that Sojourner had bought him two weeks earlier. The pajama shirt was unbuttoned, revealing his mahogany torso and hairy chest.

"You are so beautiful," Joseph said. "… like a Tutsi princess of yore."

"Thanks."

Joseph then held Sojourner's hand and then placed it on his face. He kissed her hand softly, and began to slowly rub her shoulder. He not only looked tall when standing, but also when reclining. He also seemed less lanky up close.

"So, what's on TV?" Sojourner said.

"Just the news," Joseph said, taking off his pajama shirt.

His dark eyes pierced through her, like she was a sheer,

delicate fabric. He cupped her face in his hands and kissed both of her cheeks. He then lightly kissed her lips.

"Be my sweet princess, Sojourner," Joseph said, in a breathy voice. "I want you to be only mine, forever."

Joseph raised himself on his knees. He towered over Sojourner, like a giant warrior king about to claim his throne, but his hands were as soft and fragrant as a woman's.

He proceeded to rub her deep, brown nipples gently, making circular motions with his index finger. Sojourner watched him do this, and she felt her body relaxing. She looked down and saw her nipples thicken and point straight at Joseph.

"Come and feed me," Joseph said.

He touched one of her nipples with his tongue; then, he engulfed it in his mouth. He sucked on her nipple like a baby. She grew wetter.

She looked into his eyes and touched his face, then his shoulder, allowing her hand to explore the lean yet solid muscles of his long arms. She kissed his smooth lips, which still contained the scent of the wine he'd imbibed earlier. His tongue then stealthily slipped into her mouth, like a serpent.

In one swooping motion with his hands, Joseph removed his pajama pants. She stared at his erection; it was like artwork in its clarity and smoothness.

"Come here," Joseph said, grabbing her torso with his hands and guiding her to mount him.

Sojourner positioned herself over Joseph, feeling a little awkward. As Joseph penetrated her deftly, the pleasure was intense. Joseph gently rolled them both over and mounted her. Atop he increased the speed and force of his movements. Sojourner saw her toes pointing to the ceiling, as Joseph moved deeply into her body. She was like a boat, being propelled smoothly to harbor. With a tickling giggle in her heart, Sojourner was relaxed. Joseph's long body was peacefully still, as he lay atop her.

They returned to their lives in Washington, D.C. Joseph was busy with his career at Livingston and Richards, and

Sojourner was devoting most of her time to completing her Masters of Arts.

CHAPTER TWENTY-FOUR

One evening, Joseph was invited to the Sub-Sahara Room to have a drink with some Rwandan friends of his, Ibrahim and Moses. The three men sat at a table in the nightclub conversing, drinking, and listening to Rwandan music. While there John's brother, Blaise Hakizimana, showed up in the nightclub.

"Look. John invited that damned bastard, Blaise," Ibrahim said.

"Well, they are brothers," Joseph said.

"How can you be so calm, Joe? He's a damned extremist," Moses said.

"There's a time and place for everything," Joseph said.

Joseph thought to himself. He had a vague memory of Blaise and John's father. There was a rumor that their father was a member of the political party that killed his father. However, John had always been a loyal friend to Joseph in the United States. When Joseph first came to D.C. to attend law school, it was John who offered him a place to stay while he searched for his own apartment. John also helped him to get part time jobs delivering newspapers and working as a waiter in an expensive Georgetown restaurant.

They watched as Blaise sat down on the other side of the nightclub, with a friend of his. Blaise was a tall man, who defied the stereotypical Hutu build and features, but his brother, John, was the opposite. John approached Joseph's table.

"My friends, are you okay?" John said. He looked at Joseph.

"I see your brother is in town," Joseph said, staring at John.

"Yes. He's here for some sort of military conference, just for a week," John said, looking down at the table.

"Is he still killing innocent civilians?" Ibrahim said.

"I don't know what you are talking about," John said, defensively.

"You know damn well what he's talking about. Thousands of Tutsi people are being killed in Rwanda. The military does nothing, and probably supports it," Moses said.

"My brother came here to have a drink, and that's all," John said. He then walked back to the bar area.

Just then, Joseph felt a tap on his shoulder. He turned and saw Christine Mbang, smiling at him.

"Ça va, Joe?" Christine said.

She wore a purple dress and black leather boots.

"I'm sitting over there with my friend, Joe. Let me know when you're leaving. I need a ride."

Joseph stood up and greeted her with the perfunctory French style two light kisses on each cheek. Ibrahim and Moses nodded at her politely.

"I'm not going straight home, Christine. I'm going to stop at the office for a while," Joseph said.

"Oh, okay. Anyway, we'll talk later," Christine said.

She went back to the table that she shared with her girlfriend.

The men sat drinking and discussing Rwandan politics when suddenly Blaise approached their table.

"You are Joseph Kalisa, yes?" Blaise said.

"I am. And you are Blaise Hakizimana?" Joseph said.

"Yes. It is a pleasure to see you again. I could hardly believe it when John told me who you are. This is an honor. I remember your father," Blaise said.

At that statement, Joseph stared up at him and narrowed his eyes. His lips curled, and his fists clenched.

"What do you remember about my father?" Joseph said.

Blaise looked cautious.

"That he was a professor at the National University. Our father told us about Monsieur Kalisa," Blaise said.

Blaise and Joseph locked eyes.

"Did he tell you how he was killed?" Joseph said.

Blaise took a step back.

"It was horrible. Mistakes were made during that time," Blaise said.

"Mistakes?" Ibrahim said. "The massacre of innocent civilians by ignorant and brutal mobs is what you call 'mistakes'?" Ibrahim said.

"Killing your own countrymen, while the old colonial masters stood around, laughing. So typical," Moses said.

"Your father was a part of that party, wasn't he?" Joseph said.

"My father is a good man, not responsible for that," Blaise said.

Joseph's mind started to slip into the past, and he remembered the night he was ousted from high school. The school officials were identifying students based on their Tutsi ethnicity. Blaise was there, in the same dormitory with Joseph. He remembered that Blaise was often mistaken for a Tutsi, because he was tall and thin. Blaise became angry at the implication that he was a Tutsi. This amused Joseph. The night Blaise was singled out. He shouted loudly that he was a Hutu. Blaise pointed to Joseph and indicated that Joseph was the epitome of a Tutsi. All of the attention focused on Joseph. When Joseph protested, he was knocked unconscious.

"I don't have to take this shit. I'm a Captain in the Rwandan Armed Forces. I was just trying to be civil to you," Blaise said.

"Who can be civil to a bunch of arrogant cockroaches," Blaise's companion said.

The companion was a short man with snarl on his broad face.

"That's right. We, Hutu, rule now, anyway," Blaise said, smirking.

Joseph lunged at Blaise. He swung and punched Blaise in the eye. Blaise stumbled. Then he swung back. The force of the punch landed on his Joseph's mouth. Blaise's companion jumped in, and Ibrahim and Moses also joined the melee.

John, some bar attendants, and a few patrons tried to break up the fight. Then Christine ran over and hit the Blaise on the head with her heavy purse. All the while the music played on in the nightclub, as curious patrons looked on. Blaise wanted to call the police, but John persuaded him not to. Christine said that she would swear that he was trying to attack her, if he called the police. John begged Blaise to let it be. All dispersed, angrily.

Christine finally got her ride home, compliments of Joseph, who had a busted lip. When they arrived at the apartment that she shared with her brother, Francois, Joseph sat on the sofa. He was in a daze. Francois was not home at the time, and they were alone. Christine helped Joseph to take off his jacket and shoes. Then she put ice on his lip and told him to hold it there. While heating up some pepper soup for him, she went to her bedroom.

She emerged from her bedroom in a long Caba dress, which resembled a long, colorful cotton gown. Joseph said that he was going home, but she insisted that he rest in her place. He was too upset and disoriented to be driving home by himself, Christine said. Joseph ate the pepper soup that Christine heated for him. Then Christine turned on the TV and sat next to Joseph on the sofa. She asked him about what happened, but he did not wish to discuss it. She said that she understood.

Joseph was about to fall asleep on the living room sofa watching CNN, when Christine gently helped Joseph, who was sleepy, to his feet and started to guide him to her bedroom.

"No. I have to go now, Christine," Joseph said, waking up.

"Joe," Christine said. "I think we both need each other."

"I've found the woman that I want to marry, Christine. I need her."

"You mean that tall, black American girl you brought here

before," Christine said, annoyed.

"Her name is Sojourner Brown, and yes," Joseph said. "You have a husband, and I intend to get me a wife."

"What is she about twenty?" Christine said.

"She's the woman I want," Joseph said.

He looked at her with a serious expression.

"Okay, Joe," Christine said. "Just be generous with me this evening. Let's just make a little love, and I no de humbug you again."

"I can't," Joseph said.

"Joe, you don't want me? You don't enjoy it, the way I do?"

"Of course, I do. But that's not the point," Joseph said.

"What is?" Christine said.

"Christine, c'mon, you have a family," Joseph said. "I have to go now. Take care."

He put his shoes and coat on; then he left Christine's apartment.

CHAPTER TWENTY-FIVE

Joseph arrived home at two in the morning. He put on his pajamas and went to bed. However, he couldn't sleep, so he got up and went to his office. He had converted one of the bedrooms of his two bedroom condo into an office. Perusing the bookshelves, he found an old copy of his father's book, Blood for the People. Sitting at his desk, he opened the book. He did not select a particular chapter, he just opened the book in what appeared to be the middle of the story. Then he started to read.

Blood for the People

"Maybe we should leave. My uncle has invited us to go to France with him," said Mother.

"I am not leaving Rwanda. I am a Rwandan, and this is my country," said Father.

"But they are going to kill us," said Mother.

"Let's persevere," said Father. "More than half of the school is Hutu now, and the people are happy about that. They seem grateful for that change."

"We should go to France," said Mother. "I don't like the way they look at us."

"Enough. I have been to France, and I do not wish to live there," said Father.

"I read it is beautiful," said Mother.

"Beautiful? It is modern. The architecture is beautiful," said the Father. "I lived there as a student. I didn't like the way I felt there though, like I did not exist. It is a place where a black man becomes invisible, or a charicature. No... Rwanda is beautiful, naturally beautiful. The hills, the greenness of everything... I am home here."

"I'm afraid," said Mother. "Things are so different now. Most of the children in your school are Hutu now, and some of the neighbors here hate us."

"I know, but most of the parents are good people. I am teaching their children. Many have brought us gifts. One woman even said that she misses the Mwami," said Father.

The Mother still looked worried, but she bowed to her husband, as a dutiful Tutsi wife does.

The mother was teaching her son how to pray the rosary when he smelled the smoke. He knew that his mother could smell it, too, because she stood up and rushed to the front yard. He ran to her side, and they both stared in horror. The son of a Hutu plantation worker, came running up to their home.

"Madam! Madam! The school is burning! The Master is there!" shouted the child. He was a boy of six, two years older than her son.

His mother screamed and ran in the direction of the school.

Joseph stopped reading his father's novel and went to bed.

Moses telephoned Joseph the following day.

"Gira Inka?" Moses said.

"Muraho," Joseph said.

"Your lip...It was swollen," Moses said. "I hope you put some ice on it as soon as you got home."

"Yes, I did," Joseph said. "Actually, Christine put some ice on it for me."

"Oh, really?" said Moses. "Very Good."

"I drove her home," Joseph said. "But she insisted that I go to her apartment so she could put some ice on my lip."

"That was kind of her. So she took good care of you, eh?" Moses said, mischievousness slipping into his voice.

"Nothing like that last night…" Joseph said. "I have to be polite because her family treated me well in Cameroon."

"Yes, you told me how her family did help you in Cameroon," Moses said. "But you helped Francois, when he first came to the U.S., right?"

"True. He lived with me for a year, until he got his own apartment," Joseph said.

"There you are," Moses said. "Debt settled."

"Yeah, I suppose," Joseph said.

"Are you going to the meeting tonight," Moses said.

"I don't know. I have a lot of work to do this evening, working on a brief," Joseph said.

"Yes. I understand. However, this meeting is important, too. We'll be discussing the Hutu Commandments," Moses said.

"I think their going to try to kill us off, my friend," Moses said. "I feel it in my gut. What hurts the most is that they're our own Rwandese countrymen."

"So much social chaos and politics… Why can't we be just Rwandese, eh?" Joseph said.

"I want that too, Joe, but we can't wish the hate away," Moses said. "If we do not act decisively, we'll see the biggest massacre imaginable. I'm going to the meeting, and I think you should, too. You have family in Rwanda, just like the rest of us."

"Yes…I do. My mother, my sister, and many others," Joseph said. "Then attend the meeting and keep yourself informed," Moses said.

"All right, then. What time is the meeting?" Joseph said.

The meeting started at 9:00 p.m. at Ibrahim's apartment

in Takoma Park, Maryland. He lived off of New Hampshire Avenue in an area popularly known as Langley Park. Moses, Joseph, and several other men were in attendance. The only two women in the apartment were Theodetta and Annette, and they were busy in the kitchen preparing food for the men.

"Let's start the meeting now, my brothers," Moses said.

He stood up and raised his hand to quiet anyone still talking. It worked.

"My brothers, I want to thank all of you for coming to the meeting tonight. Special thanks go to Ibrahm for hosting tonight's meeting," Moses said.

There were some nods of approval from the men who sat on the living room sofa.

"Gentlemen, we have an emergency on our hands; our troops are not doing well in this struggle."

There was some momentary whispering from the group.

"I know many of us are donating large sums of money to this noble cause, but our troops are suffering great casualties and things are looking dismal. Five months ago we lost Michel, and several of our military leaders. The morale of the troops is low, and the constant murders of our people continue in Rwanda," Moses said.

"What about the Hutu Commandments?" one man said.

"Yes, my brother, we're getting to that. That's the purpose of tonight's meeting," Moses said.

"Let's talk about that now," another man said.

"All right. I'm turning the floor over to Ibrahim, who will expand on that," Moses said.

He sat down on the sofa with the rest of the men, and Ibrahim stood up.

"The Hutu Commandments, my brothers... is pure hatred. Its purpose is to destroy our human rights within our country...," Ibrahim said.

"Look how the bastards put our women down, we can't have that...," a man said.

"Yes, I'm getting to that," Ibrahim said. "Belittling our

beautiful women is the very last straw."

"These 'commandments' exclude us from all respectable forms of employment. Eventually, there will be more massacres of Tutsi. That's what these commandments are leading to," another man said.

"So the bottom line is what are we going to do about it? We have to take some action, more than what we're doing now," Moses said.

"It's very true that some of us are making serious financial sacrifices to help finance this struggle. I personally am. I'm also interested in knowing how the funds are being allocated. Perhaps, we could have some input…," Joseph said.

"But what do you know about war, my brother?" one man said. "This money is being used to pay for the arms for our struggle, of course."

CHAPTER TWENTY-SIX

Sojourner felt a mixture of joy and sadness, as she stood in the Liberal Arts School section of the graduating class of 1991 on the main campus of Howard. She wore the traditional black cap and gown, with a colorful sash to distinguish her as a Master of Arts candidate. When the university president conferred the Master degrees, cheers and shouts of joy rose in the air from the crowd of graduates in her section. Sojourner had earned her Masters. She considered this a great moment in her life.

However, in the midst of the crowd, Sojourner's thoughts wandered to Sienna Jackson, the teenager whom she once tutored. An image of the girl flashed in her mind. Just that morning, Sojourner had read the local newspaper. There was a story in the Metro section about a teenager who had been murdered while in foster care. The name of the girl was Sienna Jackson. Apparently, her mother had died of AIDS, and the girl was placed in the care of a friend. Last week, she was found dead, beaten to death. The last time Sojourner had seen the girl was in the Angel of Mercy Shelter.

Sojourner stood in the crowd, twirling in her reverie, when Joseph appeared near her, holding a bouquet of flowers. Aunt Jess came to D.C. to attend her graduation, and she brought Sojourner's father with her.

"We're so proud of you," Aunt Jess said, trying to stifle her overflowing with pride.

She hugged Sojourner. Her father nodded and smiled.

That day, Joseph organized a graduation party for Sojourner at his apartment. He invited Theodetta, Annette, Moses, Ibrahim, Francois, Christine, John, and a few other people.

During her graduation party at Joseph's apartment, Sojourner noticed that Joseph was immersed in a conversation with his Rwandan friends, Ibrahim and Moses. They had shown up at the party, during which they discussed what was going on in Rwanda.

Aunt Jess was impressed with the décor of Joseph's high-rise apartment. Theodetta and Annette, cooked some Rwandan food, and Joseph purchased several cases of beverages. Christine brought pepper soup. They listened to Rwandan and Cameroonian music, and Sojourner requested a few of her favorite songs. Joseph proposed to Sojourner in front of the crowd displaying a diamond and sapphire engagement ring. Sojourner accepted Joseph's proposal. Her father spent the night with Joseph, and Aunt Jess stayed with Sojourner in her apartment. The following morning, they left for New Jersey.

It was Sojourner's first day at work as the Project Coordinator for the Vice President of Africa Now, a non-profit agency, which funded infrastructure development projects in various countries in Africa. One of the duties that initially attracted Sojourner to this position, besides from that it was a non-profit organization that focused on assistance to African nations, was the publication of the newsletter,

Africa Now Update. Sojourner looked forward to producing this monthly ten-page newsletter. The newsletter, along with an annual report, was sent to donors and members of this organization.

Sojourner had initially thought that she wouldn't get the position, in spite of her qualifications. The vice president of Africa Now, Mr. Reginald Jackson III, interviewed Sojourner. Mr. Jackson was a man in his late fifties, who appeared to take an interest in Sojourner's marital status.

"Well, young lady, I see that you received your Bachelors and Masters from Howard," Mr. Jackson said.

"Yes, sir. That's right," Sojourner said.

"Good old Howard University." Mr. Jackson said.

Sojourner smiled and said nothing.

"I went to Hampton Institute, myself," Mr. Jackson said.

"Oh, really," Sojourner said, feigning interest. "I know someone who went there."

"Booker T. Washington went there. Like, Howard, Hampton is one of the giants of historically black universities," he said proudly.

"I majored in political sciences, and I served in the Peace Corps for fifteen years," Mr. Jackson said. "I see you have a Masters of Arts, but what practical experience do you have with African Affairs?"

"I have had a serious interest in African history and African issues, since I was young. It has become a passion for me. And I have done quite a bit of academic research on African affairs and history, too. My thesis did require a lot of research on the topic of African history. I have brought a hard-bound copy of my dissertation for examples of this," Sojourner said.

She reached into her leather bag and pulled out the dissertation. Then she handed it to Reginald Jackson, who then perused through the dissertation and nodded.

"Very interesting," Mr. Jackson said.

"I've also published a book of poetry, in which many of my poems are in reference to aspects of African history," Sojourner said.

Again, she reached into her bag, and pulled out a paperback book of her poems.

After several more pertinent questions about her qualifications, Mr. Jackson asked Sojourner a question in reference to her marital status.

"Are you married?" Mr. Jackson said.

"I'm engaged," Sojourner said.

"You know, this position requires some travel and over time.

"I need a great deal of dedication from the individual in this position," Mr. Jackson said, looking serious.

"I'm very dedicated to issues involving African development; that's why I applied for this position."

Sojourner was uncertain whether or not Mr. Jackson would hire her, in spite of her qualifications. So she decided to bluntly speak her mind. She was engaged, and he seemed to be interested in flirting, or impressing her with his Hampton Institute background.

CHAPTER TWENTY-SEVEN

A few days later, Sojourner received a call early one Friday morning as she was scanning the The Washington Post job advertisement section.

"Hello, Miss Brown, my name is Lucinda Peterson. I'm the Personnel Manager for Africa Now, and I'm calling on behalf of Mr. Reginald Jackson, our Vice President. How are you today?"

"Hi Ms.Peterson, I'm fine," Sojourner said, pleasantly surprised.

"We would like to offer the position of Project Coordinator for Africa Now, to you. Mr. Jackson was very impressed with you," Peterson said.

"Oh, that's good news," Sojourner said. She stood up, smiling as she held the telephone receiver in her hand.

"Will you accept the offer?"

"Yes, I will."

"Great, I'll let Mr. Jackson know. You should be receiving an offer letter via U.S. mail, within a few days."

Sojourner was doing a victory dance in the living room when Rose suddenly walked in from her bedroom.

"Girl, what are you dancing for? I don't hear any music."

"I just got the job that I wanted, the one with Africa Now."

"Oh, congrats, Girl," Rose said. "What are you doing there?"

"Project Coordinator is the title," Sojourner said.

"Well, Congratulations," Rose said.

"Thank you, Rose."

Sojourner sat down on their old sofa and sipped her herbal tea, satisfied.

"I'm singing at The Marriott Hotel on 13th Street next Friday, in the lounge," Rose said proudly.

"Really, fabulous!" Sojourner said.

"Could you and Joseph come?" Rose said.

"Sure, if you want us to. I'll call Joseph to see if he's available. He's been so busy at the law firm," Sojourner said. "I can't wait to tell him about my job offer."

"About the rent situation, I'm sorry to hold you up, Soj. Jamarr said that he was going to move in with me, and that we could split the rent, but then I busted him sleeping with Janelle," Rose said.

"Men seem to have a problem sticking with one woman," Sojourner said. "I've been suspicious of Joseph and another attorney at the law firm, actually?" Sojourner said.

"Yeah, but Soj, he's still great. He's a hard working man who treats you very good, a gentleman. I told you to fight to keep him," Rose said.

"Yes, you did say that," Sojourner said. "And that's what I'm doing."

"Now, Jamarr is a different story," Rose said. "He's not worth fighting for. He lied to me about his connections in the music industry. He doesn't have a steady job. And he's selling drugs, too," Rose said.

"Now that is definitely bad news. That's dangerous, deadly even. Don't even touch that kind of lifestyle," Sojourner said.

"Yeah, you're right. But I didn't see the light, until I caught him cheating two weeks ago," Rose said. She was sitting down next to Sojourner on their living room sofa. "Damn Bastard busted my lip."

"Yeah. I remembered your lip was all swollen, but you said didn't want to press charges," Sojourner said. "What actually happened?"

"Well, I found out he was sleeping with my so-called friend, Janelle," Rose said, frowning.

"Oh, no he didn't," Sojourner said, indignantly.

"Oh, yeah, he did. He was screwing that bitch," Rose said.

"Gross!" Sojourner said.

"I was in Janelle's neighborhood, getting my hair done. So I figured I'd stop by her apartment and say 'Hi' to my girl, you know. Her roommate, Sharon, answered the door. I go in and sit down on the living room sofa, and Sharon goes to tell Janelle I was there. Before Sharon can open her mouth, guess who comes out of Janelle's bedroom?" Rose said.

"Jamarr…" Sojourner said.

"Yep," Rose said. "And I let that fool have it. I hit him with my Louis Vitton bag, and Janelle came out of the room in her bra and panties, girl. I pushed her down to the floor, and she shouted at me. Then I smacked Jamarr, and I pulled the chain that I gave him. It broke, and he went off and punched me in the mouth," Rose said, looking down at her hands.

"Oh, my God, Rose," Sojourner said. "…Then what happened?"

"I told Sharon to call the police. Then Jamarr said he'd fuck us all up if Sharon dared touch the phone."

"Lord have mercy," Sojourner said. "What a lousy dog!"

"He called me last week, saying he was sorry. He didn't want

Janelle, and he loved me, begging me on the phone, but I told him he was a crazy, nasty, trifling Nigga," Rose said.

"Well… now you have to move on with you life, Rose," Sojourner said, sitting back on the sofa.

"Yeah, I will… I just met a really nice guy at my last singing engagement at the Joplin Restaurant, in the Howard Inn Hotel. He's a medical student at Howard," Rose said, smiling. "His name is James Jenkins, and he's from the south."

"Oh, that's nice," Sojourner said.

Sojourner was a little worried that Rose was moving too fast into another relationship, but she said nothing to spoil Rose's fun.

"Please come next week, Soj. I would love for James to meet you and Joseph," Rose said. "You guys are so professional, real buppies."

Sojourner thought this statement was ironic. She remembered that for a long time, Rose thought that she was a bit of a hermit and a bookworm. That day, Rose thought that Sojourner was the toast of the town. Sojourner chuckled.

That evening, Sojourner telephoned Joseph at his apartment.

"Hey Baby Love, how are you?" Sojourner said.

"Oh, my princess, I'm so glad to hear your voice," Joseph said.

"Well, if you wanted to hear my voice, why am I calling you, instead of you calling me," Sojourner said.

"My princess, I don't want to unload my burdens on you, but I'm absolutely swamped with this Cameroon project at the firm," Joseph said. "I'm sitting here surrounded by piles of paper, all briefs that I have to read. This project is critical to the international team."

"Don't stress yourself, Baby Love. Just wanted to share some good news with you," Sojourner said. "I got the job with Africa Now."

"Excellent, Princess," Joseph said. "What is the position

title?"

"It's Project Coordinator," Sojourner said.

"Congratulations! We must celebrate," Joseph said.

"I would like that," Sojourner said. "But, I don't want to interrupt your work."

Sojourner was lying. She did want to interrupt his work; she wanted to be with him that evening.

"If I had my way, we'd be together right now. You know I have asked you to move in with me," Joseph said.

"I kind of wanted us to be married first, you know," Sojourner said.

"Then let's get married as soon as possible. I've already proposed, Princess."

"I know... Could you spare a few hours next Friday at 8:00 p.m.? Rose is going to be singing at the J.W. Marriott in D.C. She has asked if we could both attend; it's important to her," Sojourner said.

"All right, Princess, I'm at your service, forever. I'll be there next week to pick you up, okay?"

"Thanks, Baby Love," Sojourner said, making kissing sounds into the telephone.

CHAPTER TWENTY-EIGHT

The following Friday Joseph picked Sojourner up, and they drove downtown to see Rose perform at the Marriott. Joseph also wanted them to celebrate Sojourner's new job, by going to the Sub-Sahara Room, after Rose's show.

Joseph and Sojourner ordered drinks in the lounge. They briefly discussed the Cameroon case. He told Sojourner that he was representing a multinational company's interests in an immense rubber plantation in Cameroon.

A conservatively dressed black man arrived alone at the lounge, wearing a tailored navy blue suit. He stood out because he was alone, and like Sojourner and Joseph, he was amongst the youngest of the people in the lounge. Sojourner figured that he was probably, James Jenkins, the man that Rose had spoken of earlier. He sat down and glanced at his watch.

At 9:00 p.m., a small band assembled itself on the small stage of the lounge. They started to tune up a bit, and then played some familiar instrumental tunes. Then the guitarist introduced Rose. She then emerged from an exit near the rear of the stage. Rose was wearing a long, gold-toned, close fitting gown. The gown was beautiful, hugging her voluptuous, creamy beige body. She stood on the stage and welcomed everyone. She waved in the direction of Joseph and Sojourner, and in the direction of the young man who was sitting alone at the table near them. As Sojourner had suspected, the conservatively dressed young man was the James Jenkins that Rose had spoken of last week.

For the next thirty minutes, Rose sang a succession of contemporary tunes. She sang Anita Baker's "Caught Up in the Rapture of Love," Phyllis Hyman's "Somewhere In My Lifetime," and other love ballads. During her intermission, Rose walked over to Joseph and Sojourner's table and greeted them; then she thanked them for coming. Next she went over to the table where James Jenkins sat and greeted him. Rose seemed to be explaining to James who Sojourner and Joseph were because he then waved at them and smiled. Rose motioned for him to join them at their table, and he did. Then she went behind the stage to take a break and prepare for the next set.

During the brief intermission, Joseph, James, and Sojourner made small talk. Just before the intermission was over, Jamarr entered the lounge. His evening attire was out of sync with that of the other patrons in the lounge, not to mention his age difference. Coincidentally, Jamarr sat down at the very same table where James had sat earlier. He sat alone at the table, staring at the stage, frowning. Sojourner glanced at Jamarr quickly and winced slightly, sensing trouble.

The band started playing again, and Rose emerged from

behind the stage. She stood on the stage and smiled at the crowd. Then she noticed Jamarr. Rose's smile wilted; then she seemed to remember that she was on stage, and Rose smiled again. She started to sing her next set of songs, with a slightly decreased level of enthusiasm than she'd displayed earlier.

When Rose finished her act, she dashed backstage, which was unusual, given her earlier effervescence. James Jenkins seemed to notice that Rose's demeanor had changed. James glanced over at Jamarr, whom he did not know. Joseph looked at Sojourner, as if to ask her what was going on. Sojourner sipped her wine and said nothing.

Rose emerged from behind the stage. She'd changed her clothes, and she was wearing a black cocktail dress. Rose said good-bye to the band members and walked toward the table where Sojourner, Joseph, and James sat. She ignored Jamarr. James stood up and kissed her on the cheek. Joseph raised his drink to her and smiled. Sojourner sat there cautiously anticipating an explosion. From the corner of her eye, Sojourner saw Jamarr coming.

"How come I don't get a fucking kiss?" Jamarr said, with his voice raised.

"Nobody invited you, Jamarr!" Rose said.

"What the hell is going on?" James said.

"Don't worry about him, James," Rose said. "Leave, Jamarr!"

"Okay, give me my fucking ring back, bitch!" Jamarr said.

"I'm not giving you shit," Rose said. "Let's go James."

"What's with the name-calling, Man?" James said loudly, pointing his finger at Jamarr.

"Nigga, I'll kick your punk ass, if you don't get yo finger out my face," Jamarr said.

"No you wont either," Rose said. "Come on, James."

Rose reached for James's arm.

Jamarr stood between them, blocking James.

"Move dammit!" James said loudly.

Jamarr snickered at James.

Joseph and Sojourner stood up silently.

Joseph motioned for Sojourner to stand back a little.

"Hey! We don't want any trouble," Joseph said.

"Mind your Goddam business, Man!" James said.

"Jamarr, don't talk to him like that!" Sojourner said.

Sojourner could barely believe herself.

"The pretty bookworm here done found somebody that looks like her brother, only taller," said Jamarr, sarcastically.

Joseph stared at Jamarr threateningly.

Jamarr started to speak; then Rose broke in.

"Leave us alone, Jamarr," Rose said. "You had your chance and fucked up big time," Rose said.

"I want my damn ring back!" Jamarr said.

Two security personnel from the hotel approached them and asked if there was a problem. Rose explained to them what had happened. Jamarr broke in and told them she had his ring. The security personnel said that Jamarr would have to leave the premises because he was causing a disturbance. Jamarr glared at the security guards.

"Jamarr, here, take your damn ring," Rose said, reaching into her purse. She shoved it at Jamarr, and he grabbed it.

Rose then stepped around him, and motioned for them to follow her.

Sojourner, Joseph, and James following Rose out of the lounge and into the hotel lobby. Rose reached for James' hand, but he placed his hands in his pockets, avoiding her reach.

"Rose you put on an excellent show this evening," Sojourner said.

"Thanks, Soj," Rose said, looking wistfully at James, who was avoiding her glance.

"Joseph and I are going to the Sub-Sahara Club in Adams Morgan. We hope you'll join us. It's a nice club," Sojourner said.

"Oh, that sounds nice. Let's go James," Rose said.

James shrugged apathetically.

"Oh, come on James. We'll have fun," Rose said.

"Yes. Let the lady have some fun, after that spectacular performance this evening," Joseph said.

"Damn sure was a performance and a spectacle, too," James said.

"Look, James. I didn't invite, Jamarr. We broke up, and I told him that I didn't want to see him again. It's not my fault that he showed up."

There was a brief silence.

"Please, James let's put this behind us. Let's go out with Soj and Joseph. They're great people," Rose said.

"Okay, then. Let's go. I'll follow you, Joseph."

"All right," Joseph said.

The couples both walked to their respective cars in the parking lot. Rose drove with her seemingly reluctant date, following Joseph and Sojourner to the Sub-Sahara Room.

CHAPTER TWENTY-NINE

On a sunny Saturday morning in September 1991, Joseph and Sojourner got married. Sojourner was filled with a quiet joy, as Joseph drove them to the Arlington County Circuit Court for a private ceremony. She wore a tailored, white linen dress and cream colored leather pumps. Her hair was styled in a neatly cut page boy style. In her ears were tiny ceramic daisy earrings. Joseph wore a beige suit and brown leather Italian shoes. She was filled with adoration for her husband.

After getting married, Sojourner said that she wanted to go to the African Art Museum to see a new exhibit there. Joseph drove her to D.C. and parked on Constitution Avenue, in front of the Department of Commerce. They strolled leisurely to the African Art Museum. She felt very contented, as she held her husband's hand. She was Mrs. Joseph Kalisa, Sojourner thought. They entered the African Art Museum, strolled past the front desk, and descended the staircase to the exhibits on the lower level. One of the exhibits contained artwork relating to mother and child images in African art. They looked at one sculpture after the next of African women nursing their infants.

"Princess, I'm hoping we can have a child soon. You'd make a good mother," Joseph said.

They were standing in front of a sculpture of a mother breastfeeding her infant.

"You think so, Joseph?" Sojourner said.

"You are quiet, kind, and affectionate... I want us to have children," Joseph said.

"We just got married, Joseph. Let's enjoy each other first," Sojourner said.

"We can still enjoy each other, Princess... Please think about it. It's important to me," Joseph said.

Joseph held Sojourner's hand firmly, displaying a relaxed smile. His eyes, effortlessly penetrating, made her feel anchored in his love. Sojourner was glad to be Mrs. Joseph Kalisa. Most of the time, Joseph's approach with her was patient. They drove over to Georgetown and had lunch at the Citronelle restaurant.

Lunch was followed by a visit to a posh jewelry store in Chevy Chase, Maryland. Joseph purchased a stunning pair of diamond and sapphire earrings to match her wedding ring.

That evening, a dinner was held in their honor by Joseph's friend, Ibrahim and his wife, Annette. Moses and several other Rwandans, including Theodetta, attended. Other guests were Francois and Christine, Joseph's Cameroonian friends.

After their marriage, Sojourner moved in with Joseph at Le Petit Trianon. She discovered the hard way that Joseph, unlike her, was very neat. He would raise his eyebrows and his handsome face would be filled with disdain as he commanded Sojourner to pick up behind herself. One morning, while they were both dressing for work in the bedroom, Joseph complained.

"Princess, you really need to learn to hang up your clothes, rather than letting them pile up on the dresser drawer," Joseph said.

Then he shook his head in disapproval.

"Sorry Baby Love. I'll hang them up this evening when I return home, okay?"

"You said that yesterday, didn't you?" Joseph said, irritated.

Sojourner was in their bedroom, getting ready for work. She glanced at Joseph. Her dream man was not always Mr. Nice Guy, Sojourner thought.

Most of the time, Joseph and Sojourner were happily married, and it was a romantically blissful experience for both of them. They were an upwardly mobile black couple in D.C., and they enjoyed the privileges of their lifestyle. Joseph and Sojourner went to work related and personal dinners, parties, and events. However, they had their share of couple squabbles, too.

One morning, Joseph came home at 8:00 a.m. in the morning. The smell of wine was on his breath. This was the second time he had done this. She got out of bed and yelled at him, but even drunk, he could stand up straight and look like a prince. Sojourner was enraged. He attempted to pacify her with loving words, but Sojourner refused to listen. Instead, she packed an overnight bag, and drove her car to Rose's apartment, the same one she once shared with her. Sojourner recounted what had transpired, and Rose listened patiently; then she responded.

"Girl, my Mom told me that's how men are. Shit, you remember what happened with me and Jamarr?" Rose said.

"Yeah. That was horrible," Sojourner said.

"Well...That damn James Jenkins, the med student, moved

out as soon as he passed his Medical Board exams," Rose said.

"What an ungrateful jerk!" Sojourner said.

"He moved in with me, right after Jamarr made that scene at my singing engagement. You remember."

"Sure, I do," Sojourner said.

"James and I split the rent, and things were going okay. I thought maybe we'd get married one day, like you and Joseph. But James always made excuses, like he had to focus on his medical studies, and on and on," Rose said.

Sojourner sat on their old sofa, listening to Rose.

"Then James passed his medical boards and started staying out for days, and not coming home. We stopped having sex, so I figured he was seeing someone else. When he finally came home, I asked him and he admitted that he was. James was seeing another doctor, a resident at Georgetown University," Rose said.

"I'm sorry about that. It just shows that he wasn't worthy of you, Rose," Sojourner said, trying to console Rose.

Rose shrugged her shoulders, the expression on her face was sad though.

"I'll get over that dog."

"Rose, let's go out tonight, you and me," Sojourner said. "Let's see a show and go to dinner."

"That sounds like fun," Rose said. "I'm off today, so why not. What show do you have in mind?"

"There's a production of Romeo & Juliet at the Kennedy Center. I've wanted to see that. We could do dinner at a nearby restaurant," Sojourner said.

"You and your Shakespeare plays, girl. You are such a proper thing!" Rose said, chuckling.

"Well, you know me."

Sojourner was glad she had made Rose laugh a little.

"But seriously, Soj, I can't afford all that. My next singing engagement isn't until next week, and my Woodies paycheck can barely pay my share of the rent. My new roommate is a real bitch. She explodes if I don't have my share of the rent on time. You were the best, girl."

"This will be my treat, for both of us," Sojourner said.

"Dang. Thanks, Soj," Rose said. "Soj, I know Joseph made you mad coming home late, but work things out with him. You both make such an attractive couple, and he's a very nice man. You're doing well in your new job, and he's a corporate attorney in a big firm. And you look so cheerful and happy with him, most of the time. With Jamarr and James, they had me crying way more than laughing. Believe me, I know what bad is when it comes to men... Joseph's a dream come true, girl," Rose said.

Sojourner nodded in agreement.

Rose gladly loaned Sojourner black cocktail dress and some costume jewelry to wear. During intermission of the performance, they stood sipping wine in the large lobby of the Kennedy Center. Both women received stares from men of all ages. However, the more stares Sojourner received, the more she thought of her impeccable husband, Joseph Kalisa. Sojourner and Rose had a good time that evening together, and by the end of the evening, they had just about forgotten about their grievances.

CHAPTER THIRTY

One day Joseph came home from work, and passionately kissed Sojourner. He was normally even tempered, and passionate kisses were usually reserved for their bedroom.

"Princess, I have just been delegated the team lead for the Cameroon case," Joseph announced.

"Oh, that's fabulous, Baby Love," Sojourner said. "What an achievement."

"Princess, my work is being recognized," Joseph said.

He smiled and embraced her.

This recent success was like an aphrodisiac for both of them, Sojourner thought. Joseph slipped his hand in her white lace negligee, gently pulled out one of her small breasts. He sucked on her ebony-colored nipple. Bending his knees, Joseph searched with his hands, for her underwear. When he found them, he removed them. Sojourner assisted him by gingerly stepping out of her panties.

He helped her to remove her negligee. Sojourner stood before Joseph naked. He smiled a wide, approving smile, and he undid his tie and shirt. Sojourner helped him with this and placed the tie and shirt carefully on the sofa. Joseph started to remove his pants, when the telephone rang. They looked at each other. Then Joseph reached over and answered the ringing phone on the coffee table.

It was Betsy McShane. From what Sojourner could hear of the discussion, Betsy needed to discuss something with Joseph immediately.

Sojourner stood there, naked, in front of Joseph, as he talked on the phone. He observed Sojourner as he spoke with Betsy. Sojourner put her hands on her hips and pouted. Joseph winked at her, and licked his lips, playfully.

"All right, Betsy, I think you're right," Joseph said. "We can have a meeting to come to an agreement on how to best handle this dilemma. We can meet in the eighth floor conference room in an hour. See you, then." Joseph hung up the phone.

"You work six days a week, so why do you have to give up your evenings, too?" Sojourner said.

"Try to understand, Princess. Betsy is a strong ally of mine at the firm. She is a partner in the firm, and she's the one who suggested that I be appointed as team lead for the Cameroon case. My knowledge of Cameroon culture and fluency in French law helps, but Betsy's support is the driving force behind my rapid advancement within the firm."

"What about our time together, Baby Love? You should have thought of an excuse to put it off until tomorrow."

"You're my wife, Princess. When my career goes well, it's your benefit just as well as mine," Joseph said.

Sojourner silently picked up her negligee and slipped it on. Then she went to the kitchen to set the table for dinner. She prepared baked salmon in a lemony butter sauce, broccoli, and Rice-A-Roni for dinner.

Sojourner went to bed late that evening, annoyed that Joseph still wasn't home. She'd called him at the office earlier and left a voice mail for him, and he returned her call and indicated that his meeting had just ended. He would be home soon.

Alone in their bed, Sojourner drifted off to sleep. In her dreams, she saw Betsy McShane walking into their bedroom. Betsy was completely naked. She was slightly plump and pale, like one of those ancient Greek goddess statues. Joseph, who was lying next to Sojourner, said nothing as Betsy climbed into bed with them. The three of them were in bed together. Their naked bodies touched each other, with Joseph's long body in the center of the bed. Betsy sat up and stared at Joseph's erection, admiringly. Then she mounted Joseph and moaned with keen pleasure. She reached down and rubbed the hairs on Joseph's chest, with her plump alabaster hands and red nails. At first, Sojourner was paralyzed with shock at this sight. She couldn't believe that Joseph was not even resisting Betsy's advances. A visceral sense of hysteria grew within Sojourner, and she burst into action. Sojourner reached over Joseph pushed Betsy McShane off of him. Betsy fell to the floor. A struggle ensued between the two naked women, while Joseph watched calmly.

Sojourner woke up. Her skin was damp with perspiration. Thank God it was just a dream. It seemed so real. Sojourner did not want to believe the implications of this dream. She lay there in their bed alone, until Joseph very quietly entered their apartment at 3:00 a.m. in the morning.

"Where the hell have you been?"

"After the meeting Mike Randolph suggested we'd go out for a drink, Princess," Joseph said.

Sojourner turned on the lamp on the nightstand and sat up in their bed. She stared up at Joseph and folded her arms. He grinned. His clothes looked the same as they did when he left, but his tie looked a little askew. Sojourner got up out of the bed and stepped closer. He still smelled the same, except for the wine on his breath. He'd clearly had more than one glass. Sojourner could smell the scent of wine, floating from Joseph's mouth. Mentally, she searched for obvious clues that he had been with another woman.

"My team and I went to Donovan's Pub," Joseph said. "We didn't leave the office until after 11:00."

"Donovan's Pub? Where's that?"

"On Connecticut Avenue, near Woodley Park."

"Until 3:00 a.m.?" Sojourner said.

"No, Princess, until about 1:30 a.m. It's 3:00 a.m. now," Joseph said.

"It took you an hour and a half to get home?"

"Princess ... I had to drop Mike off at home; he had taken the Metro train to work. Can we end this interrogation and get some sleep. I have to work tomorrow," Joseph said.

"What's really going on, Joseph? Tell me the truth."

"The truth is right now I'm developing a splitting headache."

"Well, that serves you right for whatever it is you're doing out there 'til 3:00 a.m. in the morning."

"What I'm doing out there is attending my professional career, which consists of not only my training as an attorney, but also my social skills as a gentleman. Please understand that this will benefit both of us, Princess," Joseph said, undoing his tie.

Sojourner stormed out of the bedroom and went to the kitchen. She made herself some Valerian tea and sat on the sofa in the living room. Sojourner wanted so much to believe Joseph's story. But what about her dream? Maybe she was being paranoid? After she finished her tea, she went back to the bedroom. Joseph was sound asleep, snoring lightly.

CHAPTER THIRTY-ONE

In April 1992, Sojourner's doctor informed her that she was pregnant, during her annual pap smear. Sojourner knew that Joseph would be happy, since he was the one who insisted that they have a child soon. He had told her that he wanted them to have a baby as soon as possible. He convinced her after a while, and Sojourner had stopped taking her birth control pills. When she told Joseph that she was pregnant, Joseph was elated.

One evening, while Sojourner and Joseph were eating dinner, Joseph announced that his cousin, Theodetta, would be coming to live with them. It would be just until she finished her medical residency. Joseph said Theodetta was having some difficulty with her landlord again, and she had asked if she could stay with him temporarily. He explained that Theodetta was almost finished her medical residency, and her stay would probably last just a few months. Sojourner was annoyed that Joseph didn't ask her permission. He simply announced it as a done deal.

"Have you already told her that she can stay here?" Sojourner said.

"Yes," Joseph said.

"So you are telling me your cousin will be living with us, not asking me if she can?" Sojourner said.

"Well... Is it all right with you, Princess?"

"What am I supposed to say now, Joseph? You already told her she can stay here."

"You don't understand... We have to help her. Someone was killed in her apartment complex," Joseph said.

"Oh my God. What happened?" Sojourner said.

"She arrived home late and saw police cars in front of her apartment building. There was yellow tape in front of the building... A body was being taken out. So she sat on a bench and waited until the commotion was over..." Joseph said.

"And then what happened?" Sojourner said. Sojourner took a sip from a tall glass of water and listened to Joseph.

"When the police left, everyone was allowed to go into the apartment building, so Theodetta went to her apartment. After she entered, she went to the kitchen to get something to eat…and she saw drops of blood on the floor. She looked up at the ceiling, and blood was dripping from the apartment above her. It turned out that was the apartment where a man was killed. Apparently, there was so much blood that it seeped through the floor and into Theodetta's apartment," Joseph said.

"God have mercy. That's gross," Sojourner said. "Did she tell the landlord to relocate her to another apartment?" Sojourner said.

"She asked for another apartment, but he had no other vacancies at the time," Joseph said.

"Oh, I see," Sojourner said. "Then, of course, she needs to get out of that place. She's welcomed to stay here, then."

Theodetta showed up at their apartment with several huge suitcases. She glided into their condominium with a regality that was a bit daunting to Sojourner. Joseph moved Theodetta into the second bedroom, which Joseph had reserved as his office. Joseph then purchased a new bedroom set for Theodetta, and some new sheets. Theodetta was taciturn, but civil, with Sojourner. However, she spoke with Joseph in Kinyawanda, every chance she got.

As Theodetta, unpacked her clothing, Sojourner walked into her room and greeted her. Theodetta smiled and returned the greeting. Sojourner then noticed an old photo album sitting on top of Theodetta's suitcase, and she asked her if she could look at it. Theodetta said yes. The photo album was filled with old photos of Theodetta's family, which included her parents and Joseph's parents. Sojourner looked at photographs of the Rwandan Royal family, which were accompanied by Rwandan nobles.

"Oh, what a beautiful lady," Sojourner said. "Who is this, Theodetta?"

Theodetta momentarily stopped hanging her clothes in the closet, and glanced over Sojourner's shoulder. Then she continued to unpack her clothes.

"That's my mother," Theodetta said.

"Your mother looks so elegant," Sojourner said.

"She is a Rwandese princess," Theodetta said. "Rwandan royalty were trained from birth to exude dignity," Theodetta said.

"It's good that they could maintain their dignity with so much oppression going on during the colonial days," Sojourner said.

"For centuries, we were respected and cherished, even after the Europeans came," Theodetta said.

"But eventually that changed, didn't it?" Sojourner said.

"Yes, eventually. However, when they first came to Rwanda, the Europeans chose us to administer of their colonial policies. It seemed that they preferred to work through the Tutsis, at first. Maybe it was because we already had an organized society that we controlled, when they came. During the early colonial years, we were the chosen group," Theodetta said.

Theodetta seemed to be going into a trance as she spoke.

"Did Rwandans resist Colonialism?" Sojourner said.

"They had guns and advanced weapons, so we had to yield to them. We learned their language and were eager to go to their schools. We finally had to adopt their religion, even though we had one of own. We were forced to do their will."

"As black Americans, or African Americans, we adopted the religion of our masters, too," Sojourner said. "Too bad, Africans could not unite to prevent the devastation of slavery and colonialism."

"Africans unite? That's a joke," Theodetta said, sarcastically.

"Yeah ... During slavery in America, we had the plantation system. Slaves were divided into groups, there were the field slaves that did all the back breaking farm work and the house slaves, who worked in the masters house. However, both were slaves, and both could be beaten, sold, or killed whenever the master desired. They were all in the same boat for the most part," Sojourner said.

"We Rwandans didn't think of ourselves as slaves of the whites, but I suppose the comparison makes sense. It turned out that we were, in a way," Theodetta said. "The Tutsis ruled Rwanda, but really the Europeans ruled the Tutsi."

"But the Hutu control Rwanda now, right? What happened?" Sojourner said.

"Overnight, the Europeans took the side of the Hutu people. Just like that," Theodetta said, snapping her finger.

"And that was the beginning of the end for the Tutsi monarchy, right?" Sojourner said.

Theodetta nodded, sadly.

Sojourner went to her bedroom and brought back some extra hangars to give them to Theodetta. Theodetta resumed hanging her clothes in the closet. When she finished, she made up her bed, with the new sheets that were purchased for her.

"So, what's it like there now, in Rwanda?"

"We are at the mercy of merciless, vengeful, and murderous people, our fellow Rwandans. We who were once the backbone of Rwanda are no longer safe there. That's what's going on now."

"What happened to you in Rwanda?" Sojourner said.

"They burned our house down. Houses were burning everywhere, homes of Tutsi families," Theodetta said. "People were screaming and running."

"My God. That's horrible. I hope African people can come together and get past all the tribal divisions one day. Tribes are used as a tool to divide people up," Sojourner said.

"Actually, it's not really a tribal system in Rwanda," Theodetta said. "There is one language and one culture. It's more like racism."

"Racism?" Sojourner said. "But Rwandans are all black

people, Hutu and Tutsi. I don't understand," Sojourner said.

"Well… you wouldn't," Theodetta said.

"Anyway, there are too many divisions in African societies. There's almost no national unity, or African unity in general," Sojourner said.

"African people don't understand that kind of talk, Sojourner. You are talking about Pan-Africanism. Most Africans have never heard of Pan-Africanism. Most of us are so factionalized that we cannot see beyond our own town, or ethnic group, much less have a national identity," Theodetta said.

She sat on her newly made bed and sighed.

"The aspirations of great men like Kwame Nkrumah, W.E.B. DuBois, Marcus Garvey, and thousands of other visionaries shouldn't dry up and scatter like ashes in the wind," Sojourner said.

Theodetta closed her eyes and shook her head.

"Impossible dreams …," Theodetta said.

Sojourner sighed and continued to flip through the photo album.

"Who are these guys?"

The men in the next group of photos wore white toga-like cloth over white shirts and neat pants; some of them were obviously above average height and very attractive. They were marching in a procession in which the King of Rwanda was being carried on a tipoy.

"They are noblemen, young men from the finest Tutsi clans," Theodetta said.

"Clan?" Sojourner said. "Now that's a word that does not sit well with me," she said, chuckling.

"Why? A clan is just a group of families," Theodetta said.

"Do you know any of these people?" Sojourner said.

"Yes. One is an uncle, and another an aunt," Theodetta said.

"Really?"

"Yes," Theodetta said, with a hint of indignation.

The phone rang and Theodetta sprang to her feet to answer

it.

CHAPTER THIRTY-TWO

Theodetta settled in their home. She would come home from her rounds at the hospital at about 3:00 a.m. in the morning and turn on the kitchen light and proceed to prepare a meal. Sojourner could smell the food that she cooked, and she could see the light filtering under the door of the bedroom where she and Joseph slept. She was annoyed, to say the least.

One day, Sojourner complained to Joseph about this situation.

"Baby love, it disturbs my sleep when Theodetta comes home from work and starts cooking a meal and turning lights on at three a.m.," Sojourner said.

"Princess, Theodetta is a resident intern, so she works very odd hours. And as for the cooking, I suppose she's hungry when she gets home," Joseph said calmly.

"Yes, I know this, but this wakes me up. We both have to work during the day and have to get up early in the morning. We need to be fresh and rested, so we cannot afford to have our sleep interrupted."

"My sleep is not interrupted. It doesn't bother me, but I'll talk to Theodetta about it," Joseph said.

A few days later, Sojourner awoke early in the morning to prepare breakfast for her and Joseph. She went to the kitchen to prepare some oatmeal, tea, and toast. As she entered the kitchen, she noticed that there were dishes in the sink. There was a plate with spaghetti sauce stains on it, as well as a few strings of spaghetti. One glass, a fork, and a pot were also in the sink. The glass contained the remnants of some orange juice. This had happened before, Theodetta leaving dishes in the sink. Without thinking much about it, Sojourner went to

Theodetta's bedroom. She knocked on the bedroom door, and there was no response. Sojourner was contemplating giving up and going back to the kitchen, when she heard Theodetta talking on the phone in the room.

Theodetta was speaking in Kinyarwanda and was engrossed in the conversation. Sojourner knocked on the door again, and waited for Theodetta to answer. Theodetta stopped talking and opened the door.

"Theodetta, can you please wash you own dishes," Sojourner said.

"What?" Theodetta said.

"You left dishes in the sink, when you came home last night," Sojourner said.

"I'm going to wash the dishes that I used. You don't have to come and tell me to do it. I am not a child," Theodetta said, closing the door in Sojourner's face.

"What's the matter, Baby love?" Sojourner said, as she poured tea for Joseph.

Joseph had just entered the dining room dressed in a suit and looking dapper. He didn't look serene as he usually did.

"Theodetta met me in the hall, and she told me about what happened this morning. You told her to wash her dishes?" Joseph said.

He looked at Sojourner waiting for her response.

"Yes. I did. Look in the sink, Joseph. How much effort does it take to wash a few dishes? She left them in the sink with food stains and spaghetti strings on them," Sojourner said.

"Princess, sometimes she works a twelve or fourteen hour shift at the hospital. Maybe she was very tired," Joseph said.

"Why are you making excuses for her?" Sojourner said.

"Theodetta is my cousin. Our mothers are sisters. I want Theodetta to feel comfortable and welcomed in my home," Joseph said.

"Oh, so this is your home only?" Sojourner asked. "This isn't my home?"

"I meant our home; that goes without saying. You are my wife, so my home is your home," Joseph said.

"Yeah, right," Sojourner said.

"Princess, these are minor things, some dishes in the sink," Joseph said.

"When I first moved into this apartment with you, you were constantly making critical remarks about my poor housekeeping, but it's okay for your cousin to move in and leave dirty dishes in the sink," Sojourner said, raising her voice.

"I'm not saying that it is okay. I'm saying we need to be patient with her, not to complain about her every little imperfection," Joseph said.

"She's constantly on the phone talking, and I say nothing. I come home from work, and there's a group of people sitting in the living room, drinking beer and soda that I bought. Again, I don't make a peep," Sojourner said.

"I have to go to work now, my Princess, and so do you," Joseph said. "Theodetta will wash her dishes. All right?"

Joseph picked up his briefcase. Sojourner folded her arms and stared at Joseph. He kissed Sojourner on the cheek and quickly left for work.

One weekend in June 1992, Joseph and Sojourner gave a dinner party for Theodetta, who had just completed her resident intern training. She was a full-fledged doctor now. Almost everyone who attended the party was Rwandan. Theodetta and Annette prepared some Rwandan dishes. Sojourner's favorite was Isombe because it was a healthy and hearty dish. Sojourner prepared macaroni salad, a garden salad, and fried Flounder. Joseph purchased cases of beer, wine, and a few bottles of liquor and soda. Sojourner had spent all morning cleaning the apartment.

Joseph played Rwandan music and conversed with his guests. He introduced Sojourner to all she had not previously met, since they had a court marriage, and no formal wedding. It was Joseph's dream that they could get married in Rwanda one day, so that his mother could have the pleasure of arranging a traditional Rwandan wedding. There was a group of men who sat together, engrossed in their conversation. Joseph had introduced them as Moses, Ibrahim, and Thomas. Two of them were as tall and lean as Joseph, and one was a short man and heavy set.

Sojourner overheard a few of the men's comments in between her activities in the kitchen area.

"I'm going to Uganda next week. My uncle has a ranch and we'll be training there, you know. Moses and Ibrahim said they plan to come, too. You should come with us, Joe," said one of the tall serious men.

"It's critical that each of us consider military service. The troops need our help. They need bodies, disciplined and educated men like us. Otherwise, our families back home face something horrible. The Hutu Commandments were a warning," Moses said.

"Sojourner and I are expecting a child. How can I just leave her to go to war?" Joseph said.

"War? We are saving our people. They won't allow us to peacefully repatriate. And you know what they're planning to do to us?" the man said.

"Hush… Let's not talk about this right now," Ibrahim said.

Sojourner had just opened the door to let John in. He was carrying a bottle of champagne in one arm. Sojourner greeted him warmly and announced his arrival to Joseph.

Sojourner noticed that there were cold, uncomfortable gazes following John as he entered the apartment. Even Theodetta, who had been previously all smiles and glory, took a step back. Her smile wilted, and then it tightened into a grimace.

As Sojourner noticed all of this, she remembered that John was Hutu, while Joseph and the majority of their guests were of Tutsi. Nevertheless, Joseph stood up and greeted John with a cordial smile. He led John to a chair that was across the room from the group of men with whom he'd been actively conversing.

Ibrahim got up to go to the bathroom, and Sojourner overheard his comment to Joseph.

"Why'd you invite that Hutu bastard?" Ibrahim whispered to Joseph.

"He's my friend, Ibrahim," Joseph said, whispering.

"His brother is in the Rwandan Army. How can you trust him," Ibrahim said, continuing to the bathroom.

During the dinner party Sojourner busied herself in the kitchen and dining room areas, arranging trays of food on the dining room table, keeping the kitchen clean, making sure there were enough drinks, and greeting guests as they entered the condo. Theodetta was busy talking with her Rwandan friends, and Joseph was discussing with the tall and stoic men on the sofa. Sojourner didn't know most of the guests, and she felt a little awkward. Many of the visitors spoke in Kinyarwanda, or French, so she couldn't understand the conversations that were going on around her.

Sojourner did recognize Joseph's friend, Francois, and his sister, Christine. Francois greeted Sojourner and asked her about her job. She asked him about his career as a scientist. Christine even tried to be friendly and compliment Sojourner on being such a serene and African-like hostess. Christine told Sojourner that she looked like a Rwandan. Sojourner smiled and commented that she considered that a compliment. However, there was something about Christine's presence that made Sojourner uneasy.

Joseph made a speech congratulating Theodetta for completing medical school and her residency. She stood up and thanked him for his support, for always being there for her whenever she needed him. He then introduced Theodetta's fiancé, Maurice Gakwisi, who was one of the tall, quiet looking men with whom Joseph was conversing.

Sojourner had invited Rose to the dinner party, but Rose hadn't shown up yet. Just as Sojourner was beginning to lament to herself that she would have no one to talk to the phone rang again.   Sojourner unenthusiastically reached for the phone, assuming that it was just another call for Theodetta, probably someone asking for directions. However, to her surprise, it was Rose. She was in the foyer of the lobby waiting to get buzzed into the building.

This was Rose's first time visiting Sojourner, since Sojourner had moved out of the apartment that they once shared. Rose glanced around the apartment, clearly impressed with the environment.

"Girl, this apartment is fly," Rose said.

"Thanks, Rose. I'm so glad you made it, girl."

Then Joseph greeted Rose.

"Hello Rose. It's so good to see you, again," Joseph said, shaking her hand.

"Wow! You guys have a fabulous place," Rose said.

"Thank you. Please make yourself comfortable. I'm sure you and Sojourner have so much to catch up on," Joseph said, before returning to the sofa where his friends sat like secretive warriors.

During the course of the dinner party, Sojourner introduced Rose to several of their guests, including Francois. Rose and Francois talked for a while, and they seemed to be attracted to each other.

CHAPTER THIRTY-THREE

Joseph, Moses, and Ibrahim went to the gym four days a week in the evening. Each day Joseph would go jogging early in the morning. He started out jogging one mile and worked his way up to five miles over the course of six months. His gym membership included the services of a personal trainer who worked with him several days a week, showing him how to properly lift weights. He made progress and his lean body grew more muscular and his neck thickened.

Joseph noticed that Sojourner was pleased with his

increasingly athletic body. She'd playfully tap him on the rear end when he walked by in their apartment. It was time to tell his wife what he intended to do, Joseph thought.

He and Sojourner had gone to bed early one evening after a long day. He rubbed her growing belly until his wife fell asleep, but Joseph could not sleep. So he got up and read a brief in his office. Then he became sleepy and decided to watch some TV for a while before going to bed. That's when he heard his father's voice.

Falling asleep on the sofa, Joseph heard his father's voice. He hadn't heard his father's voice almost twenty years, but this voice was clear.

"Joseph...*vien ici*," his father said.

That's when Sojourner appeared before him. She was standing, in front of the sofa, staring at him. She apparently had awakened and came to the living room looking for him. CNN was on TV, but he was not watching the TV. Sojourner sat down next to him and touched his shoulder.

"Baby Love?" Sojourner said. "You okay?"

"I hear my father, Princess," Joseph said.

"You were sleeping, Baby Love," Sojourner said.

"I don't think I was sleeping, Princess. I heard him," Joseph said.

"Remember last week you had a dream about your father, standing in front of the university where he taught?" Sojourner said. "You're thinking about him again, and you had a dream."

Joseph shook his head.

Sojourner sat back and rubbed her swollen belly.

"I must return to Rwanda to fight," Joseph said.

"We're expecting a baby," Sojourner said. "Baby Love, please don't go there."

"There's going to be another massacre...," Joseph said. "I have to do something."

"You already donate money to help with the cause," Sojourner said. "You're helping that way."

She was on the verge of tears.

Joseph stared at his pretty wife, his eyes moved to her swollen belly.

In December of 1992, Joseph was sent to Cameroon with his team of attorneys from Livingston and Richards. They worked on a big case there for three weeks. Sojourner was eight months pregnant, and she feared that Joseph would miss the birth of their first child. She had discovered, via ultra sound, that she was carrying a boy.

When she conveyed this information to Joseph over the phone, he was ecstatic. Joseph promised that he would not miss the birth of his son, Joseph Kalisa III, whom they had already named. He was true to his word. Joseph did not miss the birth of his son. Two weeks later, in the delivery room, Joseph held Sojourner's hand, as their first child was born. However, he had to return to Cameroon a few days later, to finish up the case there.

Sojourner received a letter from Joseph a few days after he returned to Cameroon.

> *My Princess,*
>
> *I have made considerable progress with the Cameroon case. I believe that I have guided my team members toward an amicable negotiation. We aren't far from a settlement. I'm proud that the settlement will address the needs of both parties. It is important to me that I not allow myself to be, as you would often say "used as a mere tool for the further exploitation of Africa." (Smile)*
>
> *Being in Cameroon brings back memories for me. As you know, it was in Cameroon that I attended Yaounde University.*
>
> *I had explained to you that my father was killed in 1973. My father was on his way home from his office at the National University of Rwanda. He was stopped by a group of men who murdered him. I was sixteen years old.*
>
> *Although Rwanda is my homeland, my life there as a child, and during adolescence, was often miserable. As a Tutsi, I was constantly on guard for fear of being attacked or ostracized by my Hutu countrymen. I even started to feel self-conscious about my height. Every inch I grew, I dreaded. My looks and height would have assigned an elite status to me*

in the colonial days. Maybe that was the problem though.

The Rwanda that I lived in the 1960s and 1970s was often a terrifying place for me and my family. It was like the "Jim Crow" period that black American's experienced in America. I've read about how black American men were routinely "lynched" in the Jim Crow South of America, and the bloody riots in the north during the late 19th century and early 20th century. But in my homeland of Rwanda, I believe that our experience as Tutsis was often similar. I could be brutally killed just for being a Tutsi.

After my father was murdered, my mother was very afraid. My father had worked hard and was a respected professor. If they could kill him, then who was safe? I attended the Lycee, and I was constantly being singled out for punishment by school administrators for no apparent reason. There were times when I cursed my height and the thinness of my nose and body, which marked me as a Tutsi, and singled me out for ridicule and discrimination.

Once I was beaten by a mob of Rwandans on my way home from school. I was nearly beaten to death, by several men. I remember that my shirt was bloody, and I lost consciousness. What saved me was my sister's friend, Laurent.

Laurent was the son of a Hutu family. He loved my sister and wanted to marry her, but my mother was too angry with Hutu people to consent. However, after Laurent saved my life, he was allowed to marry Teresa.

One evening, I was sleeping in my dormitory with many other students. Suddenly, the doors burst open and several men walked in and began to look around. The schoolmaster walked alongside a group of other Rwandan men. The men asked him to identify the Tutsi students. Several students were identified, including one who was actually not a Tutsi at all. He insisted that he was a Hutu, and he pointed at me. I was then pulled from my bed, too. I protested, and I asked them why they were doing this to us. We had done nothing wrong. I was then struck with a club, and I fell unconscious. When I regained consciousness, I realized that I had been expelled from school.

My mother pleaded with father's friend, who was also a professor at the National University, to take me with him back to Cameroon. He did. There, I attended Yaounde University.

After two successful years in the university, I met an American girl. She worked for the American Embassy in Yaounde, Cameroon. Through her parents, she helped me to secure a scholarship to Princeton University. There was a special fund there for African students interested in the liberal arts. Her family assisted me in securing a visa, and the rest you know already.

There, so please do not say that I never want to discuss my past with you.

How is little Joseph? I love you and my son, and I miss you both so much.

Yours Forever,
Your Husband Joseph.

After the Cameroon case was successfully wrapped up, Joseph returned home. Sojourner met him at the airport with their infant son. She stood at the gate A1 at Dulles Airport, waiting for Joseph to arrive. She was holding their son.

"Baby Love!" Sojourner said, waving at her husband as he entered the baggage claim area.

"My Princess, and my little prince!" Joseph said.

They kissed and embraced.

"Give him to me," Joseph said, as he put his suitcase down and held out his hands for his son.

She gently placed the infant in his arms. He was wrapped in a soft, light blue blanket.

"BabyLove, I'm so glad to see you. It's hard when you're away," Sojourner said.

"I know," Joseph said, kissing his son.

Joseph spoke softly to the infant.

"My umuhungu."

CHAPTER THIRTY-FOUR

In July 1993, Joseph III was crawling around their condo. Joseph was happy that his career was going well at Livingston and Richards. He actively engaged in several international cases at the firm. Sojourner had just started a new job as an English instructor at Montgomery Community College in Takoma Park, Maryland. Joseph was very proud of this, his wife, the college instructor. She had resigned from her position as project coordinator with Africa Now a month before their son was born. Before resigning from her position with Africa Now, Sojourner had complained to Joseph that her boss said that he couldn't do without a project coordinator for six months. This was after she requested a six month maternity leave. According to Sojourner, Mr. Jackson had become quite obnoxious ever since she announced that she was expecting a baby. Mr. Jackson became strict and critical of her work. Sojourner endured this for a while. However, during her eighth month of pregnancy, she had enough. She and Joseph agreed that she should stay home with their infant for at least six months after the birth, before returning to work. She wanted to breast feed their son and focus on the child, and Joseph encouraged her to do this.

A month later, Sojourner's father died. He had another stroke and did not survive it. Sitting on her bed holding little Joseph, Sojourner cried. Would he forgive her for not visiting him before he died, she thought?

She had promised to visit him at Aunt Jess's home, but she did not. Instead, she sent him a Kwanzaa card with a photo of her newborn son. Then she felt Joseph, wrapping his arms around her and his son. They went to New Jersey to help with the funeral arrangements.

The funeral was held in an elegant funeral home in Atlantic City. The funeral home was owned by a family which had been in the business for several generations. Sojourner, Joseph, and Aunt Jess worked with the funeral director to make sure the protocol was dignified. Many family members and friends showed up. A few local winos, friends of her father, showed up, too. Aunt Mae showed up with her daughter Mimi and Uncle Jobe.

The menu at the wake, which was held in a local hall, included several big platters of fried chicken, macaroni and cheese, collard greens, old fashioned potato salad, macaroni salad with shrimp, sweet potato pie, upside down pineapple cake, and much more. One of Sojourner's aunts, Aunt Louise, looked at Joseph, nodding her head slowly.

"Baby, you sure are a beautiful man though. But you need to eat something. Ann, make Joe a plate," Aunt Louise said.

Joseph smiled.

"Yes, Aunt Louise, I'll make him a plate," Sojourner said.

Sojourner picked up a paper plate and select collard greens, potato salad, and a slice of sweet potato pie.

"Put some ribs and fried chicken on the plate for him, Ann," her aunt whispered to Sojourner, not wanting to be overheard. "He's a on the lean side, girl."

"He doesn't like to eat too much meat, Aunt Louise," Sojourner said.

"Don't like to eat too much meat?" Aunt Louise said.

"Nope," Sojourner said.

"Lord, no wonder he's thin," said Aunt Louise.

"He's not that thin," Sojourner said.

"I know, I know. He looks strong anyway though," Aunt Louise said. "How about some of that catfish over there?"

"Maybe."

"I think we need some more paper plates," Aunt Louise said. "Plates are running out."

"I can go and get them," Joseph said. Joseph had overheard Aunt Louise, as he sat in a chair, holding his baby boy.

"Baby Love, just relax with little Joe. Aunt Louise and I will go and get the paper plates and stuff. There's a supermarket next door. We'll only be a minute," Sojourner said.

Joseph and their son were left in the company of Sojourner's brother, Langston, Uncle Jobe, and her cousin, Larry. Langston got up to get more food, momentarily leaving Joseph with Uncle Jobe and Larry.

"Ann sure has done well for herself, God knows. We all proud of her... Wish her Mama could be here to see it," Uncle Jobe said.

"If only they could have detected the cancer earlier," Joseph said. "Breast cancer can be treated, if discovered early."

"...cancer? Well, I don't think that killed her faster than them drugs she use that day," Uncle Job said. "Damn shame how they found her."

Joseph's eyes widened for a moment, but he was silent.

"Uncle Jobe...now you know better, talkin' like that," Larry said. "Excuse our uncle please, Joe."

Joseph nodded, but he was silent.

Langston came back with two plates of food.

"Joe, I brought some more collard greens for you," Langston said.

"No, thank you. Bon Appetite," Joseph said.

"Why you excusing Uncle Jobe? What he say?" Langston said. He looked at Uncle Jobe suspiciously.

"I ain't said nothin' bad. Don't yawl start botherin' me," Uncle Jobe said.

"Talking about Aunt Nora..." Larry said.

"Who was talking about my Mother?" Sojourner said. She had just returned with Aunt Louise.

"Uncle Jobe," Langston said.

"What did you say, Uncle Jobe?" Sojourner said. She was staring at him.

"Nothing bad, baby," Uncle Jobe said, smiling.

"He said Aunt Nora used drugs," Larry said.

"What! You got your nerve, coming here to spread your venom. You damn bum!" Sojourner said.

"Wait a minute, gal! You can't talk to me like that. You still my little niece," Uncle Jobe said, standing up and pointing his finger at Sojourner.

Joseph stood up, holding little Joseph.

"Uncle Jobe, please. This is a family occasion for mourning," Joseph said softly.

"I didn't mean no harm, Joe, but Ann can't talk to me like

that…calling me a bum!"

"Who called you a bum?" Aunt Mae said. She had heard the raucous and approached them.

"Ann did," Uncle Jobe said, looking at Sojourner.

"Oh, now you done went too far, Ms. High Class," Aunt Mae said. "You're too good for everybody now, right? Got all them fancy degrees and…"

"He was bad mouthing my Mother, Aunt Mae! And I'm tired of you ranting at me. I've worked for what I have, and I've never said I'm better…you say that. I come home to my family to bury my father. This is what I get….Uncle Jobe talking about the past…in front of my husband and child!" Sojourner said.

"Jobe Brown, you a damn fool," Aunt Mae said, turning to Uncle Jobe.

Little Joseph started to cry and Joseph kissed the child's forehead.

After the funeral and wake, Langston asked to come and stay with Joseph and Sojourner for few months. Sojourner said no, but Joseph said yes. Joseph said that he did not mind and would welcome her brother. The brother returned home with them, and Joseph noticed that Sojourner had little patience for Langston. Joseph, on the other hand, did not mind the Langston's presence. Sharing his home with people whom he considered close family members was not hard for Joseph. He noticed that Sojourner, however, was exasperated with Langston.

With Langston's encouragement, Joseph started watching sports programs regularly on TV. He'd loudly cheer for the Redskins, something he had not done before Langston showed up in their apartment. He would also inquisitively observe Langston watching BET and video music channels. Langston and Joseph would have conversations. Joseph would jokingly remark, that he might as well learn more about basketball, since so many people seem to believe that he was a basketball player anyway. Langston could not believe a man as tall as Joseph did not play basketball. He and Joseph started watching games together.

Langston, on the other hand, wanted to learn about soccer, a sport with which Joseph was very familiar. During the World Cup season, Langston and Joseph would sit and watch soccer games together, while little Joseph sat with them on the sofa.

Sojourner had occasionally considered asking Langston to move out of their apartment because he was sloppy, often unemployed, and sometimes belligerent when she confronted him. Joseph had come home from work one day and saw her shouting at Langston. Later on that evening, Joseph reminded Sojourner that as Langston's older sister, she was like a parent to him, especially since their parents were deceased. After seven weeks with Sojourner and Joseph, Langston moved back to New Jersey to live with his girlfriend.

CHAPTER THIRTY-FIVE

In October 1993, Joseph received a call from Rwanda. It was his sister, Teresa. After the call, Joseph explained to Sojourner that Teresa was upset. According to Teresa, the government was planning another massacre of the Tutsi population. Teresa was scared. Even though her husband was an influential government official, she believed that eventually she would be killed, too.

Teresa and their mother had been publicly insulted and nearly attacked during a brief outing. She was called a "cockroach." According to Teresa, this was happening to Tutsi people all over Rwanda.

At work, Joseph's colleagues were talking about the Battle of Mogadishu, which was fought between forces of the United States against Somalian guerrilla fighters in early October 1993. The results were disastrous, and left public opinion against military intervention in Africa conflicts.

He also told her that Moses and Ibrahim had been trying to persuade him to join the rebel army for a while. By training, he was a lawyer, not a soldier, Joseph thought. Joseph kept himself in shape by taking advantage of his gym membership at work and jogging regularly. However, Joseph wondered if he was fit enough to be a soldier?

Joseph's friend, John, went home to Rwanda in January of 1994. When John returned, he visited Joseph and Sojourner. John looked worried. He said that he knew something horrible was going to happen, and he didn't want to be in Rwanda when it started. John was a Hutu whose brother was in the Rwandan Army. John didn't agree with his government's treatment of the Tutsi minority. He brought a letter from Teresa, Joseph's sister. Joseph read the letter to Sojourner.

Dearest Brother,

Laurent and I visited our neighbor, Augustine Nzaramba, and his wife Monica. Monica and Augustine have six children, ranging from two years old to twelve years old. It was a good day, it seemed. There was the sound of children playing and the aroma of cooking food surrounded the house. Augustine's family lived in a three-room wooden house with his wife, Monica, and their six children. The couple greeted us warmly and respectfully led us into their crowded home. The small house was filled with children, as well as Augustine's teenage sister, Gertrude, who lived with him and Monica. As we entered the house Gertrude smiled shyly and led the children out of the house. The baby remained indoors with Monica. Monica called in her oldest child, a lean boy named Jean. She gave him some Rwandan francs to go to the purchase some soda from a local soda stand.

We sat on an old sofa, and Laurent and Augustine talked. I then noticed that the voices of the children outside were suddenly lowered. Jean re-entered the house, tearful. He was holding one bottle of soda. Monica emerged from the room and approached her son. She asked the boy what had happened. Laurent and Augustine stopped talking. Our attention was focused on the child with the lean body, a tear in his eye.

Apparently, he was verbally abused and cheated while purchasing the sodas from a local makeshift soda stand. The son of the soda stand-owner had insulted Jean. Jean paid for two sodas, but was only given one. When he asked for the other soda the boy called him a cockroach, "inyenzi." Jean demanded that the boy either give him the other soda, or give him his change. Then the boy told Jean that his father had said that the Tutsi's would all die soon. No one at the soda stand came to Jean's defense, and the boy was older and broader than him, so he gave up and came home.

Laurent stood up. He wanted to go to the stand to confront the person who had cheated Jean. Augustine pleaded with Laurent that he must not confront the perpetrator. This was happening to Tutsis regularly. Disrespect was becoming routine, and basic rights were often violated. Very often, if a brave person demanded to be treated justly, he could be secretly killed at night.

Monica retrieved two small freshly washed glasses and poured our soda into the glasses. We finished our soda. The atmosphere was somber. Monica called Gertrude and told her to bring the children into the house. Laurent discreetly handed Augustine some Rwandan Francs, when he thought no one was looking. Augustine thanked him profusely and looked emotional.

Laurent said that on a night like this, it would be good to have a drink at a local café. Augustine shook his head. Going to a café at night would be a dangerous activity for a Tutsi. Augustine suggested that we should be home before darkness falls, since I am a Tutsi woman.

Laurent and I left Augustine's house. As we walked back to our car, I noticed that there were people everwhere. Some people were staring at us, resentfully. Because of my height, I stood out. The physical trait of height and thinness takes on a strange meaning in Rwanda. Even my Hutu friend, Georgette, has been mistaken for a Tutsi. Because of this, she was harassed as she walked home from her job at the hospital.

The next day Laurent and I went to a café for lunch. While we were in the café, Laurent was openly insulted by a Rwandan waiter. The waiter called him a traitor for marrying a Tutsi "whore." Laurent stood up and said that his wife was the best that the world had to offer.

A group of raggedy ruffians gathered outside of the café. They stared at Laurent, who stared back at them defiantly. I thought we were going to be killed right there.

The man at the next table was a colleague of Laurent's, a Hutu man. He grabbed Laurent's arm, and he told us to follow him to his car. We did. His driver was waiting there for him. He drove us home. From then on, I rarely ventured out.

I think of our three children, Aime, Valentina, and Innocent. I do not want them to be hurt, but each day I fear for their future.

One day, our children were playing in the front yard of our compound. There was some noise in the front yard, so I went out to see what the

commotion was about. There stood my neighbor, Cecilia. She was
shouting at her children. She pointed excitedly at my children and said
that they should not play with the inyenzi children. I was shocked because
our children played together for years. Cecilia was never an enemy. I had
thought her to be a good woman, but evil swallows up good so easily.

Nevertheless praying my rosary each morning, I hope for the protection
of our gracious Virgin Mary, Mother of the Word Incarnate. I believe she
will intercede to protect us.

Love,
Teresa.

After reading his sister's letter, Joseph was visibly disturbed.
Joseph knew that his sister, Teresa, was normally a calm
woman, who carried her burdens without complaining. The
despair in Teresa's letter made Joseph realize that the situation
in his country could no longer be handled by contributing ten
percent of his income to the rebel forces. Joseph decided that
it was time for action.

CHAPTER THIRTY-SIX

Theodetta visited Joseph and Sojourner one Saturday. She
had her son, Prosper, with her. Theodetta had gotten married
and had a child. She gave birth to a son, Prosper, two months
after Sojourner had little Joseph. Sojourner was preparing
dinner in the kitchen, and she overheard Theodetta and Joseph
having an intense discussion in the living room.

"They are implementing those Hutu Commandments, Joe,"
Theodetta said.

"I know... Teresa wrote me a letter, letting me know how
bad things have gotten," Joseph said.

"It's obvious that they're planning a massacre, Joe. I feel it
in my bones. They want to kill us all. I don't understand why,
but I believe it," Theodetta said.

"Calm down, Theo," Joseph said.

"Remember, you are a Tutsi. They're killing Tutsis in Rwanda as we speak. We have to do something, Joe," Theodetta said.

"I know I am a Tutsi! You don't have to remind me of that, Theo!" Joseph shouted.

"I'm going home to get my mother," Theodetta said.

"Wait… I'm joining the rebel army," Joseph said.

"The rebel army? How effective are they?" Theodetta said.

"That's not fair, Theo. They're trying. They're so outnumbered," Joseph said.

"I don't have time to wait for them, Joe," Theodetta said. "Can you and Sojourner take care of Prosper for me while I'm gone? Maurice is in school in Virginia, and I don't think he can manage with Prosper while I'm gone."

"Of course, we will take care of Prosper," Sojourner said.

"Oya! You can't go to Rwanda; it's too dangerous," Joseph said.

In late February of 1994, Theodetta went to Rwanda. She entered Rwanda via Uganda to visit her mother. She was confronted by a group of men and murdered, while returning from a visit with an old school friend.

Many Rwandans who lived in the D.C. area visited Joseph and Sojourner's apartment. They stopped by and brought food to condole with Joseph and Maurice, Theodetta's husband.

Sojourner had just arrived home, with little Joseph and Prosper. Joseph was sitting on the sofa in the living room.

"Baby Love…Are you all right?" Sojourner said. She was helping the toddlers to remove their coats.

"Princess, I'm joining our forces. I'll be leaving soon. When I return, I'll bring you and Joseph with me to visit our family in Rwanda. Maurice will do likewise with Prosper," Joseph said.

"Joseph, how can you think about leaving me alone with two babies to care for? Everyday is a struggle for both of us to raise these babies, so how am I supposed to do this by myself?"

"I've checked some things, and I think you'll have what you need to take care of the boys, at least until I return. You are working, so you'll be all right. I'll show you how to manage the bills."

"Don't abandon me, Baby Love," Sojourner said.

"I'm not abandoning you, Princess. I can't stay here while my mother, sister, and family are murdered. They've killed Theodetta, and there's a huge massacre about to take place. We have proof of that. Are you asking me to do nothing about that?"

"No...You should do what you can," Sojourner said. "I'll support your decision."

"Princess, I've done all I can to assure your comfort in my absence."

"I know, but I'm scared I'll lose you, Baby Love. It's like a suicide mission, a small rebel army up against a national army," Sojourner said. She sat down on the sofa.

"I know it seems impossible...but I won't give up. I want to fight, like those 'Warriors of Yore.'"

Sojourner turned on the TV with the remote control.

The boys stood watching Barney.

"Joe and Prosper, come here," Joseph said. Joseph held his arms out, and the boys hurried to him.

"You must be good boys and listen to your mother. Do you understand?" Joseph said to them.

The two boys nodded in unison.

Sojourner shook her head and sighed.

CHAPTER THIRTY-SEVEN

"I have to return to Rwanda, Betsy. I've booked my flight already," Joseph said.

They were sitting in Betsy's office in the firm.

"Are you visiting your family, Joe?" Betsy said.

"...There's a national emergency. Everyone in my family

could be killed, thousands of Tutsi people actually. There's going to be a huge massacre…I have to go and help stop it."

"What are you going to do, Joe? You're just one man. It would take an army to stop something like that," Betsy said.

"Exactly."

"Are you joining an army?"

"Yes."

"Oh, my God, Joe. You have any military training?"

"No."

"None?"

"None."

"You could be killed, Joe."

"I know… I don't know when I'll return Betsy. I hope that I'll be welcome to return when I do."

"You're wife is okay with this?"

"My wife supports me."

"I'll talk to Pete about this," Betsy said.

"Please Betsy. The issue of joining the army must be just between us. Tell no one."

"Okay."

Betsy spoke with Peter Shininsky, and Peter refused to hold the position indefinitely in Joseph's absence. According to Betsy, Peter said that Joseph was the lead attorney for African cases. If Joseph would not be available to handle his cases, then someone else would be designated. Either Joseph stayed and handled the cases, or turn in his resignation. They would be glad to give him an excellent reference in the future. Joseph turned in his resignation from Livingston and Richards. He was later informed that the team lead slot was given to Jacques Bovary, whom Joseph knew had been eager for the position for a while.

It was March of 1994, and Joseph and Sojourner were in an

airplane, hovering over Uganda. Joseph and Sojourner had taken the boys to New Jersey to stay with her Aunt Jess for a week. Sojourner would accompany Joseph to Uganda, where he would depart to join the rebel forces on their mission into Rwanda.

Sojourner felt a poignant sense of triumph. As the plane descended slowly Sojourner's anticipation grew. When the wheels of the airplane touched the African soil, she was filled with excitement. She was an African American, experiencing a part of her heritage. Tears welled up in her eyes. Looking out the window, Sojourner saw the urban skyline and green, terrain of Kampala, the capital city of Uganda. Joseph looked at Sojourner and touched her hand. As the plane taxied on the runway, most of the passengers started to stand up to grab their carry-on bags from the overhead compartments.

Joseph and Sojourner were enveloped in the warm African air as they exited the plane. They entered the Entebbe International Airport and looked around. The airport building was not impressive, but it was different from the one at home in the U.S. First, there was no air conditioning. Second, Sojourner saw that she was surrounded by faces in all shades of brown, from the lightest to the darkest. Sojourner felt a sense of peace with her being. In Africa, the darkness of her skin was natural. She felt liberated in a sense.

Many of the women and men wore traditional African clothing. Some wore western clothing, dresses and suits. In the U.S., it was very cool at the time, but in Kampala the weather was hot and humid. Sojourner had worn a coat to JFK airport. However, here, no one wore a coat in the airport, although a few of the newly arrived travelers did hold coats in their arms.

As they walked toward the baggage claim area, Joseph started to wave at a Ugandan couple who cheerfully waved back at him and Sojourner. They were Edith and Samuel Miremba. Joseph had told Sojourner that Edith was the sister of his friend, Moses. Edith, a Tutsi woman from Rwanda, had married Samuel, a Ugandan man. Together they lived in Kampala. There was another person with the couple, their driver. Joseph introduced Sojourner to the couple. Then they proceeded towards the baggage claim area, where they picked up their suitcases. The customs officers looked through their luggage carefully. When they found several bottles of wine, the chief of the officers insisted that we pay a duty for the bottles of champagne. However, Joseph settled this matter by politely explaining that he had brought the champagne as gifts for his friends, not to sell them. Then he presented the chief customs officer with two of the bottles of wine. The customs officer then smiled, accepted the gift, and allowed them to continue.

They exited the airport. She stared at the lush green landscape. A Land Rover was parked in front of the Airport. It was the couple's truck. The young man who accompanied the couple started to load their luggage into the vehicle. They then entered the truck.

As they drove around the city of Kampala, Sojourner gazed at the African urban landscape. They drove through the city. She looked out of the car window, trying to see as much of the capital city as she could. The business and government districts had streets lined with modern office buildings. On these buildings were the signs of corporations, banks, and government agencies. This was an aspect of Africa that Sojourner rarely saw on TV back home in the USA. The people in the capital city were dressed in western clothing styles, as well as some traditional African fashions. Some of the ladies were dressed in colorful traditional outfits that were elaborately designed and colorful. Crowds of African people walked up and down the streets of Kampala, attending to their businesses. Like many people who live or work in cities, these people seemed preoccupied and busy. However, there was not a sense of impersonal anonymity that usually persists in large cities. Most of the men and women had a natural gracefulness in their manner. Many took note of their surroundings as they walked through the streets of the capital. There were small groups of people conversing. Street vendors sold a wide variety of merchandise and goods, souvenir T-shirts, miniature ivory sculptures of animals, ivory jewelry and combs, fresh fruit, and many other things.

The chauffer then drove though a residential neighborhood within the capital city. This neighbor contained a mixture of modest and grand homes. There were a few large, villa-like homes, with a Mercedes, or a large sport utility vehicle, parked in the driveway. In spite of the many attractive homes in this neighborhood, many of the streets were not paved.

As they drove toward the outskirts of the capital city, the attractiveness of the houses decreased. They passed a large neighborhood, where the wooden houses were cabin-like in size and design. The streets in this neighborhood were all unpaved. The truck bounced up and down as they entered deep put holes on the unpaved streets of the neighborhood.

Sojourner saw signs of poverty, and the clothing that most of the people in this area wore was simple, and, for some, raggedy. Children played in the dusty streets without shoes, and sometimes without shirts. A toddler ran alongside shack-like homes that bordered the dirt road, barefoot and dusty. Sojourner thought about Joseph and Prosper. Was it just chance, that they were not running up and down in the muddy streets of this land, barefoot and hungry?

Young women balanced buckets of water on their heads, as they went about their chores. A few chickens roamed freely in the dust and mud. One group of elderly men sat on cardboard boxes in front of a wooden shack discussing loudly, as very small, shoeless children played nearby in the dusty streets. The dust from the unpaved, dirt roads rose up as they drove by this animated scene, and Sojourner sneezed.

"Roll up your window, Princess," Joseph said. Sojourner did as Joseph requested.

CHAPTER THIRTY-EIGHT

Uganda, March 1994

Sojourner and Joseph spent a few days with Edith and Samuel. The home of the Ugandan couple was small, but cozy and modern. They brought many gifts for the couple, their children, and their house servant.

One night, Sojourner and Joseph lay side by side in the bed of the guest room together. She was drifting off to sleep when she felt Joseph's fingers gently lifting her nightgown. Sojourner smiled to herself. But how could they make love in this room, with their hosts possibly within earshot. It was midnight and the house was completely dark, so why not, she thought. With Joseph's assistance she slipped out of her gown. In the darkness, she found his sweet mouth. He found her breasts and sucked them. Between her legs, he used his mouth to silently drive her wild with pleasure. Moments later, they were on the floor, cushioned by Sojourner's thick, beach towel. On her hands and knees, she felt Joseph enter her. It was so delicious that she struggled to muffle her groans. His hands traveled over her back and reached for her breasts. She gave herself completely to their needs, and they went on like that for a while. Joseph moved gently, then harder and harder, and Sojourner closed her eyes and allowed her mouth to drop open. Sojourner whispered words of encouragement to Joseph. They moved faster, and both received that for which they strived.

The following morning, Samuel and Edith drove Joseph and Sojourner to the town of Masaka, Uganda. Joseph sat silently, looking out the window. He was obviously deep in thought. Sojourner wondered what was going through her husband's mind.

Four men in military fatigues met them, near a picturesque, white cottage-style building, surrounded by luscious green grass and acacia trees. Sojourner recognized three of the men. One of them was Theodetta's widower, Maurice. He was the father of Prosper. The others were Ibrahim, Moses, and one other man. Each greeted Joseph with a hearty handshake. Maurice waved at Sojourner and approached her respectfully.

"*Bonjour Madame* Sojourner. How are the boys?" Maurice said.

"They're fine. They're with my aunt in New Jersey," Sojourner said.

"Thank you, Madame. Please thank your aunt for me. I will be able to get Prosper when we fulfill our mission. I'll bring him back with me then," Maurice said, smiling.

"That's fine, Maurice. Good luck to you," Sojourner said.

Joseph picked up his suitcase and prepared to depart from his wife. Sojourner touched his arm, and stared at him. Joseph embraced her.

"You must go home now ... my Princess."

She breathed in his fragrance again. It was the same fragrance she breathed in when she first saw him at Livingston and Richards. The same glorious face stared back at her, but this time the face was filled with emotion and adoration.

"I don't have a home without you, Baby Love? My home is with you," Sojourner said.

"My Princess, we built a home together, go and tend to it," Joseph said.

"I don't want to leave you here."

Joseph just shook his head, and then he kissed her.

"If we could be here, near where you are. The U.S. won't miss me, anyway," Sojourner said.

"But it is still your country, my Princess," Joseph said. "It's like you once told me. African American's have paid more than their share of blood, sweat, and tears for America. They helped to build America and to make it great. You have to continue to stake your rightful claim there."

Sojourner sobbed.

"*Ne pleurent pas ma princesse douce.*"

He kissed her again.

"Look at me, my wife. I'm a Tutsi man from Rwanda, and I'm not wanted in my own country either. My family and friends could be massacred by their fellow citizens. But it's still my country, and I'm going to fight for my people's right to exist there. It will be a better place...I will bring you and Joseph home with me."

"I love you, Baby Love...The boys and I are waiting for you," Sojourner said. She tried to compose herself.

Joseph joined the men. They had solemn expressions on their faces as they entered the cottage house. There was a large military vehicle parked in front of the house.

Then Edith and Samuel guided Sojourner back to their Land Rover. As she was driven back to the couple's home, she stared out the window, thinking to herself. Why was a massacre going to take place in Rwanda? From all the photos that she had seen, Rwanda was an aesthetically beautiful country. The landscape was green and fertile, and the climate was warm. What else did a people want?

On the plane ride back to America, Sojourner thought about the plight of Rwanda. In America, it was called black on black crime. There were frequent discourses on how to prevent this violence, or at least minimize it. An epidemic of homicide was an enormous problem. Sojourner believed that all agreed that it was shameful occurrence.

When Sojourner reached the U.S., she drove to New Jersey to get Joseph and Prosper from her Aunt Jess.

On April 6, 1994, the president of Rwanda was assassinated. After that, Rwandan militia groups roamed the streets, killing at will. Roadblocks were everywhere. Rwanda had turned into a living hell. Sojourner watched on the quick news reports that gave bits and pieces of what was happening in

Rwanda.

At home in the apartment with little Joseph and Prosper, Sojourner was horrified and dejected by the lack of action being taken by the United Nation forces that were still present in Rwanda. It was because of the presence of the UN forces that so many people in Rwanda believed that the massacres could be halted. But the genocide proceeded with strong momentum.

When she heard that the UN had reduced its presence from 2,500 troops to a few hundred troops, Sojourner called the offices of her local congressmen to pressure them to address the issue of the massacres in Rwanda, but all she received were pacifying words and empty promises to bring up the subject on the floor of Congress.

What about the law library of the law firm where Joseph had once worked, Sojourner thought? Was not there some international law that was being broken here? What was the purpose of all those international law books and procedures, if those laws could not save lives in the real world? Where was the rest of the world, anyway?

Sojourner then telephoned Betsy McShane, who in turn contacted a friend of hers who worked at the White House. The friend informed Betsy that the President was not discussing the Rwandan issue due to his busy schedule, with so many other international issues. Betsy relayed the message to Sojourner.

Her husband was no longer in the safety of Washington, D.C., Sojourner thought. He was a soldier in a tiny rebel army, which hoped to prevent the extermination of its people. Sojourner sobbed while watching the evening news. Little Joseph and Prosper played in the living room, as she silently cried.

She received a letter from Joseph two weeks later.

Uganda, March 30, 1994

My Princess,

Believe that I am with you now, not that I have gone away to a perilous place of bloody strife. Take my spirit home with you to my son and to Prosper. Hold them in your arms, the absence of which creates a void in my heart. I could not bare the sight of you waving goodbye to me last week. I want to be with you, my Princess. I want to bring you and our son back to Rwanda with me, but Rwanda is not a place for you right now.

For now, show them the pictures of their ancestors, on the walls of our home there in D.C. With or without me, I want their feet to one day touch the fertile soil of their Rwandan ancestors. As a soldier, I will fight to save my people, but the priorities for me are my Mother, my sister, Teresa, and her children.

Today, I'm in a kind of military boot camp, with hundreds of other men. Our training starts tomorrow, I cannot disclose my location, in case this letter is intercepted. My troop is scheduled to move toward the border of Rwanda in two weeks. The most fervent prayer possible will be needed to prevent a complete human disaster.

Whatever the outcome, my Princess, I envision that we will live forever in the royal palace of our imagination.

Yours Forever,
Joe.

CHAPTER THIRTY-NINE

Kigali, Rwanda, April 14, 1994

Before the telephone line was cut, Teresa had frantically tried to telephone Joseph. The last time she had spoken with her brother he had told her that he intended to join the rebel army, since he was forbidden to return to Rwanda. Sojourner answered the phone when Teresa called.

"*Bonjour! Joseph est la? J'ai besoin parler avec Joseph!*" Teresa said.

"*Bonjour! C'est Teresa?*" Sojourner said.

"*Qui. C'est moi,*" Theresa said.

"*Comment allez vous?*" Sojourner said.

"*Il est mauvais, ma soeur,*" Teresa said; her voice was getting shaky. She started to sob, audibly.

"Are you okay?" Sojourner said, reverting back to English.

"No… I not good," Teresa said. "Please help! We need help!"

"Joseph should be entering Rwanda with the rebel forces," Sojourner said.

"Help Now! Everyone be killed," Teresa said.

She started to sob on the phone.

"Oh, God! Don't cry, Teresa," Sojourner said.

Then Teresa's telephone line went dead. She would not be able to make any more phone calls for help.

Teresa spoke very little English, so she had difficulty explaining to her sister-in-law, Sojourner, that she believed she and her family had only hours to live. Teresa was hopeful about her brother being somewhere in Rwanda, but the bodies were pilling up in the streets, and she figured that it would only be a matter of hours before hers and her family's would be added to the piles. The dead bodies surrounding her family's compound reminded Teresa of what awaited her beyond the front door.

Teresa hung up the phone solemnly. Talking to her American sister-in-law would do her no good, she thought to herself. She was in Rwanda, and Sojourner was in America, safe. Would she and her children be killed, with her husband, Laurent? They would probably not spare Laurent. They considered him a traitor, since he was married to her, a Tutsi. He loved and protected her and their children, Teresa thought. Teresa could feel the terror in her bones, as she could hear the gunfire and screams of agony outside the window.

It was night time, and Teresa cautiously peeked out of the window in the front parlor of her small house. She saw that several houses were on fire. The fires leaped into the air, like hell fires. The smell of smoke filled the air of the town, and the smell was followed by human screams of absolute terror and agony. These were the screams of men, women, and children, who despite their desperate efforts, could flee no farther than a few feet from their doorstep.

One of the burning houses was only two doors away from Teresa's home. Teresa knew the family that lived in that house. It was a Tutsi family, Monica, Augustine and their six children. Monica was a hard working woman, who had worked as a nurse in a local hospital. Augustine, her husband, was a handsome drunkard who spent most of his time looking after his three cows. He would even sometimes abuse Monica, after drinking too much banana beer. Teresa watched over the years as Monica bore child after child, while struggling to meet the needs of her children and husband. Helpless and horrified, Teresa listened as Monica's family was being murdered.

Monica's family rushed out of the house. They were immediately surrounded by machete wielding Rwandans, their neighbors and fellow citizens. In the darkness, Teresa could see only shadows. However, from what she could hear, she surmised that Augustine was first attacked and killed. Before he died, Teresa heard him vehemently pleading with his killers to spare his wife and children.

"Felicien? It's you? My wife helped your wife to during the birthing of all your children. Spare her and my children… I beg, my friend," Augustine said.

"Shut up, cockroach!" said a man. "Time to die!"

In those last words before his death, Augustine had redeemed himself, in Teresa's eyes. An ordinary man seemed like a martyr at that moment. He did not die a drunkard, but a loving father and husband. He did not plead for his life, but his wife and children's lives. She grinded her teeth together, as she heard more screaming. From what she could hear, then the killers slaughtered the children, except for the oldest girl. There was the crying and shrieking of the rest of the children as they were killed. Teresa's hands trembled and tears wet her cheeks, as she listened to the crying and begging of Monica for her children's lives. As the screams subsided, she heard the shrieks of Monica and her daughter, stripped of their last shred of dignity, as they were raped by the killers of their family.

Through all of this homicidal madness, one could hear the killers talking and laughing. Most sounded drunk. It was like an evil spirit had descended on them, squeezing all goodness out.

Laurent was not home, so Teresa was especially vulnerable. He had given two thousand dollars cash to distribute to his "colleagues" that day. Joseph had sent her ten thousand dollars in American currency a month ago. That bought them a delayed execution. Each day, Laurent had to pay off his comrades to keep them from bursting into his home and murdering his family. However, what was going on in her neighborhood was enough to convince Teresa that her family would not be spared for long.

Teresa's eldest son, Innocent, who was fifteen years old, crawled over to her and pulled her gently away from the window. His grandmother, brother, and sister were hiding in the bedroom. It was difficult for Teresa to stay in the bedroom with so much noise and madness going on outside. Together, they crawled to a corner in the parlor.

"Is uncle coming, Mother?" Innocent said, whispering.

"Yes. Your uncle is coming," Teresa said.

Teresa grabbed the smooth hand of her teenage boy and looked into his eyes. He was a well-behaved and a helpful son, who excelled in school. School was suspended now. The entire country had shut down most normal functioning. Killing was the focus.

Raising her children was a supreme labor of love for Teresa. In the past, it had tested her patience. Each child had a unique personality. One was easy to handle, while the other two were a regular challenge. They were a joy to behold, she thought. How could all those years of nurturing and hard work to raise her children end with her watching them slaughtered mercilessly? Their precious lives held so much promise for the future.

"Don't fear to die, my son," Teresa said. "God loves us. If we die, we will be welcomed into his kingdom."

"But if God loves us, why would he let them kill us?" Innocent said. "Why does he allow people to kill and rape everyday? Can he not send the angels to protect us, as he did in the Scriptures? No one comes to help us, Mother," Innocent said, angrily.

Teresa closed her eyes and thought of her two handsome boys and her pretty little girl, Valentina. It seemed that they were doomed to die very soon, since children were not being spared in the massacre taking place around Rwanda.

Teresa had discovered that her husband was compelled by the Rwandan militias to participate in the killings, and she was enraged with him. Laurent, a muscular man of medium height, had gestured wildly when she confronted him about this.

"Teresa, I have no choice. Many Hutus have killed their wives, even some government officials. It's crazy, but they expect us to do this... They have come to kill us many times, but it's because I participate that they've not insisted to kill us. That and the money we give them," Laurent said.

"I can't believe a man would kill his wife because someone told him to," Teresa said. "Oh, Laurent, my dear, how can you kill innocent people?" She was crying.

"What do you want me to do?" Laurent said.

"Don't kill like those others!" Teresa said.

"I just told you, Teresa! Everyday they tell me that they are going to come here and kill all of us. The only thing that stops them is that I participate in the work."

"Work? How amazing that you call it work! It's just murder. That's all. You are all nothing but a bunch of cursed murderers!"

"As long as they think I'm supporting them, they will leave us alone."

"No, Laurent. They will not leave us alone. They have killed the Prime Minister, and those U.N. soldiers, so they won't stop with us."

After a night of listening to monstrous screams, wails, and groans outside the window, Teresa saw her husband enter the house slowly at dawn, carrying a bloody machete. His shirt, which was white in the morning, was now tan with dust and splattered with blood stains. He looked at Teresa, and then he retreated quickly into their bedroom. The children looked at their father with fearful eyes.

Kigali, Rwanda, April 15, 1994

Teresa rose early the next morning to the melodious sounds of birdsong and roosters crowing. She looked furtively out of her parlor window. It was a bright sunny day, and the banana trees in her front yard were swaying gently in the breeze. More bloody human corpses were lying about the neighborhood. Gangs of merciless militia members had roamed the streets last night, searching out victims. Among the bodies was the corpse of a young man. Examining the body, she saw the body of a once tall and thin Rwandan man.

There was a stray cow ambling down the street. Militiamen gathered at a nearby roadblock, ignoring the cow. During these violent times, it was more dangerous to be a human being in Rwanda, than to be a cow or a tree. The trees and animals were not being hacked to pieces, or gang raped, but this was happening to human beings in Rwanda. Teresa imagined that somewhere in Rwanda the apes in the forests were peeking through the bushes, staring at the vile madness of their human neighbors. The buzzards and dogs took advantage of this nihilistic slaughtering festival to have easy meals of fresh human flesh. She felt envious of the birds singing in the trees. They were free. Teresa held her rosary and prayed for a rescue of some sort.

CHAPTER FORTY

Kigali, Rwanda, April 16, 1994

Blaise looked out the window of the armory. The terrain of this section of Kigali was a world of electric green, juxtaposed by orange tinted earth. Little houses dotted the landscape. He saw militia groups roaming the dusty streets with machetes. Murderous looks were on their faces. There were innumerable roadblocks throughout the city and country. It would be almost impossible for anyone to escape them, Blaise thought.

Blaise knew that he looked like a Tutsi. He was six feet two inches tall and had a nose like a Muzungu, but he was not a Tutsi. Everyone he knew in his family was a Hutu, but his mother once whispered to him that his great-grandmother was a Tutsi. As a boy, Blaise hated roll call in school. The teacher made them stand up and identify themselves by ethnicity. As soon as he said "Hutu," his teacher would shout at him.

"Stop lying. You are a Tutsi," said one teacher, who was new to the school.

The other students laughed at him, except for the very few other students who really were Tutsi. He noticed that they were silent. His father went to the school to confront the teacher. He told him that his son was definitely a Hutu. The teacher apologized.

The same thing happened when he went away to the Lycee. Everyone, who did not know his family, thought that Blaise was a Tutsi. While socializing with his friends, some Hutu boys would shout at him.

"Lousy Tutsi! We'll get you," one boy said. He stood with group of rag tag youths standing on the side of a dusty dirt road.

"I am Hutu," Blaise said.

"Liar. Look how they lie!" the boy said.

He remembered the day he was almost kicked out of school because he looked like a Tutsi. A group of men were identifying students who were Tutsi, and they made Blaise get out of bed. Blaise quickly reminded them that he was Hutu. Then he pointed out someone whom he knew was a quintessential Tutsi, Joseph Kalisa. Joseph had looked at him with the hurt gaze of a deeply betrayed person. Blaise knew that what he did was wrong. Joseph was known to be a studious and affable person, and Blaise had played soccer with him. But he betrayed Joseph and caused him to be expelled from school. That was probably why Joseph was very hostile the last time he saw him in the nightclub in Washington, Blaise thought.

The militias were going to kill Teresa, Joseph Kalisa's sister, Blaise thought. A colleague of his had told him. Laurent was running out of American dollars, and every Tutsi family in his neighborhood had been killed. Blaise wondered if he should stop them. Then he remembered what had happened to one of his colleagues who showed mercy toward a Tutsi family who was fleeing into the Mille Colline Hotel for refuge. The compassionate man allowed the family to successfully escape into the hotel. For his mercy, the soldier was beaten bloody and derided by other government soldiers. Then the soldier was demoted. Blaise knew that he'd worked hard to attain this position, enduring jokes about his stereotypical Tutsi appearance. No. He would not intercede to save Teresa, and her princess mother.

He thought of his brother, John. John had telephoned Blaise

a few days earlier. He begged him to protect Joseph Kalisa's sister and her family, including their princess mother. Blaise, who was surrounded by his fellow government officers during the call, could not respond honestly. Instead, he shouted that he was a good Hutu who would stand up for Hutu dominance. John then told him that he was a sick maniac, just like the rest of his Rwandan Army comrades. It was ironic how John rejected Rwandan government politics, since John looked like the stereotypical Hutu, Blaise thought. John was short and muscular, with a broad face and nose. Blaise admitted to himself that very often one could not tell a Hutu from a Tutsi these days. Few people could. Centuries of intermarrying had blended features of both groups in Rwanda.

It was interesting how one's position in government depended on how absolutely inhumane one was willing to be to keep it, Blaise thought. He was proud of his status as a captain in the Rwandan Armed Forces. His latest assignment was the overseeing of an armory in Kigali. Blaise was, however, still plagued by guilt for what he had to do to retain his station in life. He killed people regularly. As a soldier, killing was a way of life for him. He had killed rebel soldiers in the forests bordering Rwanda, but that was war. Watching Rwandan civilians descend into a killing spree was different. The most disturbing part of that was seeing a few women participate in the killing. This defied Blaise's notion of the definition of womanhood and changed the way he viewed women. However, he noticed that his colleagues in the army did not seem to have these pangs of conscience. Many killed enthusiastically and seemed to have no regrets. He almost envied them for their callousness. He had done well in life. His house was bigger than most in the town, and his father had been a bourgermeister. His brother, John, was a businessman in the U.S.

Blaise heard the screams of the teenage girls in the barracks. How many times did he warn his subordinates to stop bringing those poor souls into the barracks, Blaise thought?

It was strictly against military regulations. Maintaining order in the armory was becoming very difficult, since the recruiting standards were getting lower and lower. Two of his most recent army recruits were nothing but incorrigible ruffians, Blaise thought. The standards used to be much higher. As for him, he had had his fill of distraught, terrified, and weeping adolescent girls. He wanted a relaxed, happy woman who could reciprocate his love.

He beckoned a subordinate soldier and requested that he fetch some banana beer. That was the way to bear all this wicked madness, to drown in drink, Blaise thought. Hell, everyone was doing it.

CHAPTER FORTY-ONE

Parc Nacional Des Volcans, Rwanda, April 17, 1994

After two decades abroad, Joseph was marching into Rwanda as a soldier in a small rebel army, carrying an AK-47. He resented the term "rebel." He thought to himself. Why were they considered rebels? Rebelling against what, the massacre of innocent civilians? He had seen the lakes bordering Rwanda, filled with the bodies of Rwandan people. The water was red from blood. He was not a rebel. He had never been the rebellious type. His mother sent him away from his native land only to save his life, not to rebel. He became a soldier to save the lives of others, to prevent the extermination of his people.

With a troop of five hundred soldiers, Joseph walked through a jungle. There was a thick mist covering the forest floor. The troops began to trek up the mountains, which was also covered with a dense forest. The rain started to pour heavily, and the soldiers' fatigues were soon soaked. Along with the rest of the rebel soldiers, Joseph walked through muddy puddles. He noticed a baboon, perched on a tree. It yawned lethargically. Then one of thousands of hanging vines brushed against his wet face. He was tired, and the journeying was just beginning.

The rebel soldiers were all tired and hungry from days of trekking through the terrain of the park, carrying guns, artillery, and supplies. His legs and his feet ached. It had been a long time since Joseph had to relieve himself without any modern conveniences. Joseph hated squatting to defecate in the forest. Initially, there were several boxes of toilet tissue, but the troop had finished it. It was strange, using toilet tissue in the middle of the rain forest, with no toilet in sight. The food rations had dwindled to almost nothing, and the soldiers were encouraged to improvise by finding wild fruit and edible plants in the forest. Joseph had almost forgotten what his uncle had told him long ago about which plants in the forest were edible and which were not. He often had to rely on the knowledge of the more experienced soldiers, who reminded him of what was safe to eat.

In spite of his lack of military experience, Joseph was able to keep up with the other soldiers and to trek through the forest with little difficulty. He had taken care of his health in the United States; he had a healthy diet, and he exercised regularly. His marriage to Sojourner increased his overall physical and emotional health. Joseph thought about Sojourner and smiled. The love they made in Uganda was breathtaking, Joseph thought. He replayed the scene in his head, as he heard the incessant hum of the forest insects.

Many of the rebel soldiers in his troop were the characteristically tall, lean, Tutsi men, but most were not. Two of the soldiers were Hutu men. Nonetheless, there was a sense of solidarity and purpose among the soldiers. The men were silent most of the time, each one immersed in his solemn thoughts. Joseph saw Captain Alexandre Nkusi talking on a portable military telephone; the captain looked somber as he hung up the phone. The news must have been very bad because the captain rarely showed his emotions.

The rebel soldiers had been informed of the atrocities taking place in Rwanda. Also, there was the Captain's radio. Listening to Rwandan radio stations, which broadcasted and encouraged the nationwide killing spree in Rwanda, they received real time updates on the massacres. These rebel soldiers knew that as they marched toward the interior of Rwanda, their fellow Rwandans were hacking many of their family members to a bloody and agonizing death. For some of them, their wives, sisters, mothers, and other female relatives were being raped, or murdered. They had seen bodies floating in the beautiful lakes bordering Rwanda. This was a lonely band of silent soldiers, doing what seemed to be the impossible. Their people made up a small segment of the population of Rwanda. Joseph thought to himself. How could such a small army defeat the madness of a massacre in progress? Still the soldiers marched on, with Joseph Kalisa in their midst.

A silverback gorilla, sitting peacefully in the mountains was all that Joseph could see, as he stood silently with the other rebel troops. Captain Alexandre looked through his binoculars and quickly signaled to his lieutenant. The Rwandan government army troops appeared in the distance. Hundreds of them were moving slowly up the mountain, apparently unaware of the presence of the rebels. Joseph's torso seemed to freeze, and he counted every breath. His fingers gripped his AK-47. So outnumbered, Joseph thought. They were organized, and they had some advanced weaponry, so perhaps all was not lost. He would follow the captain's instructions and not move or shoot until the rocket launcher team fired. The hope was that the Rwandan army would temporarily scatter. The rebels would take down the government troops who scattered. But they would not move in on the enemy because they did not have the numbers to sustain close combat. The surprise attack would have to suffice under the circumstances.

When the Rwandan army was dangerously close to the

position of the rebels, the captain ordered his rocket launchers into action. The first shot resulted in a huge flame that tore through the forests of the mountainside. As anticipated, many of the government troops scattered. The snipers took down as many of the government retreating soldiers as they could. Then Joseph, along with the other rebel troops perched on the side of the mountain, aimed his gun and fired at the scattering Rwandan army troops. Joseph's first shot was a waste, but the second hit a government soldier in the head. No time to feel regret or triumph, Joseph fired off a round of shots taking down several government soldiers. His captain was satisfied with the number of casualties inflicted on the opponent. He ordered the rebels to retreat. The rebels retreated into Kisoro, Uganda, just outside of the border of Rwanda. The soldiers could not pursue them very far into another country.

CHAPTER FORTY-TWO

Washington, D.C., April 21, 1994

Scream. That's what Sojourner wanted to do, but she didn't. Both boys had begun to cry in unison as Sojourner bathed them. She put their rubber ducks into the tub and persuaded them to be quiet. Then Prosper and Joseph started to splash water all over the tub and the bathroom floor.

It had been a long day. After picking the boys up from the Happy Land Day Care Center, she secured each of the toddlers in his car seat. Prosper was crying, and Joseph kept saying that he was hungry. One of the workers in the day care center had told her that Joseph was fighting with the other children that day, while Prosper had been whining all day. And neither boy was completely potty trained. So what was she supposed to do? Her routine was wearing her out, Sojourner thought. She had a new appreciation of her mother, who had raised her alone. Guilt crept into her chest.

Sojourner had judged her mother harshly. She had once felt justified, but not anymore. There she was, with her Masters of Arts degree and a dignified job, driving a Mercedes Benz to her posh address in D.C. She had the nerve to complain. How had her mother, who was a high school drop out, survived raising children on minimum wage...with a drug addiction?

Prosper and Joseph sat on the sofa watching the Rugrats cartoon, as Sojourner cooked dinner in the kitchen. She then feed the boys and allowed them to play with their toys in the living room. She changed the channel to CNN and watched the evening report. The anchorman announced that the Red Cross estimated that hundreds of thousands of Tutsi people had been killed in Rwanda, since President Juvenal Habyarimana of Rwanda was assassinated on April 6, 1994. The reports described the massacre as being carried out by local militias armed with machetes, as well as neighbors killing neighbors because of tribal differences. How could so many people be killed in fifteen days, Sojourner thought? It was April 21st, and the massacres started only two weeks ago.

Sojourner remembered that her husband had said that the difference with Hutus and Tutsis was an ethnic, or racial, issue and not a tribal one. He said that Rwanda had one culture, shared by both Hutus and Tutsis. To Sojourner, both groups were black Africans, so how could it be a racial issue? As the news described the carnage of neighbors hacking each other to pieces at a phenomenal rate, she began to cry. Where was her husband amidst all that madness, she thought? Then she realized that the boys had both come to her side; they were staring at her silently.

In her dreams, Sojourner had seen Joseph walking through a forest, carrying an AK-47. Her debonair husband was a guerrilla soldier. It was surreal.

Ruhengeri, Rwanda, April 25, 1994

Joseph's troop was in the midst of their second battle as they struggled to advance into Rwanda. Although the rebel army was well armed, they were far outnumbered by the Rwandan Army and the militias, which roamed the streets of Rwanda's cities and towns.

He aimed his gun and fired at several Rwandan Army soldiers. The worst part of this soldier business was killing people, even if the people were cold-blooded killers, Joseph thought. During his first few weeks of combat, Joseph was slow to pull his trigger. Then he remembered the lakes and streams, with the human bodies. He decided that kill he must. Joseph's resolve to perform his duties as a soldier became harder than concrete as his troop marched through the towns of Rwanda. What he saw there were the corpses of people strewn all over towns and villages. At first, he could not believe that he was looking at the bodies of people; then he looked closer. He smelled the horrible stench. It was real. Men, women, children, and newborns had been slaughtered mercilessly. Latrines were filled with the bodies of human beings, sometimes whole families, which had been forced there by attacking militias. The sight of these atrocities broke his heart, but instantly strengthened his determination to continue wholeheartedly with his mission. Tears streamed down the cheeks of Joseph's face until his eyes were completely dried out. Raising his gun, he pursued the perpetrators of the genocide with controlled passion and focus.

Stealthily, his troop entered the small border town in Rwanda; the town was almost deserted. The dusty, garbage-filled, unpaved streets were silent. Some of the dead were clothed, and others were partially clothed. The wind blew wild and carelessly and dogs roamed from corpse to corpse, sniffing. Everything was a shambles. It was like hell had come to the surface of the earth, Joseph thought.

CHAPTER FORTY-THREE

Murambi, Rwanda, May 15, 1994

Joseph Kalisa's troop entered yet another ravaged town, filled with ransacked shacks. The green hills were covered with the bodies of people who lived, struggled, and dreamed just like their human neighbors all over the world. He entered the town with hundreds of other rebel troops, marching single file and holding AK-47 guns. The rebel troops marched deep into the interior of Rwanda to once again confront the Rwandan Army. Joseph fought a despair that surrounded him like a suffocating and poisonous fog. Joseph grasped the beaded rosary around his neck. He recited the prayer of Saint Michael the Archangel as he marched.

"Catholic bullshit," a soldier said. The soldier's name was Thomas Rubibi, and he was walking directly in front of Joseph. The soldier had glanced over his shoulder when he heard Joseph whispering the prayer.

"What do you mean by that?" Joseph said, stunned by the caustic remark.

"Look at that church over there," the soldier said. He pointed to an abandoned, ransacked Roman Catholic Church in the center of the destroyed town. Joseph glanced at the church quickly and kept marching.

"That church is filled with the bodies of hundreds of Rwandan Catholics who believed that they would be protected in that church," the soldier said.

The troops were marching single file in a long procession through the streets of the town. The soldier continued his tirade, as Joseph listened quietly, marching behind him.

"Lured there by the parish priest himself, those people were butchered like cattle… And what did the priest do? Nothing. What did the Catholic Church do?" Thomas said.

"Is the Church to be blamed because Rwandans slaughtered

Rwandans?" Joseph said. "Rwandans killed Rwandans."

"Yes. But these same Rwandans claimed to be Christians … followers of the Catholic faith," Thomas said. "Why couldn't the Church intercede? One word from the right person could have saved thousands of lives in many churches like this all over Rwanda. To them we are not worth even one of their words, are we?"

"Those people who were murdered in those churches are like martyrs… They are with God now," Joseph said.

"God?" Thomas said. "What does he care!"

"He cares. He allowed even his own son to be tortured and murdered for our sake," Joseph said.

They entered the church and saw hundreds of putrid, rotting human corpses were there. These were the remnants of the families seeking refuge. He gazed at the sight of the corpses all around the interior of the church, then at the statue of Jesus on the altar. The stench was almost unbearable.

"Jesus was here when this happened, you know," Joseph said.

"What are you talking about?" Thomas said.

"The girl we found hiding nearby, the one who had been hiding amongst the bodies in this church. She said that one of the fathers had given mass before the militias broke in and killed everyone. He had just blessed the bread. So Jesus was physically present in this room, as the killers entered," Joseph said.

"How does that make him present, Joe?"

"It's transubstantiation," Joseph said. "When the bread and wine are blessed, the bread and wine are transformed into the Body and Blood of Christ."

"Oh, so Jesus was here, was he?" Thomas said, sarcastically. "And… what did he do?"

"So…eventually, there will be justice, Thomas," Joseph said, softly.

Thomas sucked his teeth and turned away from Joseph.

Joseph stooped down and looked at what appeared to be the body of a child. He began to pray, holding his rosary.

"Our Father who art in Heaven, Hallowed be...," Joseph said, before being interrupted by Thomas again.

"Look Joseph. Your foolish prayers are nonsense. Do you hear me? Look at your brothers in faith!" said Thomas, gesturing to the corpses surrounding them. "That infant and his mother, half-eaten skeletons now....they lay under the gaze of your sweet Jesus. Oh, and how many dead mothers in this building are clinging to the feet of Mary...in vain."

Joseph shook his head and stood up, kissing his rosary. He walked away from Thomas.

Captain Alexandre opened a door to a room in the church where more corpses lay, protected from the marauding packs of dogs, who fed on the corpses in the main part of the church. The soldiers walked in; Joseph and Thomas milled in with them.

Joseph kneeled to pray over what appeared to be the rotting corpses of a mother and her infant, impaled together by a long metal rod through her chest and the infants back, the skeletal face formed an expression of utter surprise and horror. Her mouth was open, and her hands were reaching for her infant. Her once bright pink dress was discolored by the dried up pool of blood that she lay in. A rosary was around her neck.

"My Lord Jesus! Oh, my Lord and my God!" Joseph said, a tear ran down his cheek.

"Haven't you seen enough to let you know that Jesus isn't interested in your prayers? He didn't listen to the mother lying there with a pole shoved in her chest and her baby's chest. You think he's going to listen to you?" Thomas said, standing behind Joseph.

Joseph stood up and faced Thomas. "'Get behind me, Satan!'"* Joseph said.

* *The Holy Bible*, Matthew 4:10

"Quoting the Scriptures are you," Thomas said, sardonically.

"Shut up! Let me do this my way," Joseph said. Joseph threw his hands up in the air, and the rosary he held flew up in the air and down to the floor, near yet another pile of fully dressed, rotting corpses.

"Good. That's where it belongs," Thomas said, pointing to the rosary on the floor.

"Stop it, Thomas! That's enough," Captain Alexandre said, walking over to them.

Captain Alexandre stood between the Joseph and Thomas, who were staring at each other, on the verge of a fight. Thomas walked away, cursing to himself.

Captain Alexandre picked up the rosary for Joseph, who was rubbing his forehead, closing his eyes momentarily.

"There you are," the Captain said, handing the rosary to Joseph.

"Thank you, Captain," Joseph said, nodding to the captain.

The captain sighed and spoke.

"I agree with Thomas, Joseph," said the captain softly.

Joseph looked at the captain and gripped his rosary tightly.

"I have to hold on to my faith, Captain. I think it's the only thing that will enable us to rebuild what we've lost."

The captain smiled sadly and nodded. Then he walked away.

It was time to clear the area around and in the church. Thousands of bodies would need to be picked up and stacked in orderly rows inside the church. Some of the bodies were whole, and others had been hacked to pieces. The stench was sickening, but the soldiers continued with their grim task.

Several soldiers vomited and fell to their knees, for they were from the area surrounding this church. As children, they had been baptized in this church, attended mass with their families. They knew that the innumerable piles of rotting corpses could contain the earthly remains of their family, friends, and neighbors. A black, floating layer of flies hovered above the corpses.

As he picked up an arm, Joseph wondered if his own family had miraculously survived the genocide. Since there was no electricity or phone lines working in the demolished and ransacked town, he and his fellow soldiers could not make phone calls to other parts of Rwanda, or the world. And who would they call anyway? Most of the population of Rwanda was probably fleeing out of the country to avoid retaliation, hiding, or dead. Even before the genocide, most Rwandan households did not have electricity or running water, much less a phone line. Phone lines were normally restricted to government officials and companies.

Kigali, Rwanda, May 20, 1994

Joseph's troop had already fought four battles in the last seven weeks. Joseph and the other troops looked almost emaciated in their fatigues. Many of his fellow soldiers had been killed in the previous battles. He had watched one of his fellow soldiers die right next to him, and he managed to drag the dying man behind a building. Holding him in his arms, Joseph prayed over him. He was amazed that he was still alive, having been shot at so many times.

The wind blew, wild and carelessly, circulating the strong odor of death and decay. Many of the perpetrators had fled, yet a few were still hiding in various places about the town. The rebel soldiers walked through the town, holding their rifles, keenly aware that the earthly fate of many of their family members could be found in the many mutilated corpses lining the streets and roads all over Rwanda, or thrown in mass graves. The general of the rebel army constantly lectured his soldiers on the importance of self-discipline, focus, and emotional control. He told them that to be effective, the soldiers must avoid emotionalism, in spite of the horror before them.

Marching with the rest of his troops, Joseph walked past the corpse of a partially clothed woman near a shack-like house. The woman's breasts had been mutilated. It was likely that she had been raped. Her legs were spread apart. He averted his eyes from the corpse of the woman. He did not want to see the horror that had been inflicted between her legs.

Joseph thought of his sister, Teresa. Was she already dead? He had promised to help her, but he knew he was probably too late to save her and her family. Who could he save, Joseph thought? The rebel army was still outnumbered by the Rwandan Army and the militias. Maybe Thomas was right, he thought. No one else thought enough of them as human beings to intervene. He and the other rebel soldiers would do what they could.

A small subdivision of their troop ran for cover in the streets of Kigali. The Rwandan army threatened to destroy the fragile presence of the rebels in the capital of Kigali. The militias still ruled much of the country. Joseph wondered how they would succeed, as he stood next to his fellow soldier, Thomas.

"I live for revenge, you know," Thomas said.

"I live to stop the killing, not revenge," Joseph said.

"How can you say that? They've shown no mercy, no humanity at all," Thomas said.

"Remember what the girl we found told to us. She said that one of the priests was good. He was a Hutu priest, and he provided mass for the townspeople and refused to open the doors and let the militia in," Joseph said.

"One good man out of thousands of killers...What about the other priest, in that same church? He escaped and allowed the militias to do what they wanted to do," Thomas said bitterly.

"What was he supposed to do? Maybe they threatened to kill him... Everyone can't be evil," Joseph said.

CHAPTER FORTY-FOUR

Kigali, Rwanda, May 25, 1994

In Kigali, Joseph's troop had merged with other rebel troops and set up a large, organized camp. Everyday refugees, genocide survivors, poured into the rebel military camp to escape the murderous militias. They walked into the camp and prostrated themselves before the soldiers, thanking them and calling them heroes. Joseph and his fellow soldiers were grateful to see that some Rwandans had survived this nightmare. Hence, their efforts weren't in vain. The survivors looked horrible though, Joseph thought. Their clothing was terribly soiled and worn thread bare. He pondered their situation. Some of the women who entered the camp, had been once beautiful and neatly dressed before the massacres. However, they stood before him skeleton-thin and unwashed for months since the killings had started. Women, who before the genocide had many children, came with one child, or no child at all. Many were widows who had witnessed the humiliation and murder of their spouses, as well as the slaughter of their children. Some had hidden themselves under piles of rotting corpses, in insect infested swamps, or in a kind Hutu neighbor's house. And there were the children. From toddlers to teenagers, with deep wounds from machetes, they walked into the rebel camp like little ghosts.

Joseph was assisting in the organizing of the armory one afternoon, when he was approached by one of the women in the camp.

"Excuse me, Sir," an old woman said.

"Yes, Madame" Joseph said, stacking a pile of rifles.

"You are the son of Joseph, the University professor, and Madame Antoinette of Kigali, yes?" the woman said.

"Yes, I am," Joseph said.

"I'm Claire Bizimana," the woman said.

Joseph stared at the old woman, but he didn't recognize her. He had been out of Rwanda for so long. Then he remembered. The woman was a neighbor to his sister, Teresa, and her husband, Laurent. He spoke.

"Madame Bizimana?" Joseph said.

"Yes. You are a very big man now. You've come home to save your people. We thank you," Madame Bizimana said.

"Madame, what happened to my mother, my sister, and her family?"

The woman looked at the ground. Then she looked up at the sky, shaking her head.

"Madame Antoinette would be so happy to see you today. You and these soldiers are such heroes, you know," Madame Bizimana said. Her wrinkled face struggled to smile.

"What happened to my family, Madame Bizimana?" Joseph said, staring at her intensely.

"I believe Laurent was forced to kill by his colleagues, but it seems that he persuaded the other killers not to harm his wife and children. I don't know how he did it, but Teresa survived the first few weeks of the killing. One night, I peered cautiously out of the window, and I saw Teresa send her daughter, Valentina, out the house with a Hutu woman. I was surprised. Then I realized that the woman was Laurent's sister, Evangeline. As a Hutu, Evangeline could walk the streets, but since there were so many roadblocks all over, I don't know if she and the child survived. Hutus who show kindness to Tutsis are often killed by the militias. I myself was hiding with an American businessman who stayed behind. I was his housekeeper; he was a kind man who refused to abandon me and my children when the killing started. I could hear much of what was going on. They turned on Laurent. They wanted him to kill his Teresa, but he would not let them. Poor Laurent... The killers even had threatened to rape Teresa, which is what they often did with their female victims. Laurent armed with a gun, killed several of the militiamen, who had only machetes. More militiamen came in, this time with guns. They shot Laurent and everyone in the house. Compared to most others, they had a merciful death. Still, I thought about the horror of them killing Madame Antoinette...a Tutsi princess..."

Joseph stared down at the dusty, reddish earth beneath his feet. He was too late to save his mother, his sister, and her family. Joseph nodded at the woman; then he turned and went back to the barracks.

There he sat alone on his shabby cot. Tears were streaming down Joseph's face, rolling over his lips and into his mouth. He swallowed the salty liquid.

"Forgive me, Father," Joseph said. "I tried to save them, but I'm too late. I'm too late!"

Placing his head in his hands, Joseph cried. Then he buried his face in his dusty pillow to muffle the sound.

CHAPTER FORTY-FIVE

Kigali, Rwanda, June 1994

Captain Alexandre Nkusi dispatched Joseph's troop to fight a division of the Rwandan Army in the city of Kigali. The rebel army wanted to consolidate its control of a small section of Kigali by attacking one of the collapsing government's armories. It was an extremely dangerous mission because the rebels were still outnumbered. The captain hoped to penetrate one of the few strong holds of the Rwandan Army. As they moved through the city of Kigali, the rebel soldiers saw Rwandans fleeing the country in large numbers. Streams of Rwandans poured out of the city hastily, carrying as much of their worldly possessions as they could carry. The captain commanded the rebel soldiers to not kill those who were fleeing. It was reported that many of these people who were fleeing had participated in the massacres, but also that many of them had not. However, all of them feared the revenge of the rebel army.

The attack started near nightfall. Amid abandoned houses in a neighborhood in Kigali, Joseph's troop was dispatched to capture an armory. It was a rectangular building, and it contained some barracks to accommodate the government soldiers. The social chaos of the nationwide massacres in Rwanda affected the discipline and focus of the government soldiers. Many of the government soldiers tended to be inebriated.

The rebel troops intended to surround the armory, which was guarded by government soldiers. Stealthily, the rebel soldiers advanced. They were one half mile away from the armory.

One of the four rebel snipers was perched on a building across from the armory. Quietly, the rebel soldiers advanced from opposite ends of the same street. As they got closer to the armory, Joseph could hear evidence of chaos within the armory. There was the sound of men arguing within the building, followed by the sound of a man wailing in pain. High pitched, terror filled, screams of a women could be heard coming from the barracks.

Soon one third of the rebel soldiers were slowly surrounding the perimeter of the armory. Two of the four towers that surrounded the armory were empty. Under optimal circumstances, each tower should have had at least one soldier, but the government army's control and morale were disintegrating. The rebel troop meant to take full advantage of the opponents' weakening state.

A watch tower soldier suddenly spotted the rebel soldiers around the perimeter of the armory. The government soldier fired his gun, but he missed the first and second time. He shot one of the rebel soldiers on his third try. The rebel soldier fell, and the others quickly ducked for cover. Joseph peered into the darkness and realized that it was Maurice, Prosper's father, who went down. Before the soldier in the tower could shoot another, the rebel sniper fired one shot and killed him.

The rebel soldiers opened fire on the soldiers in front of the armory. The government soldiers returned the fire, killing several rebels in the exchange of gun fire. More soldiers ran out of the armory, but the rebels continued to advance in spite of the casualties. The captain gave orders for the snipers to hone in. Then more government soldiers went down.

Death did not exist in their minds as they charged in the direction of the Rwandan Army. The sweetness of this moment would lie in pulling the trigger and watching the enemy die. Joseph himself killed more than he could count.

Then a small reinforcement of Rwandan Army troops arrived and ran in the direction of where the rebel troops where shelling the armory. One of the rebel soldiers advanced with a rocket launcher. A hole was blown threw the main door, and a part of the entrance was ablaze in a growing conflagration. After that, many of the government soldiers abandoned their post and ran away. Some stayed, disoriented, but still fighting. A squad of the rebel soldiers threw grenades through the windows.

The flames leaped into the air, and the soldiers guarding the armory dwindled slowly. Many were trying to salvage what was left of the arms, depositing them in trucks and driving off fast. Joseph's troop shot at them as they tried to escape. Joseph and Moses stood near each other, alternately shelling and ducking for cover, with other rebel troops.

There was still gunfire exchange and bodies falling around Joseph. Men were dying everywhere on both sides. Joseph continued to fire his AK-47 and to duck for cover near the building. Joseph saw a group of naked young women burst out of the building amidst the flames and chaos. With their breasts bouncing and private areas exposed, the women ran in Joseph's direction, as though they preferred the mercy of a quick bullet to what they had endured in the armory. However, the women were not shot. The rebels offered them what protection they could under the circumstances.

Government soldiers were running in the opposite direction, toward a vehicle. The rebel troops moved closer as the government soldiers were retreating. There was the sound of many soldiers running, carrying guns and ammunition. Then Joseph saw a familiar person emerge from the building. The retreating man was tall and lean, with a familiar gait. The flames from the burning building illuminated the area near the armory, and he quickly recognized the face. It was Blaise Hakizimana. Joseph aimed and fired. Blaise fell.

The flames reached for the night sky above the armory. Joseph felt like someone had hit him in the head with a metal stick. Then there was the sensation of a hot liquid pouring slowly down his neck and back. His eyes were open, but he saw nothing. Before he became unconscious, he realized he'd been shot.

When Joseph awoke, he was back in the barracks. Miraculously, the bullet entered and exited the surface of his head, and the gunshot wound was not fatal. Another soldier explained to him that the armory was almost destroyed, and the government troops had abandoned it. The rebel troops were in control of what was left of the armory. Joseph was glad with this news, and he fell asleep.

As he slept, he dreamed that his mother and sister were calling him. They were standing in front of Laurent and Teresa's home. As he approached them, they disappeared. In their place was a girl. The girl was Valentina, Teresa's daughter. When he awoke, Joseph believed that the child could still be alive somewhere in Rwanda. He was determined to find out where the child was.

Joseph lay on the cot in the infirmary section of the barracks. He had to go to Teresa's home. He could feel their spirits calling him, but was this a land where spirits talked? Surely the spirits were too outraged and angry to communicate with the living, Joseph thought. The living were not worthy of such a communication. It was late June, and most of the militia activity had been quelled by the rebel army forces. It was time to venture into the city of Kigali to look for Teresa's home. Accompanied by seven other soldiers, with his AK-47 slung over his shoulder, Joseph entered a Humvee vehicle and drove off through the dusty streets of Kigali.

As Joseph drove with his fellow soldiers through the city of Kigali, he saw what seemed like a wasteland filled with destroyed homes. Some of the homes were blown up with grenades, and others were left intact. The collapsed homes were overgrown with rubble and bush. The stench of rotting human flesh was thick in the air, as there were open mass graves and piles of corpses in throughout the city. Hell had really come to earth, Joseph thought.

He finally located Teresa and Laurent's home. With his fellow soldiers, he entered the house. The house was empty. Apparently, it had been used by the militias after they murdered Laurent and Teresa's family two months earlier. This was evidenced by the bloody machetes that were piled in a corner of the home. The bodies had been removed, but there were still blood stains on the floors and walls. Joseph walked slowly through the home. It was a mess. The killers were probably on the run, Joseph thought.

He kneeled and touched the floor, where there were dried up blood stains.

"My sweet, Mother," Joseph whispered. "Sleep peacefully in the arms of the angels. They will take you to God."

Silently he cried, as he stared at the stains. Then when he was overwhelmed with emotion, he bellowed.

"All Mighty God! Why?"

CHAPTER FORTY-SIX

Washington, D.C., June 1994

Sojourner had heard nothing from her husband. The boys cried each night. The O.J. Simpson case was the subject of every conversation, it seemed. She was shocked to see the white Ford Bronco in a high speed chase with the LAPD. She watched the scene a dozen times in a day. It was a nightmare that no one could escape. However, her husband was involved in another nightmare...in Africa. Sojourner had finally found a TV channel with some news coverage of the events in Rwanda. It quickly mentioned that approximately 800,000 people had been murdered in ten weeks in Rwanda. That was it, a few seconds for those 800,000 people. Each day, the TV coverage of the O.J. Simpson arrest dominated the news.

Chaucer's *The Canterbury Tales*, was the topic of her lecture. Sojourner was teaching summer classes at Montgomery Community College. Sojourner felt faint as she walked to her office after class. She had a migraine headache and nausea. Worry had caused her to neglect herself. She was getting dehydrated and weak. Not knowing if her husband had survived the madness in Rwanda, along with her responsibilities, was taking its toll on Sojourner.

As she fed the boys that evening, she received a phone call.

"Hello," Sojourner said.

"Good evening Madame," the voice said.

"Hello. Who's calling, please," Sojourner said.

"This is John Uwayezu, Madame Sojourner. I'm Joe's friend, remember?"

"Oh, yes. I remember."

"Have you heard anything from Joe?" John said.

"No. I haven't. I've been worried sick for months now, John. Have you heard anything?" Sojourner said.

"Only what I see on the news. It seems like all the phone lines in Rwanda are down," John said.

"Please let me know as soon as you hear anything, John. I don't know what I'll do if anything's happened. Don't know if I have the will to be without him," Sojourner said.

"Don't give up. Joe's a fighter. How are the children?" John said.

"They're fine. Thank you."

"Let me know if you need any help, please," John said.

"I'm okay. Thank you for calling, John. I appreciate it."

That night, before going to bed, she checked on the sleeping boys. That day, the day care center director said that Prosper had an "accident." The day before, little Joseph had an "accident." When would this potty training madness end, she thought? Sojourner was beginning to think her maternal skills were woefully lacking.

Alone in her bed, she closed her eyes and ascended to the realm of her dreams. She stood in front of the Smithsonian Castle in Washington D.C., the neatly landscaped gardens before her. The Museum of Asian art was to her right, the Museum of African Art to her left.

Joy blossomed in Sojourner's heart, as she saw her husband, Joseph, approach her. They embraced. Holding hands, Joseph and Sojourner walked toward the Museum of African Art. They entered the African Art Museum, passing the information desk, and descending a staircase to their right. When Sojourner and Joseph reached the bottom of the staircase, Sojourner realized that they were suddenly in Rwanda. This was not the Rwanda that she envisioned from the television news reports, the Rwanda of the summer of 1994. It was a Rwanda that was rarely mentioned, free of fear. It was filled with human smiles and vibrantly green, hilly terrain. This was pristine Rwanda, tropical, the one she had read about as a child. Steam seemed to rise from the base of the earth to the top of the tree filled landscape.

Sojourner awoke the following morning. It was time for another busy day with little Joseph and Prosper. The sleepy toddlers whined as she tried to dress them. She was in the room that her husband once called his office. It had been converted to a bedroom for the boys. The phone rang. Who could that be at this hour, she thought?

"Hello," Sojourner said. She balanced the phone between her shoulder and her ear, while she pulled the T-shirt over Prosper's head.

"*Muraho*, my wife…" Joseph said.

"Baby Love! It's you… Thank God!"

"Princess…I'm glad to hear your voice. How are our boys?"

At the sound of Joseph's voice, Sojourner started to cry, tears of joy.